Radcliffe Road
Forbidden Love in a Garden Shed

Betty Valentine

I0673784

FIRST EDITION
Published in 2025 by
GREEN CAT BOOKS
19 St Christopher's Way
Pride Park
Derby
DE24 8JY
www.greencatbooks.com

Dedication

For Judy who loved the idea of being in this book, and for Velcro, my much-missed furry writing assistant

With grateful thanks to:
Den and Carla for their friendship encouragement,
cocktails and gin. Spa Sirene at the Royal Yacht Hotel
-where I plough up and down in the pool to get my ideas,
and the Lockes coffee house St Helier where I refuel
afterwards

Introduction

Dear reader as yet unborn,

My name is George, and I think my work here is pretty much complete.

The end of the road is coming. Circling the drain, as the young people say. It is a good analogy to describe my current situation. I have a dodgy ticker and a dodgy hip, to accompany all the other things that a man in his nineties has to deal with. As well as all that, I am heartbroken, and I do not want to hang around for much longer in this fast-paced world that I don't understand.

Most of my generation are dead or completely gaga. I will miss the family, of course, but they have their own lives to get on with and I will be happy to go.

I have been working through the pages of my diary and pulling out the plums to make a history of my life. I am not being arrogant; someone has asked me to do it and reluctantly I have agreed.

For the avoidance of confusion, you need to know that I called my original diary 'Dave'. He has been my companion and my sounding board since 1958. Both of us are a bit dog-eared and Dave is keeping Sellotape in business. He will be coming into the coffin with me on my final journey. If there is an afterlife, at least I will have something to read.

The first residents of the newly built and recently occupied Cedars Retirement Community, aka '*The Home*', or '*God's Waiting Room*' as we say around here, have been asked if they would like to write down their life stories for a time capsule, which will be placed under the sensory garden. It will be opened in 100 years, when we oldies are nothing but dust. From Chapter 1, you will find my life story as I can recall it, with a little help from Dave.

I am lucky, because I have Dave to remind me of what I did, and thought, and felt. Over the years, I wrote many a note in him, but it all needed weeding, something I used to be rather good at in the old days, ha ha. After all, nobody wants to read "Vera B called round for a cup of sugar in 1968 and stayed nattering away for an hour", do they? She was a bloody tiresome woman anyway.

I have had plenty of time for the project because I have been ill and confined to my room while recovering. Apparently, it was a UTI - you know, a water infection, which I thought was purely a women's thing, until I got one myself.

It sent me a bit loopy at first. All those toxins building up in the blood can do that in an old person. Terry said I was talking absolute rubbish about seeing the angel of death and a man with a gravy boat strapped to his chin, as well as other random imaginings that I remember very little about.

At one point, I saw my wife, Eileen, sitting on the bed. We had quite the conversation it would seem. She looked well considering she has been dead for decades. Henry was there, but only in the doorway. He blew me a kiss and whispered,

'Go to sleep, Georgie,' which I did.

When the drugs kicked in, I started to feel better. Everyone said it was a blessed relief because they had all been worried about me. They fail to realise that I do not feel at all blessed, because I want to go. Life is a heavy burden for me now. If I could have followed Eileen out of the door, I would gladly have gone with her and Henry, to wherever they are waiting.

I'm not bitter or crabby. I smile and eat up my greens like a good boy, well a few mouthfuls anyway, but it is an effort. I am a colouring pencil at the end of its life. Small and hollow and not much use to anyone really.

My recovery time has been purposeful. The family clubbed together and bought me a laptop computer for my birthday, and I have been transferring my written notes into the time capsule document that our Helena set up. These laptop things are absolutely marvellous. It saves everything automatically in case I press the wrong button or do some other stupid old-man thing and wipe the lot.

I am going to sleep now, but I will probably be awake again in a few hours listening to the random gruntings and toothless snorings of my fellow inmates. There is an old girl up the corridor who could rival a snoozing brontosaurus in volume. No wonder they call this place Jurassic Park. Mind you, us oldies can shift when it's dinnertime. You cannot hear yourself think for the sound of sticks and hurrying Zimmer frames when grub is up. It's like a geriatric M25 out there sometimes.

Tomorrow I will read through what I have pulled together, then I can die in peace, knowing I have told our story.

What a funny, unhappy fellow I was back in 1958, scribbling away alone in my shed. Who cares if Dave is made of paper, he has been a jolly good friend to me.

Regards, George.

Prologue

Dear Diary,

You don't know me, but I hope that we will become friends.
On New Year's Day I reached that grand old age of 40. My son,
Terry, gave you to me as a Christmas present, so I am going to
fill you in with all my comings and goings, if I have any.

I see you have a sturdy lock, but I doubt that it will be
needed. Only people with secrets and interesting lives need to
keep their thoughts hidden. I am very dull, so we won't be
needing the key. I am going to keep you here in the shed on my
allotment, because it is the one place that I can truly be myself
with no marital supervision from her indoors.

Oh dear, now I don't know where to start. I have a pen and
a quiet half hour to think with no interruptions, so that will
be helpful. To be honest, you could end up empty because my
life is pretty tedious at the best of times. I am quite frankly the
Invisible Man of Radcliffe Road, without the panache of the
actor Claude Rains or indeed the film-star salary.

I promise not to overload you with long lists taken from
my life, but just this once I will indulge myself with an
autobiography.

My name is George, George Andrew Fielding Potter to be
exact; I never use the Fielding, which was my mother's maiden
name. Most people call me Little George. I'm the nervous one
with the stutter.

I am nobody special, in fact as I said before, I am pretty
much invisible. The sort of man you would probably pass in

the street and completely fail to notice unless I happened to say something.

Most of my life I have found it difficult to speak. I know what I want to say, but something prevents me from doing it clearly. I am like a record with a scratch. Sometimes I can go along quite nicely but if I am tired or under stress, the record keeps jumping.

From my earliest years, people have assumed that I don't have much to say, or that anything I did say would not be worth waiting around to hear. With you, dear diary, I can speak out as clearly as anyone else and not be judged. I like that idea. It gives me confidence - something I have always lacked.

Eileen, my wife, gets very fed up with me and that doesn't help. She is not one to suffer fools gladly. In her eyes, I certainly appear foolish. I am not stupid; I just have a bit of trouble getting my point across sometimes. People dismiss me, which is a shame because I think a lot about the world, and I sometimes have opinions that might prove to be interesting.

It isn't a problem at home, because Eileen does all the talking anyway. I am a stuttering appendage, good for carrying boxes and providing food for the table. According to Eileen, that is where my usefulness ends. If she ever learns to carry her own boxes, I will probably be eaten up, like some male praying mantis who has outlived his function.

My allotment is my salvation away from the house. I grow a bit of fruit, all our veg and the roses that Eileen likes. We have two children, Sally who lives away and Terry who will start at Cambridge this year. We are both very proud. Eileen said he has inherited her brains and not mine. She is probably right.

Sally is not my natural child. Eileen was widowed at 21. Her first husband, a scaffolder, fell from a building and broke his neck. I met Eileen when Sally was a small girl. I am the only dad she has ever known, and I have always thought of her as my own daughter. We were very close as she was growing up, a fact which irked Eileen from the beginning.

Sally and Eileen tend to brush each other up the wrong way. They have never really seen eye to eye. Sal is arty and a bit of a free spirit, but, like Eileen, she is stubborn and she knows her own mind. Over the years it is me that has stopped them from killing each other. Two express engines on the same line and headed for an almighty crash. The problem with standing on the rails as a buffer is that you tend to get hit by both trains.

My boy, Terry, can be just as stubborn if he has a mind to be, but generally he is easy-going in nature. I like to think he is more like me, but he has grown up to look an awful lot like Frank, Eileen's Irish father that she never knew.

If I am going to be honest from the beginning, I would like to talk frankly about my mess of a marriage. Eileen and I have had our happy moments, but they have been just that - moments. We don't hate each other, that would require emotion and quite frankly neither of us could be bothered with the effort. We don't love each other either. We just exist in a dull, grey place, separately but together behind the green front door of number 13 Radcliffe Road, marking time before the inevitable happens to one of us.

We were thrown together in some troop canteen at the beginning of the war. She was lonely and I was a virgin who did not want to die without doing 'it' at least once. Both of us were young and scared and somehow over the course of one night,

Terry happened. So, before I knew it, the marital handcuffs were on and we were marching down the aisle. A week later, I was off to North Africa for five years.

When I was demobbed in early 1946, I returned to a wife I hardly knew, a stepdaughter who only remembered me from the letters and drawings I had posted home, and a son I had never even seen.

They were a unit, Eileen and the children. There had never been a dad on the scene and Eileen was very much used to having things her own way. It was tough on all of us.

When they met me at the docks, it was obvious that we had some work ahead. Sally gave me a hug and called me Daddy because she had obviously been tutored in what to say. Like a child in a school play, she read her lines and then retreated behind her mother. Terry burst into tears and refused to have anything to do with me at all until I produced a stuffed camel, which he promptly named Malcolm for some utterly bizarre reason known only to himself.

I remember so well all the feelings I had when I saw them from the boat - crippling fear mostly. I was afraid I might let them down or that they might reject me as a cuckoo in the nest that Eileen had created. Could I learn to love them, and would they learn to love me? I was relieved to have someone to share the moment with. So many had nobody there to welcome them home.

To me, they were a forlorn group of strangers standing under an umbrella in the pouring rain. Eileen wearing a silk headscarf tied under her chin, waving fit to bust. Sally in a brown mac, her dark hair in a long plait tied with a green ribbon, The bow had become so wet it was hanging down her back like seaweed. She was tall and skinny, so different from the chubby blonde toddler I just about remembered. Then there was Terry wearing wellingtons, an oversized duffle coat that had obviously been Sally's, and a blue school cap. He was wrapped up for the cold like a robin, his face a mass of freckles to match the brightest red hair I have ever seen on a young child. There he was, my own son, five years old and until that moment I'd had no idea that he was ginger. A funny looking coot, he had ears like a taxi with the doors open (we had them pinned back when he was seven) and a serious look on his face as Eileen lifted him up to show him who his daddy was. The fact that we missed so much still makes me angry. No child should have to have their own father pointed out to them. I didn't know them, and they hardly knew me, but we were going to be a family and I was determined to do my best for them all. My commanding officer was standing next to me at the rails looking for his own family.

He laughed and said, 'Is that your boy, George? The sturdy little fellow in the Wellington boots?'

I had to choke back a tear as I nodded that he was indeed mine. What had really got to me was him calling me George instead of Sergeant Potter. The war was truly over. At that point I had no idea that a new one was just beginning.

We left for home on the train, with Terry holding Malcolm and wearing my army cap. Eileen did try, we both did, and for a month or two we played happy families. The crunch arrived when Terry asked me to read him a bedtime story instead of Eileen.

My wife didn't say a word, but I could tell she was hurt. I had no idea of what to do because I was well and truly in the *middle, that cuckoo in the nest, stuck between Eileen and my new family.*

It deteriorated from there. I refused to fight her for the children's affection, but I was a novelty and of course they were interested in me.

I wanted them to see me as their dad, but Eileen clearly felt pushed out, which made things difficult. If I said one thing, she would say the opposite, just to be awkward, and that is one of the reasons I got an allotment in the first place. It gave us some space at the weekends and in the evenings. The children liked to help, and Eileen got a bit of time for herself to get her hair done or to do whatever she wanted.

Eileen is odd - a mixture of fire and smoke. She will tell you exactly what she thinks of you if you displease her. I could not count the times she has done that to me.

In other ways she is ridiculously modest, and she hides behind a curtain of respectability. She is the kind of woman who will not hang panties and stockings out on the line unless it is dark. She will get up extra early to whip the offending items in again before anyone can see them.

My undies can wave to the world, and she wouldn't give two hoots, but her own are kept secret. I have no idea if she thinks that some pervert will gain pleasure from a quick glimpse of her matronly pants swinging in the breeze, but it is a subject best avoided if you don't want a lashing of tongue pie from my mrs, and she serves it up in pretty generous portions, believe you me.

We Potters live at the very end of Radcliffe Road, in a row of solidly built Victorian red-brick semis with white windowsills. Boxes made for the lower middle classes to inhabit. We are bordered on one side by a fence, which divides us from the allotments, and we have a neighbour down the right-hand side. I say that, but weirdly number 13 is not semi-detached at all. We are an oddity, an after-thought by the developer when he realised he had got his sums wrong and had space for one more house squeezed in at the end. We are detached from the semi next door, but not by much, just an alleyway where we keep the bins.

The street itself is lined with pollarded lime trees, which are lumpy and ugly and thoroughly suburban. We have a hedge out the front now, as do all the other houses. Once upon a time, I am told, there were rather smart railings, but they were all snipped off during the war to be made into Spitfires or some such thing. You can still see the little stumps of metal where the bolt cutters, or whatever they used for the job, did their work.

So that is us, living a quiet and eminently respectable existence like all the other residents of our road. Nobody would dare to put a gnome in the front garden for fear of censure. Heaven help us if the grass remains uncut or the windows not receive their weekly washing.

We keep ourselves to ourselves around here, and any gossip is generally channelled via Eileen's friend, Vera, in the post office. What goes on behind our front doors stays there, and any unseemly bedtime shenanigans are strictly lights out and think of England - at least ours are!

On that subject, this week, because it was my birthday, we had a spot of the old marital naughties. Eileen has it all regulated. I am rationed to my birthday and once if we are on holiday, as well as extremely occasional congress at times of her choosing throughout the year.

I cannot say it was unpleasant, but as usual it was in silence with the lights off. I will take what I am offered, but for her it is purely functional, like worming the dog.

I so wish she could enjoy it too, or at least give the impression that I am pleasing her. I would never force my attentions upon my wife. In our early days I did my utmost to try to give her some degree of pleasure, but I soon realised that my efforts were not generally appreciated. I like to think I am a kind man. I genuinely tried to talk to her about it, to see if I could understand what the problem was.

I have heard of chaps who expect regular deliveries of nookie whether the Memsahib is in the mood or not, and they will ensure that they get it. I would never entertain the thought. For one, Eileen would probably lay me out flat and secondly, I know that somewhere deep in her past there are many unhealed wounds.

I wonder if she was the same with Arthur, her first husband. I expect she may have been. Occasionally, after a sherry or two she will relax, like the first couple of nights I spent with her. I was a virgin with no idea of what to expect and I thought that all women must be like Eileen. A chap in the army put me right on that one.

Dave Robinson told me one very long night on guard duty, that his wife was a warm and loving woman. Together they had explored the mysteries that lay between the sheets, and it had formed an unbreakable private bond between them, which they both enjoyed enormously. He couldn't wait to get back to her arms. Sadly, he never did.

So anyway, I let Eileen decide when 'tonight is the night' but I really wish that we could be a bit more loving to each other. It is pretty rotten to never have anyone's arms around you. After it is all over, she has a cigarette, I say "thank you"' and then trot back to my own bed next door, because a cuddle is out of the question.

People who are single say it is lonely. Nobody ever tells them that being married can be bloody lonely too.

I have penned the odd poem in my time. It helps me to express myself. Of course I would never dream of showing them to anyone else. Eileen and I are stuck together, and this is how I feel about it:

> *Separate lives, on separate pages*
> *existence lived, in separate cages*

The only exception to me not showing anyone else my poems was when I proposed to Eileen with a poem inside a card. She thought I was trying to be romantic, but actually I thought it would go across better than me nervously stuttering everything out like an idiot.

She read it then she teased me with "Oh, George, you are incredibly soft sometimes" but she kept the card and, of course, she said "yes". Not that she had a lot of choice because somehow during the course of our first weekend together, we managed to conceive Terry. The world has a great deal of sympathy for a young widow with a small child. An unmarried mother, on the other hand, gets zero when she is stuck holding the baby!

Well, my first attempt at a diary entry seems to have gone quite well. It feels odd to be able to open up about things. I feel quite cleansed of some of my anxieties. It isn't as if I could do it with anyone else, is it?

Thank you for listening. I know you are only made of paper, but I can pretend, can't I?

Now that we have been introduced, I think you should have a name too. Diary sounds a bit cold and formal, and I hope that you will become my friend and confidant. Perhaps Tom would do, but Tom was the name of a pushy boy who used to steal my sweets at boarding school.

Oh, I know. I have previously mentioned that I had a great friend in the army who took me under his wing until the other fellows got used to me stuttering away. He was killed at El Alamein, and I have sorely missed him and our chats over the years.

So there you have it, I will no longer call you diary, from now on you will be Dave Robinson.

Before I go, I have a confession to make. I want to be totally honest with you, and I need to do so from the beginning with no fibbing. I started with a lie, and I need to set the record straight - sorry.

Our daughter, Sally, is not just living away from home. She ran off last year. You know what young people are like. She had a flaming bust-up with her mother. Hot words were said on both sides, and Sally packed her cases and walked out.

Somehow, Eileen found out that Sally had become pregnant after a sneaky weekend away with her boyfriend, a Teddy Boy named Donny, a most unpleasant youth of whom neither of us approved. She'd had an abortion at some nasty back street clinic.

Of course, Eileen went mad. She called Sally a stupid slut who, apart from it being a sin, could have died because these places were not clean or competent, and that many girls had lived to regret it, or not lived to regret it at all, which I thought was rather more than a step too far.

Sally retorted back that it takes a slut to know one, and how everyone knew Eileen was as knocked up as a nine-pin with our Terry when she dragged me down the aisle like a little whipped dog. She followed it up by calling me a spineless coward who would have walked out years ago if I had any backbone in me at all.

I said I had heard quite enough from the pair of them, and they both had a go at me for sticking my nose in. That was rich considering it was solely me who was keeping them from spilling blood on the carpet.

Why she didn't talk to us, I will never know. She could have come to me, because I would not have judged her and she knew that. Together we could have tackled Eileen and then supported her in whatever she wanted to do, rather than her running off to some back street knitting-needle merchant. It is beyond sad that my beautiful, spirited daughter decided that she could not trust either of us to help her through this.

We thought Sally would calm down and come home, but she hasn't. As the weeks passed and they turned into months, it dawned on us that she's not coming back at all. We have no idea of where she is or if she is ok.

Eileen has told me more than once that "Sally could be dead in a ditch and we would never know". I told her not to say things like that, but of course she is right, we wouldn't know and that is truly heart-breaking.

Terry is furious with Sally because she has made Eileen cry on more than one occasion. It has upset him terribly. She was his big sister, and she has let him down and gone off to God knows where and he can't do anything to make his mother feel better about it.

If the truth be told, I am bloody annoyed with Sally too for being so stupid and selfish. I am also at my wits' end with worry and with wondering if she is ok. These fears live behind a door that is clearly labelled 'murdered hitchhiker' and sometimes 'unknown corpse'. Just a postcard to say she is alright would make a world of difference and give poor old Eileen some peace of mind. My wife has her faults, God knows, but she has been a very good mother, and she deserves better than this from her daughter.

There, the record has been set straight. If I cannot be honest with you then I cannot do so with anyone. Time to put you into a drawer, in case Terry comes in rummaging for a bit of string or something, which is a thing he sometimes does.

I will pop in again when I have something interesting to tell you. It might be a while, but I won't leave you mouldering away and forgotten in the shed like a packet of seeds that have slipped down the back of the bench.

George.

Chapter 1

Now, the first thing to happen was the departure of our neighbours, the Hankinsons, together with their tribe of cheerful but noisy children, and Chester the incredible farting dog. Billy, their youngest, told me they were going to be *£10 poms'* in Australia and that Chester was going to live at Granny's house in the country. I told him it all sounded like an adventure for them and for Chester, when I was really thinking I hope Granny kept her gas mask.

I got Sid Hankinson, who was an architect's technician, to build me a model of our house for Eileen's 40th birthday. My idea was to put a photo of the children in each window and one of her in her kitchen holding the dog.

I am sure she would have loved it, but Sally ran off before I got the chance to use it. That empty window would have been like a missing tooth, so I took it to the shed and used it to store newspapers. If Sally ever returns, I will resurrect it.

This leads me to introduce the other members of the Potter household. First there was Eric, Eileen's beloved, but terminally dim, pug. He was *'as thick as a yard of lard'*, as my grandfather used to say. I mean, he was ok. A waddly, licky fellow. No real harm in him, because malice or cunning would have taken the brains he patently did not have. I wouldn't have entirely trusted him, though, because he was Eileen's familiar. He probably yapped away to her about the rest of us when they were alone.

They were inseparable and she treated Eric way better than she did the rest of us. Then there was Daffodil, our cat. I named him that because Terry found him, a tiny ball of splodgy fluff, hidden inside a box of bulbs. We guessed that the mother cat had left him for some reason and didn't return. Daffy spent most of his time in the allotment shed with me, because he and Eric could only tolerate so much of each other before the fur started to fly. A bit like my marriage really. Daffy and I were kindred, gentle souls who disliked being bullied, which Eileen and Eric were inclined to do.

So, we were all waiting for new neighbours to appear on the scene, which they did in due course. We saw them with the agent when they looked round. A tall, balding chap of about my own age got out of a big, grey car, closely followed by what I assumed were his wife and daughter. I noticed our Terry looking at the wife. To be honest, I couldn't blame him, because she was a rather good-looking blonde, like one of the ladies from a Hitchcock film. Their daughter, a dark-haired, slim young woman, seemed to be about 20. I thought she looked a bit like Audrey Hepburn in her pedal pushers and flat shoes.

The man was interesting. He had a high forehead and seemed the academic type. Eileen was worried that they might turn out to be the 'wrong sort'. I could not see what the problem was. They looked like a perfectly ordinary family to me.

A few weeks later, on a bright, chilly morning, I met the husband. Terry and I were out in the front garden when a van pulled up. Terry was kneeling, down his hands in a bucket of water, trying to find a puncture on his bike tyre, and I was attending to the weeds around some spring bulbs. Our new neighbour seemed to be struggling to lift a crate, so I called out,

'Hey there, can I give you a hand?'

He answered back, 'Oh, would you? This one is a proper beast to lift, I think I overfilled it.'

He had a distinct accent that I recognised immediately. Between us, we heaved it up the steps and into his house.

'What on earth is in it, an elephant?' I asked, leaning against the door frame to get my breath back.

'Books,' he said brightly. 'I'm opening a bookshop in town, on Jenkin Street where the dry cleaners used to be. Do you know it?'

'Yes, I do know it,' I replied, warming to him. 'I work just around the corner, as it happens. I'm George, by the way, George Potter, and that lad out there is my boy, Terry,' I stuttered out, because I always had trouble with the T sound.

The man nodded. 'I'm Heinrich Muller, but you can call me Henry.' He held out a large hand for me to shake. 'Now how about a cup of tea, to say thank you for your help?'

Half an hour and a mug of tea later, I left when his wife and daughter turned up. I had plenty to tell Eileen.

They had definitely turned out to be the wrong sort, and Eileen was not happy - which was a bonus. I don't take pleasure in the misery of others, but sometimes Eileen jolly well deserved what she got.

Heinrich, Clara and Claudie Muller (home on a visit from her teacher training college in Scotland) were indeed the worst sort of people in Eileen's book. Educated, cultured, quiet, well-mannered and, horror of all horrors, German. I was, of course, delighted.

According to my wife, The Hun had secretly invaded number 11 Radcliffe Road, sneaky beggars, turning up in a damned great Pickfords van and trying to get in under the wire!

I told Eileen that the war had been over for a long time, and we were all friends now. She said '*Shut up, George*' like she usually did.

She'd lost her father in the first war, before she'd ever got the chance to meet him and she was naturally quite bitter. What she seemed to forget was that I'd lost my own dear father in the last war, but I bore no grudges. Unlike Eileen, I got to grow up with my dad. She'd been denied that pleasure and the pain had stayed with her, so battle lines were being drawn.

She'd told me once about the long journey she and her sister Beryl had made when they'd been children. After their mother's breakdown they'd been sent from London to an orphanage in rural Ireland. Beryl was seven, almost eight, and Eileen had just turned five. Their father was Irish, and the church thought it would be a good idea. Apparently, it was hell with windows and she and Beryl only had each other. Two small girls against a lot of cruelty and other vile things, which damaged them for life.

Eileen said she could remember the journey as if it were yesterday. They were placed into the charge of this ferocious nun. Thin as a bone, with steel-rimmed glasses pinched onto her beaky nose and her black robes flapping, Eileen thought she looked like a scraggy old crow.

It was a long journey by train and then by boat. They were told not to speak until they were spoken to, and they could see she meant it.

Eileen said they sat in that dusty third-class railway carriage with its horrible prickly seats, for what seemed like days. She was only five and scared stiff of Sister whatever-her-name-was. In desperation, she whispered to Beryl that she needed to 'go' and Beryl put up her hand and said very politely, '*Please, ma'am, my little sister needs the lavvy.*'

This provoked a response of, '*We do not mention bodily functions in public, Beryl O'Connor. If you had come from any kind of a decent home, you would know that. If your sister needs to be excused, she can ask for it herself. Now she can wait until I tell her she can go.*'

Eileen said she had never been more proud of Beryl, who faced up to this terrifying creature and said defiantly, '*Fine. When she pees her pants, you can clear it up, because I'm not doing it.*'

Apparently, this nun was like lightning. A bony hand caught Beryl around the face, leaving a mark that lasted for hours. It all went downhill after that because Eileen did, in fact, pee her pants and they arrived in Ireland with a reputation for being ignorant, dirty and from a bad family.

I suggested I take the new neighbours some vegetables round to welcome them to Radcliffe Road. Eileen encouraged me and added a jar of jam to the basket. She wanted to hear more details so she could report back to her Tuesday bridge-playing ladies, aka '*The Coven*', and her best pal, chief witch among the card playing hags, Vera Bulstrode from the post office. My Mrs was not generally a gossip, but this was a particularly juicy one and I knew she would not be able to resist.

Henry was very pleased to have a visitor because his 'girls', as he called them, had gone shopping for curtains. He told me about his plan for the new bookshop. His idea was to sell a few pastries and good, strong German coffee to entice people to call in and browse on their way to work. He was very excited and full of ideas on how to grow his business.

I told him all about my allotment and he asked me if I would give him some tips. He wanted to grow something for Clara as she loved flowers. Henry said he liked plants, but he had no idea of how to grow them because he had always lived in a city or the suburbs, where a window box full of sad dusty tulips, which everyone forgot to water, was as close to nature as you were likely to get.

As a child, I'd spent a lot of time at the family farm in Suffolk. My grandfather had taught me all about growing flowers and vegetables, and how to care for the land. I promised Henry I would show him how to grow a lily bulb in a pot for Clara. He was absolutely thrilled. I hoped he wouldn't kill it with kindness, because he seemed the enthusiastic type.

In return for the plant, he promised to teach me the finer points of chess. I used to enjoy a game every now and then with Terry, but I was a rank amateur compared to Henry. He shrugged and told me it was a question of logic and memory.

We stayed chatting for ages and Eileen was more than a bit narked when I got back. I didn't give two hoots when she gave me a proper old ticking off, because I had made myself a new friend.

Within a few weeks, Henry and I were pals. I liked him a lot. At first, he seemed shy and formal in that polite way the Germans have. It took me over a week to persuade him to call me George instead of Mr Potter.

He started dropping by when I was at the allotment on a Saturday morning, usually when I was opening my Thermos of tea around 11. I didn't think it was the tea that attracted him, it was Eileen's excellent cake. For all her faults, she was a truly magnificent chef.

She'd learned to cook when she'd gone into service in a big Irish house at 14. The household had been large, and life had been strict, but it had been an excellent way to learn. The young Eileen had been noted as a bright girl who had a good memory and Cook had seen potential in her.

She married Arthur, her first husband, at 18 and within a year she had Sally, so her training stopped. When she was widowed, she picked herself up in true Eileen style and made her living cooking for a firm catering for dinner parties, because she could work from home. Eileen was never a whiner. She just rolled up her sleeves and got on with it.

I tried to encourage her to use her talent, possibly making birthday and wedding cakes once rationing ended, but she said she didn't have time for all that as looking after me was quite enough. This was a shame, because I thought she would have made an excellent businesswoman. She had a very good head for figures and a brain as sharp as her tongue. She would have done well, and it would have given her something to focus on besides my shortcomings, which would have been a real blessing.

According to Henry, his wife Clara was almost completely deaf. She could lip read if you were facing her. Her hearing had started to fail after she'd contracted meningitis when she'd been 10. Henry told me she was very bright and creative, but she got frustrated because people tended to see the deafness first and ignore the rest. I could well understand what that felt like. There have been times when I have longed to shout, '*I am a person with a stutter - not the other way around*'. I once wrote a silly poem about my stutter; it went something like this:

My tongue is a bird
that longs to fly
sometimes it hops
I don't know why!

A few days later, our Terry took a tumble; he was knocked off his bike by the wing mirror of a lorry.

The doctors could find nothing seriously wrong with him, but he stayed unconscious. It was a terrible time. For a few anxious days, we sat by his bedside holding hands and willing him to wake up, while the heart monitor ticked away the seconds and we counted the hours. Eileen and I put aside all our differences for Terry. We didn't love each other, but we both loved our boy. Henry and Clara were very kind in giving us lifts to the hospital as they both drove. The thought of losing Terry was just too damned awful to contemplate and their support was most welcome. At some point during that awful disinfectant-scented week, we realised the new neighbours were becoming friends.

Terry did come round eventually, with a truly spectacular bruise on the front of his head, but seemingly none the worse for his ordeal. In September, we saw him off on the train to Cambridge with a new duffle coat, all his worldly goods packed into a couple of suitcases and his portable record player under one arm. He was excited but trying to be very grown up about everything. Eileen cried a bit. I gave him a hug, tucked a fiver into his pocket and told him to be sure to write to his mother every week. Our chick had flown the nest, which left the two of us bumping around in the house together. Not a pleasant prospect.

I never mentioned before, but we lost our youngest child, who'd been born about a year after I'd come home from the war. We'd still been pretending our marriage was going to be a happy one at the time she'd been conceived. Eileen had a bit of a rough time, and the baby was early. She wasn't right from the beginning, and she only lived for four hours. I remember so very clearly the bright April morning she was born. I sat in the windowless, expectant father's room smoking and playing cards with three other chaps while we waited for the off, and our offspring. The white painted walls and ceiling were stained nicotine yellow, a colour I believe became comically referred to as *Fagnolia!* I was first out of the traps, and with the hearty congratulations of my fellow inmates ringing in my ears, I went off to meet my new daughter, only to be told in the corridor that I had better hurry because she wouldn't be with us for very long. Pale and beautiful with a mop of dark hair, she passed away in my arms while Eileen was sleeping. Slipping from the world with hardly a sound, except the sobs of her sorrowing father.

Matron told me it would be much better if Eileen didn't become too attached and they wanted to whisk the baby away before she woke up. I was ready to punch the stupid woman in the face for her crass and unbelievable cruelty. I refused point blank to let them take her. We were both there when Eileen woke up, so it was me that told her our baby had died and not some uniformed Storm Trooper. United in grief, we brushed the baby's hair and put her in a lovely little dress, bootees, a cardigan and a soft knitted bonnet, all smart and ready for the undertaker, a much-loved child·who went to her rest in the outfit her mother had made for her to come home in. I would have fought a lion for her, and it was the day I realised I had truly become a father.

We called the baby Lizzie, Elizabeth Mary after our mothers. I missed out on everything with Terry as he was already at school before I got to meet him. With Lizzie, I was there for the whole of her short life. I asked the bishop, a family friend, if she could be buried with my mum and dad so that they could watch over her for eternity, and he agreed. Eileen was pleased that the baby wouldn't be alone or with strangers. It was all I could do to ease her pain.

Every year on Lizzie's birthday, I used to cut a sprig off the apple tree that we planted for her and Eileen put it in a vase in the kitchen. We did not mention her for the rest of the year, but I knew Eileen kept a pair of unused knitted bootees in a box by her bed. They were the blue ones she had knitted in case our Lizzie was a boy, who we were going to call Robert. I expect that occasionally she got them out to look at.

So, we waved goodbye to Terry, and I busied myself on the allotment and in my growing friendship with Henry. One autumn Sunday when he was visiting, we sat in a couple of deck chairs in the sunshine and enjoyed a cheeky beer. This was very high on Eileen's list of '*Things George enjoys but is not allowed*'.

Henry gave a small burp, apologised and said, 'Do you know, for the first time in years I actually feel quite settled and happy. Sitting here in the sunshine with a beer in my hand and you to chat to feels right. It isn't easy to feel accepted, and I don't have the language barrier that some people do.'

He stretched his arms up, wiggled his long fingers and yawned.

I took a swig from my own bottle and asked, 'Where did you learn English then? You must have had a good teacher, Clara too.'

'Oh,' he mused, 'perhaps I never told you, no I don't suppose I did. My grandmother was English, a Londoner as it happens.'

I listened with fascination as he told me his story.

'My Oma Lottie worked as nursemaid to a German family in London; when they returned home, she went too. Oma had a very quick ear for languages and in no time at all she was speaking German like a native. She met and fell for my opa, who was called Franz. He was a dashing young carpenter who had come to the house to fix a wobbly dining table. They married and settled down to raise their own family in a town not far from Berlin, where my mother was born.'

He finished his beer and wiped his face with the back of his hand, before he continued. 'Opa Franz died when I was a baby. I don't remember him at all. All I ever knew was my Oma who came to live with us, and she taught me and my sisters to speak English.

'Times got very hard, George. Clara and I were newly married, and we were living in furnished rooms above the baker's shop that Clara worked in. It wasn't great but it was near the university where I was studying and doing a bit of teaching to make some extra cash.'

He looked me in the eye as he said, 'I knew we had to get out, George.' He turned to me and whispered, 'Anyone at the university was marked as subversive. I was waiting for the day they came and dragged me off into the military or shot me. Deaf people like Clara were seen as defective, and a pollutant to their bloody glorious master race.' He growled with an air of disgust.

He rolled the beer bottle around in his hands. 'I was at my wits' end, George. There were so many troops on the streets that any young woman was vulnerable to attack, a deaf one doubly so. Clara didn't want to go but I said we must.'

He smiled, mocking himself. 'I was young and determined to do the right thing for my family, so I put my foot down as master of the household.'

'What happened?' I nudged.

Henry grinned. 'Oh, the usual, a plate of stew thrown at my head and she didn't talk to me for two days.'

I rolled my eyes and said nonchalantly, 'Been there myself, pal, although with my Eileen, putting your foot down generally means "yes, dear".'

Henry eyed the third bottle.

'Have it if you want,' I offered. 'Eileen would give me hell if she smelt beer on me anyway, better not risk a second one.'

'How about we share?' Henry suggested.

I gave him a thumbs up.

'We were all set to go, George,' he continued, dropping his voice, 'when a neighbour knocked on the door, an old man who collected the rents from the tenants to give to the landlord, so we let him in. You had to be damned careful who you let into your home because informants were everywhere.'

He cracked open the beer and watched as foam ran down the bottle. 'He saw our half-packed case on the table then smiled and said, *"So, you are going, I see. This is a good thing. Take your pretty wife and run as fast as you can, young man, don't stop until you are safe. Oh, don't worry I am not an informant or a blackmailer, but I have a big favour to ask you both later."* This man, who was called Herr Schneider, left us and returned about an hour later, with a sleeping baby in his arms.'

Henry, deep in thought, swigged from the bottle then passed it to me, sweat blending with the froth on his upper lip, although the day was mild. He turned and whispered something so quietly that I had to strain to hear him.

'Claudie is not our child, George; she was the favour that Schneider asked.'

I stared at him open mouthed, beer dribbling down my chin.

'Three weeks old, the newly born grandchild of Schneider's Jewish friends. She had been given to him for safety, until he could find her a loving foster home or get her out of Germany. He told us the family had money and were willing to pay if we took her with us when we left.

'We knew we would never be blessed in that way—my fault, not Clara's—a bad case of mumps when I was 12 put an end to my chances of fatherhood. We said we would take her with us, but not for money; we didn't want to buy ourselves a family, George.

'After a lot of persuading, we took the baby and the money, not for us, for Claudie and her future. We left Germany by train, telling nobody. We were a young couple sitting in a dusty railway carriage, with not much to their name besides a suitcase full of clothes and their tiny baby sleeping peacefully in a basket on the floor. No different to thousands of others fleeing persecution, except for the fact that Claudie wasn't ours and Clara had several bundles of notes sewn into the hem of her skirt.'

I was astonished and I had no idea of what I should say to him, but he wasn't finished.

'The three of us made that long, cold journey together, George. When we had to walk, I took the case, with Claudie strapped to my front, and Clara carried the formula, the nappies and the basket. On the way, we became a family. There was no way either of us would have given her up; she became Claudie Muller long before we got to England.

'When we registered, everyone assumed she was ours and that is the way it stayed. We told her all about it when she was 12.'

He ran his fingers through his thinning hair and sighed. 'Over the years, we tried to find her family but there was no trace of them, they had vanished, wiped from the pages of history by those vicious bastards. We gave her a future, but she has no past, nobody to call her own. She is rootless, George, and that is a terrible, terrible thing to do to anyone. I don't know if we did the right thing not handing her over, she should have been with her own people, not with us.'

He started to cry. A big fat tear rolled down his face, and I patted his arm and said, 'You did a very good thing, Henry. I'm sure her family would be so grateful to know she had a safe and loving home, instead of the terrible fate she could have suffered.'

Henry nodded, then he wiped his little round glasses and wandered off to look at the last of the roses because he said they calmed him down. I was beginning to think we might make a gardener of him yet.

When he was feeling better, we got down to a bit of digging which helped to distract him. I suggested that it might do him good to get an allotment plot of his own, and that I could help him get started if he wanted to give it a try. I knew full well the deep satisfaction and peace that could be gained from working on your own patch of land.

He shook his head. 'It's a nice thought but the allotment committee probably wouldn't have me, George, or they would make up some excuse, because foreigners, especially

German ones, are usually most unwelcome in small organisations.'

I didn't push him and we left it there. I could tell he was talking from bitter experience. It isn't easy to be the odd one out in an organisation and, believe you me, I knew all about that one.

I distinctly remember my interview for promotion to officer. It had happened after basic training, because I had gone to a minor public school set up for educating the sons of clergymen. They'd interviewed me and had asked me a lot of rather personal questions.

Without reading my form, the officer said, 'So you are a single man then, Mr Potter.'

I replied, 'No, I'm not single, sir. I have a wife and a daughter and baby number two is coming out to bat later on this year.'

He gave me a look and said, 'Good for you, old chap.' As if he couldn't quite believe a stuttering little specimen like me would be able to attract anyone, let alone persuade a woman to marry me and produce my offspring.

I passed all the tests, but I decided not to take a commission after one examiner joked, 'Now where shall we put you? Not communications, Potter; the war would be over before you completed a sentence.' Followed by, 'They would think the radio was on the fritz with you in charge, old chap.'

I joined another unit as an ordinary soldier and was duly despatched to the desert, where I eventually made sergeant, which was good enough for me.

Sorry, I am getting off the track here, a thing I am inclined to do if something else strikes me.

I wanted to help Henry out if I could, so I put my thinking cap on and came up with a splendid idea. I decided to give him a patch of my land that he could call his own. I had plenty, so I wasn't going to miss a slice. I thought it would make a good early birthday present. When I told Henry, he was delighted. Within 10 minutes, he was sat on a box outside the shed with a notebook and pencil, making plans for what he would plant where. It was like watching a six-year-old on Christmas morning. I gave him a key to my shed and Clara promised to knit him a striped bobble hat for the allotment. Eileen started to add a second slice of cake to my elevenses tin, which meant acceptance. It was never easy to get inside Fort Eileen, and when she let the drawbridge down and gave you cake, you knew you had made a friend for life.

I set my new gardening buddy a few tasks so he could get his hands dirty. One of our committee members had a friend with several horses. He provided us with manure and was only too pleased to be rid of the stuff. Every now and then he arrived with a lorry load. There was a special designated place where he dumped it and anyone who wanted some could go and get it. We all popped a few shillings into a tin, and it bought the chap a bottle of something at Christmas.

I grew a lot of roses, and they loved a good dressing of rotted manure, so did the veg. I generally fetched a few wheelbarrow loads, which was pretty hard work, then forked it all into the soil. Henry seemed more than keen to help. He rolled up his sleeves and got shovelling. He appeared perfectly at home in the muck. I took a breather and watched him for a bit - he was funny, stripped down to his vest whistling away to himself. It was lovely to see him so relaxed, seemingly without a care in the world.

'When Adam delved and Eve span
who was then the gentleman?'

I remembered this quote well from my school days. I think it means that shovelling crap is a great leveller.

Something that I found a bit of a chore seemed to be therapy for Henry. A chance to do a simple task with no one putting any pressure on him. He and Clara had been through a lot and if something like shifting manure for the roses helped him find peace, then why on earth not. All he wanted was to be happy and to find a place for himself in the world. He was a good person who had some bad things happen to him. He told me that they left Scotland because their shop windows were broken and truly disgusting things were posted through the letterbox, some of them on fire.

They had escaped from the Nazis and, according to Henry, they hadn't stopped running since. He told me his family were staying put this time, because he was tired of apologising for who he was, and Clara's nerves were at breaking point; she could not take any more upheaval. I promised myself that I would do all I could to help them out.

When we were done, we sat and had a brew. Henry was glowing and grubby. He had muck everywhere, on his nose and on his glasses. I hid a smile and suggested that he might like a wash under the tap before he ate his cake. He wiped his hands on his trousers, saying that he felt like a proper gardener at last. I remember thinking, *Oh well, it probably won't kill him* - at least I hoped it wouldn't.

Shortly after this, I became Fearless George Defender of the Free. I had a curt note from Colonel Reginald Braithwaite, newly crowned King of the Allotment Committee. He said it was against regulations to share a plot and that Herr Muller should wait his turn like everyone else and not jump the queue. He didn't actually write, *'Stop siding with the enemy, Potter, you traitorous dog,'* but I could imagine him saying it.

It wasn't against any rule that I knew of, and I got brave and said so. I also told them that Eileen would no longer be available for committee catering and that they could do without her cakes from now on if they wanted to make an issue out of it. *Ha, that showed them.*

There had been bad blood between myself and the colonel ever since I'd got my allotment in 1946. The rule was you put your name down, waited your turn, and whatever plot came vacant next you got it, if you were top of the list.

My plot, when it became free, was the pick of the bunch. It had belonged to the first chairman of the allotment association way back in 1920. It had a bigger and more substantial shed (because they used to hold meetings in it) electricity, a tap, and a sink. In the winter it was quite cosy.

Braithwaite thought that as ranking officer he should have jumped ahead of humble Sergeant Potter. He was directly below me on the waiting list, but rules were rules, and I got the shed. One of the other committee members told him that the war was over and he had to accept their decision. At the time, I would happily have given up the shed for a quiet life.

So, he was not exactly my best friend. He thought me a stuttering fool. He was probably right, but I was a stuttering fool with a big shed, which never ceased to annoy him, and he was a pompous idiot without one.

Only the British would get so bent out of shape over something as petty as a garden shed. Ridiculous really, but it is our nature. We are a small island, and things assume great importance when you are defending your patch, either physically or intellectually, although I am not entirely sure intellectual applied to the colonel. He just shouted a lot and expected you to do the thinking for him. I met a few like him in the army. We called him 'Red Reg' behind his back, not that he was a commie, quite frankly he would gladly have shot the lot of them. It was because of his hair and his face, which was the colour of beetroot soup.

George Potter, rebel in a cardigan, that was me. Sometimes I surprised myself. There was no way I was going to back down over the Henry thing because I knew I was in the right. They didn't have a leg to stand on and they knew it. I expect they thought I would fold up as usual and tell Henry he couldn't have his bit of land. They were wrong. It seemed I was growing a few teeth and claws as I got older. Grrr... Someone needed to stand up for poor old Henry, and that chap was me.

Eileen was impressed. She told me she was proud of me for not being a complete wimp. Not exactly a compliment, but I took it as one from her! After a few days' standoff, I was taken to one side by a member of the committee and told that Henry could stay if I didn't make a song and dance over it, and if I promised that Eileen would continue to provide refreshments! Do not threaten to come between an Englishman and his cake, because they don't like it, and Eileen did make a truly amazing Victoria Sandwich. I bet Reg was furious and chewing up the carpet. He had issued his first diktat from carrot central, (aka the allotment office) and he got overruled. That showed him, the pompous old windbag.

I was beginning to enjoy letting it all out between the pages of my diary. It was solely my domain, and I took steps to ensure it stayed that way. Eileen hated spiders and I made a point of mentioning that the ones in the allotment shed were huge and hairy, so she and her feather duster kept well away. I always liked spiders. They were generally inoffensive and got a lot of stick when they just wanted to be left alone. Maybe I was one in a previous life.

Chapter 2

Into every life a little rain must fall, so they say, and some of it landed on me in 1959. Not a deluge, just a small sprinkle.

It seemed as if the moment I gave Henry a key to my shed he started to take over. I was always a neat, orderly person as a rule, but once Henry took up residence everything became complete chaos. Piles of books everywhere, half opened packets of seeds and biscuits, and about fifty rubber bands wound around the shed doorknob, which drove me bonkers.

There were so many books in the shed that Daffy took to sleeping on the table because he could not get to his corner. We were both feeling the squeeze and it got to the point where I could stand it no longer. Eileen suggested I talk to Clara about it, hopefully when Claudie was around, so there were no misunderstandings.

I took her advice and went next door for a few words. Clara rolled her eyes, and Claudie said, 'Oh dear, it's not the first time.'

Clara just sighed as if she had heard it all too many times before.

Henry, it seemed, had previous form on this score. He was naturally messy, and he got so enthusiastic about a new project that he often forgot that there were other people involved. They promised to have a chat to him about it.

Claudie told me, 'Dad will probably be very sorry and move the books, then you can set a few rules. He has always been keen to learn but he needs reigning in sometimes.'

So, I got my shed back. We had a bookshelf each, and Daffy reclaimed his cat basket. Henry was obviously embarrassed, and he put out his hand to apologise, saying he hoped he hadn't lost the best friend he'd ever had. I went a bit pink at the ears and reassured him that it was all fine, then we had a cup of tea and a chocolate biscuit to show that everything was back to normal.

Henry laughed out loud and said, 'I love you British, you can solve anything if you have a cuppa in your hands. Just think, there might never have been a war if the Fuhrer had been a tea drinker!'

He brought me a book from his shop to say sorry for crowding me. It was about Wagner because Henry knew I liked him. How thoughtful he was; he never could stand Wagner himself. It was one of the few things we disagreed on in those early days, but we were both rather fond of Nat King Cole.

Henry was really coming along with his patch of ground and looking forward to harvesting potatoes. His joy at every leaf and flower was infectious, like a child discovering nature for the first time. He told me in a complicated world where everything moved fast, it was good to stop and enjoy the simple things in life. I was beginning to think he might be a bit of a philosopher on the quiet.

Eileen, bless her, took Clara under her wing and she persuaded her to join the WI. For Eileen, the WI was a major part of her life like her religion, and she was hoping that Clara would get involved and make some new friends. They'd been very kind to us when Terry had been ill—as well as all the lifts, Clara had left us prepared food on the back doorstep, so Eileen wouldn't have to start cooking when we got in from the hospital. I will say one thing for my Mrs, she knew when someone had done her a good turn, and she always tried to pay it back in some way.

Eileen's sister, Beryl, thought that the WI was just a load of silly housewives making jam and she considered herself far too sophisticated to join. Eileen thought that Beryl would not know a jam pan from a coal bucket, and she would be equally useless with both of them! It was true—Beryl always had the most beautifully lacquered nails and manicured hands, mainly because they had a daily woman who cleaned and cooked for them, as well as a gardener. She did not do a thing in the house, except look decorative and spend hours on the telephone to her friends.

If I remember it correctly, I spent one rainy September afternoon that year hiding in the shed. Not the allotment shed, the one at the bottom of the garden where we kept the mower. I lied and said I was doing a bit of maintenance before the winter, when I was actually reading the paper and finishing a particularly gripping novel. A lurid private eye thriller that Eileen thought was tat. She could talk. All her novels were romantic drivel.

Why was I hiding? That was easy. Eileen was making jam, which she hated doing. It made her ratty and bad tempered. She would snap like a bulldog if you got within snarling distance of the kitchen.

She could have just bought the stuff, but for Eileen it wasn't just jam, it was warfare in a jar; close combat confection, and we all suffered. Even Eric, if he got under her feet. She made all sorts of things with soft fruit from the allotment. She bottled it and even preserved some in booze for the Christmas trifle, but the rest got made into jam. We had a surfeit of pretty much everything that year.

She loved making chutneys and pickles for the WI to sell and they were very highly thought of. She made piccalilli just for me, because I loved it on a cheese sandwich. Jam, however, was her...dammit, now what do they call it...? oh yes, her nemesis.

When Eileen had reached working age, she'd been taken on at that big house in Ireland. There had been one other young girl there, named Dora. This Dora was foul and used to call Eileen all sorts of horrible names because she was from an orphanage. They had to share an attic room and a bed, which did not go down well with either of them.

Now the idea was that both girls got a six-month trial where they would learn domestic skills. At the end of the six months, if found satisfactory, the cook would take on one girl and the housekeeper the other to work as a parlour maid. If found wanting, Eileen would have returned to the orphanage in disgrace and would have ended up in a factory somewhere or working in the laundry.

When the time was up, both girls were given a chance to show off what they had learned. One of the tasks was making raspberry jam for the cook. Dora did it perfectly and was horribly smug, but Eileen burnt hers. She told me she remembered bursting into tears and running off. The cook found her and said she wasn't going to get very far in life if she dissolved every time someone did better than she did, and she needed to learn to accept defeat gracefully. Eileen told me she sniffled back that she didn't give two figs about stupid Dora. She was upset because it was such a bloody waste of some really lovely fruit and an awful lot of sugar.

In the end, the cook said that she would take Eileen anyway, because she didn't want a flighty little piece like Dora in her kitchen, and that Eileen was a good, honest hardworking girl who would listen and wanted to learn.

She had four years there and she did eventually learn to make jam. Now her nemesis was her friend, awful Vera Bulstrode from the post office. Vera B won the WI first prize for her jam three years in a row—1958 to 1960—always pipping Eileen at the post, so there was a certain amount of tension whenever the dreaded 'J' word was mentioned.

Chapter 3

1960 turned out to be quite a year. The rain fell on us. Both, literally and figuratively.

My goodness me, we had the most terrible storm, lashing rain like I have never seen before and wind like the gates of hell had just opened. The allotments were a mess and everything got flattened. Loads of things were ruined, ripped from the plant before they were even half grown.

Henry and I were out from early morning, along with all the other plot holders. Eileen, dressed in wellies and a headscarf, came to see if she could help. So did Clara, who took one look and dashed off again quick smart. She came back with a huge, flattish looking basket and started to pick up all the tiny onions and carrots, which had been washed from the ground, aubergines, peppers the size of your thumb and any abandoned courgettes, cucumbers and peas that she could get her hands on.

Henry told her gently, 'The vegetables are too small for us to eat for dinner, sweetheart.'

And she told him, 'Stop patronising me, I know what I am doing. Go and boil your head.' In German, of course, but the meaning was perfectly clear. Then she bustled off again, this time with Eileen in tow, leaving the two of us completely mystified.

When we popped home later, there were interesting aromas coming from our kitchen and I swore I could smell curry. They obviously didn't need us around, so we went to Henry's for a sneaky beer instead. When we had drunk enough to get brave and go and see what they were up to, we found them sitting on the back step, smoking away like a couple of old sailors. Rather surprisingly, there was also a bottle of homemade schnapps and two glasses. I tried that stuff one Christmas. Henry's brother-in-law used to send it over - you could have launched a ruddy Sputnik with it!

Considering my old girl didn't approve of strong drink, and Clara had to be careful because of her medication, they had been hitting the sauce pretty hard. Mind you, two glasses would probably have got you to the moon and back.

Eileen told me they had been pickling all afternoon. She was damned right, they had — and not just the vegetables from the look of it. Henry explained that Clara's grandmother was Danish and had passed on the recipe for a wonderful, sweet mustard pickle that used up any scraps of vegetable you cared to throw into it. It took about six months to mature but the wait would be worth it. There were jars of it all lined up on the kitchen table, so I hoped he was right.

Eventually he took his better half home, and I piloted mine up the stairs for a nap. She dragged me in with her. When I protested and said there were gentlemanly rules about that sort of thing (just for the look of it, you understand) she told me to shut up and enjoy it, which I have to say I did rather.

The next shower of rain fell on Henry. One Sunday morning, he got a call from the ironmongers next door, to say that the bookshop had been vandalised. He beetled off, then returned an hour later in a terrible state. Someone had been very busy pouring red paint over the windows and to finish the job they'd written absolute filth all down the walls.

The six of us, Terry and Claudie included, went down to help him out. We were scrubbing and cleaning until our fingers were raw. The paint was old and sticky, like someone had been storing it in the shed for a long time, waiting for an opportunity to use it. Maybe they had been storing up their hatred too. The police could do little except take a statement. I imagined that as most of them had served in the war, or had fathers who had; they probably had divided loyalties anyway.

We got some of it off and Terry painted over the writing in black, until we could think of a way to get rid of it. He asked a lecturer at the university to suggest something chemical that might do the trick.

Clara insisted on coming with us, although Henry didn't want her to. She told him quite plainly that she had seen it all before and was immune to it. This worried Henry greatly, because, as he pointed out, she should have felt something. Locking the pain away did her no good, as her mental state was fragile at the best of times.

Henry was very angry – well, who could blame him? I thought he just wanted to get hold of the person who did it and smack their face against a wall until they stopped howling. That was how I would feel if it were my shop. Not that I would have done it, just that I might have felt like it. He told me it was nothing to do with the perpetrator. He felt angry because a part of him thought he bloody deserved it just for being German. He was always haunted by guilt. He found it hard to even comprehend that the full horror of the Nazi final solution was carried out by his own country and fellow countrymen. I tried to soothe him with the fact that other countries also committed acts of extreme brutality for which we should all have felt the deepest shame.

He gave me a filthy look and snapped back, 'What do you know about it, George? Your side won. Nobody is going to paint your front door with dog shit, are they!'

What could I possibly say in return?

Clara apologised on his behalf, but I told her there was no need. I think she had words with him. More than a few, because he did say sorry and he thanked us all for helping him clear up the mess. They lived with national guilt every day of their lives. The guns had stopped firing, but for them, and for so many others, there was no lasting peace. He was a good man and a kind and honourable one. A rational creature who had to come to terms with the sad fact that much of the world hated him and his family, even though they had done nothing wrong personally. The whole German nation suffered collective punishment.

Everything settled down again, and life resumed its familiar and regular pattern. I was busy discovering the pure joy that a real friendship can bring. Henry became a brother to me—the feeling of closeness was new to both of us. Henry had two sisters, and I was an only child. Sometimes we sneaked off for a quiet pint when we were supposed to be at the allotment. Our treat now and again. It felt rather racy to be slipping down the pub. Before Henry had come along, I would never have dared in case Eileen found out. He made me feel brave, and anyway I liked beer. I still do.

Henry decided he was going to have a go at some home-brew that we could keep in the shed. I had a feeling it might be a disaster, with corks popping off everywhere. He had such an inquisitive nature that you couldn't help but find his enthusiasm endearing, if a trifle messy. Henry was always messy. How a man with such a clever, ordered brain could be so incredibly untidy has always been beyond me.

Schnapps aside, Eileen disapproved of drinking anything more than a nip of sherry, because her stepfather had been a drunk who'd often hit her mother until she'd left him. I sometimes wonder if that was one of the reasons Eileen chose me as a husband, because I was always quiet and compliant. I would never have raised my hand to a woman, or a man for that matter. If we ever came to blows, Eileen would have made mincemeat out of me anyway. I am eternally grateful that we never had to find out.

This subject was on my mind at the time, because a third shower of rain appeared in the form of an unexpected visitor. Eileen's awful sister, Beryl, came to stay with us. She had a shiner on her that any boxer would be proud of, because her Charlie had lost his temper and given her a fourpenny one. It was not the first time and sadly it was not the last. We all knew the routine. She would be tearful and distressed, vow that she was leaving '*that bastard Charlie*' and then go back to him. She usually hid the bruises with makeup, but this time her eye was beyond a bit of powder.

It was odd. Charlie was not usually '*a bastard*', as she called him. He was generally Mr Charm. He was not some drunken slob either. He was a bank manager, and they lived a comfortable life in Hastings. They'd never had kids, so they often indulged themselves. Every now and then Beryl would do something that made Charlie snap, and he could not control his temper, so he thumped her.

It did make me wonder what else went on beyond the doilies and lace curtains of other middle-class homes. I am sure there were many well-kept secrets. Most of us put on some sort of front, don't we? I sometimes looked at people on the bus and imagined what their lives were like behind closed door; it was a sort of game I played to amuse myself on the journey when my work friend, Ronnie Brown, was not chattering away beside me.

Our Beryl didn't want the neighbours or Charlie's colleagues from the bank to see her, and you could only bump into so many doors before tongues started to wag, so she came to us to lick her wounds.

Eileen was always a good sister to Beryl. As usual, they talked and made plans for Beryl's future without Charlie. In reality both of them knew it was never going to happen.

When he turned up all contrite and sorrowful on our doorstep, I was always dispatched to talk to Charlie '*man to man*'. I found this difficult, not because I was afraid of him, quite the opposite to be honest, I could cheerfully have wrung his neck. I was a long way from being the best of husbands, I know that, but for all my faults, I would never have considered hitting my wife. There were times when I could have strangled her, and no doubt she felt the same way about me, but that was as far as it went. Any man who uses his fists instead of his brain is, and always will be, beyond contempt. Charlie would tell me he was sorry and that she drove him to it. Life with Beryl was not easy, but he was no angel when it came to spending lavishly.

This particular time, a huge bill for some new furniture from a posh department store had sent him over the edge. I listened, just as Eileen always listened to Beryl. We offered good advice, which they always ignored, then they went home to make amends, which started the cycle anew. My advice to Charlie was always the same. Walk away if things are getting heated and set proper spending limits for both of you. He was a bank manager, for goodness' sake. Eileen told Beryl to leave him for good. Beryl always replied that she was too old to start afresh and then she reflected that their comfortable lifestyle was probably worth the odd wallop now and again. She was a silly, affected woman who put more importance on material things than she did in having a marriage with a bit of respect where she wasn't going to get the living daylights knocked out of her. Eileen knew that there was nothing she could do. If she had started on Charlie, she would have fallen out with Beryl, and her sister would have had nobody to turn to next time. We all knew there would definitely be a next time.

So, what with one thing and another, we had quite a lot of rain that year. I was still a happier man, because I had found a true best friend. Who would have guessed that would happen when I'd helped him to carry his box of books into the house? It wasn't all brilliant. Clara, who was always fragile, was going through another period of depression. Eileen told me she was very worried about her because she seemed so down. Henry described Clara as, '*The wreckage of a human being who sometimes sinks beneath the waves*'. All he could do was wait until she surfaced and hope that she would float back to him. As we moved into 1961 and my birthday rolled around, I could only hope that the showers would cease for a while.

Chapter 4

In early 1961, we had to say goodbye to our cat, Daffy. He was getting on a bit, and he suddenly developed this nasty-looking lump on his back. The vet said it was cancer, so we had to have him put to sleep. We all missed him, even Eileen.

I remember when he'd arrived. Terry, who'd been about six or seven, had rushed into the scullery all excited, with this tiny bundle of fluff in his hands. Eileen moved into rescue mode and, within five minutes, Daffy was wrapped in a warm towel and happily licking milk from an eye dropper she had found in the first-aid kit. She took him upstairs and once he was installed in a box by the bed, she would feed him whenever he cried. She told me it was no worse than having a baby, and she showed the rest of us how to do it so that we could all take a shift. He was a gentle, good-natured soul, who politely ate his mice outside the shed and never sat on the paper when I was trying to do the crossword. I buried him at the allotment in a sunny place, under the daffodils he was named for. It was where he used to sleep as he got older. Eileen said that she liked the cat because he was far less trouble than I was and kept himself to himself.

Henry made Daffy a polished cross, which was sweet of him. He was surprisingly good with his big hands, particularly with wood. He used carpentry as a way of distracting himself from his problems with Clara. She got very depressed and at times was quite confused and erratic. He worried about her all the time, and he was constantly looking for ways to help her. He decided to encourage her to write down how she felt on the good days as well as the bad ones, so he gave her a diary just like mine. He thought it might help her to unpack herself privately. I knew from experience that it helped to write out your most private thoughts and feelings without fear of someone else reading them. Once or twice there had been tears at the allotment. Watching Clara struggle was very hard on him. He opened up to me and I sat and listened to him like a good friend should. He sobbed as he told me that he was exhausted with worry. She didn't want to go into a mental hospital again, but Henry thought he might not have a choice, for her own safety. He needed to earn them a living from the shop by building the business and he couldn't do it when he was worried sick that Clara would come to harm while he was away. He told me when they lived in Scotland she disappeared for a couple of weeks and she was brought home by the police, wet and confused, with no real memory of where she had been.

Claudie came on a week's visit from Scotland. She had almost completed her course, and she was looking for a first job nearer home, so she could help out with her mother and give her father a break now and again. Despite his own problems, Henry always seemed to have time for my worries. We often talked at the shed. It felt good to be able to let it out sometimes. He found my relationship with Eileen absolutely fascinating. One time when I retreated to the shed after Eileen and I had words regarding my failure to do something or other, I found Henry already there reading the paper. He made me a cup of tea and then he said he didn't understand why we stayed together if it was always so difficult to communicate.

I sighed and commented, 'We have got into the habit of living together, I suppose. We don't hate each other, but we don't get along terribly well so we have had to learn tolerance instead, or maybe it's indifference.'

I sipped my tea and tried to calm down.

Henry smiled. 'So, you just carry on. How very British.'

I shrugged and said wearily, 'I think it's what a lot of people do; they try to make the best of things. Eileen is not a bad person, she's quite a decent old stick really, very capable and strong because she has had to be. We annoy each other because we are very different people.'

Henry smiled and said he understood.

It was wonderful to have a friend I could talk to about pretty much anything. At times, it felt like we had nobody else in the world to turn to except each other. I am not entirely sure what I would have done without him. Both of us had rather troubled marriages in different ways and it was a great relief to know that there was someone else out there who understood.

He came into my life and changed it in so many ways, generally for the better, with the exception of his maddening untidiness which was easily forgiven - most of the time! Eileen thought I was a trifle untidy. Good grief, if she had ever shared a workspace with Henry, she would have had him summarily shot by a WI firing squad, up against the potting shed.

Talking of Eileen, this is a funny thing. She embraced the television age and became hooked on a programme all about life in the North. Until that point, the television had been my domain, and she had full use of the radio in the kitchen, as she said TV was for idiots. She loved *Coronation Street* and the ups and downs of its residents. It was all a bit flat caps and, '*Two pints of mild please, Jack*' for me, but Eileen loved it and so did Beryl. They used to have these tedious telephone conversations about the characters. It completely mystified me. Way more '*kitchen-sink drama*' than *The Archers* or *Mrs Dale's Diary*, which she used to enjoy. I got shoved off my perch so that she could watch her programme. I didn't really mind. I just enjoyed a nice quiet read of my book until it finished and that awful tinny music started up.

Another amusing thing I remember from around that time, was me tearing my trousers climbing up on the shed to retrieve a yellow balloon that was caught around that silly pointy bit of wood on the end of the roof. To this day, I have no idea of its name or function, if indeed it ever had one. Henry gave me a leg-up to retrieve it, but I caught my pocket on the way down. I ripped my trousers as I slipped, knocking Henry into the mud. He laughed himself stupid. I told him to shut up, but it was pretty funny, and I ended up laughing too. We strolled home together, filthy and grinning like a couple of naughty six-year-olds. Eileen was watching the end of Coronation Street when I got in all muddy with my Y-fronts on display. They were, as I recall, a lurid purple paisley affair, an abomination of a Christmas present from Beryl which Eileen refused to hang out on the line. She was glued to a particularly gripping storyline about a gas leak. She switched off the set with a sigh as if she were counting to 10 and ran her hand over the polished top to remove any dust which had dared to settle. Then she turned and gave me the death-stare; a look she used to reserve for Terry when he came home after one of his adventures.

I cowered by the dining room door as she tutted and muttered, 'Oh my word, look at the state of you, George. Will you never grow up?' But she was smirking as she said it, and the hideous pants went into the bin.

There was a tag on the balloon string. It was from a Dutch school child. We had to fill in the back and send it to them so they could see how far it had travelled.

Henry, who was sitting at his kitchen table said, 'It's come from Kerkrade, George, a town which is right on the border with Germany. I will write them a message in German and pop it in the post, maybe they will win a prize. What are the chances of a Dutch balloon making it all the way to our shed? Life is random sometimes, isn't it?'

We never did find out if they won, which was a shame because I felt invested in the competition, after all, despite it costing me the pocket on my best allotment trousers, I was finally free of those awful pants.

We continued working the allotment together, watching the things we had planted grow and flower. Our friendship was growing deeper too. Henry became a pivotal part of my life, and I could not imagine how I ever managed without him in it.

Chapter 5

The rest of 1961 was a rollercoaster year for me. I rode its dips and hollows, and I enjoyed highs like I had never known before. It was the time in my life when I changed and started to become me.

It all began with what seemed to be a bit of an off day for Henry. This turned into a long campaign of what I can only describe as freezing me out of my own shed, would you believe.

Henry was really surly with me, like I had offended him in some way. At times he was cold and distant, bordering on the downright rude. This was not like him at all. I could not make head nor tail of his behaviour, and I began to wonder if his continuing problems with Clara were weighing him down. All I can say on the subject is that it was hurtful to be treated in this cool, off-hand manner by someone I had become extremely close to and considered to be the best friend I'd ever had. I did try to be understanding, but I was running out of ideas. If I am honest, my patience was wearing a bit thin too.

My shed was where I went to avoid conflict with Eileen, not start round two with another challenger, but every time I went to the allotment I was faced with an extremely obstinate and grumpy German bear. It got to a point where I did not enjoy being with him very much at all and I did my best to avoid the allotment when he was there. This caused me much pain, because there were lots of things that needed doing in the spring, and I hated seeing everything getting all weedy and neglected. I decided to give him a few more days to change his behaviour before I took him down to the pub and had it out with him, man to man. I never liked arguments, but I could not see any other way of dealing with it but head on.

He did get a bit better, and he even suggested a game of chess one afternoon when it was tipping it down. I wasn't going to ignore the faint hand of friendship when it was offered, so we set up the board. Henry always did take ages to make a move and that day he was particularly slow, so I started to get a bit ticked off with him for faffing around. It felt for all the world like he was deliberately trying to annoy me.

Tetchy, I drummed my fingers on the underside of the table and muttered, 'Do you think you could possibly get a move on, only I have a dentist appointment three weeks next Thursday and I wouldn't want to miss it.'

Henry looked up and gave me a slow smile. 'Do you know how adorable you are when you are being all cross and British?'

Then he leaned forward and kissed me - a real smacker it was, right on the lips!

It only lasted a second before I pulled away, stunned into silence. Henry went very pink. Then he said in a soft voice,

'I have been wondering what it would be like to kiss you, George. Until this afternoon, I never had the courage. Now I have, I can tell you that it felt absolutely wonderful, and I don't regret it for a single moment. Just recently, I have realised that I care about you far more than just friendship and I need to know if you feel the same about me?'

He rolled his eyes, then continued, 'It's pretty soppy, I know, but lately I have been dreaming about you, the sort of dreams a fellow could never tell his wife. I know I have been a bit of a pig to you and for that I'm sorry, but I have been torturing myself with guilt. I love you, George. There, I said it, and I need to know if you love me back because it is killing me not knowing.'

I recovered my voice and then I asked him, 'What the bloody hell do you think you're doing? I'm truly sorry, Henry, but this has got to stop, right now. I don't know where you got the idea from, but I'm not that sort of a chap. I'm a regular Joe, always have been about that sort of thing and it isn't for me, OK. Let us be very clear, if you feel the need to jump up and kiss me every time we play chess, then you are jolly well going to have to find a new opponent.'

Henry, his face turning beetroot, mumbled, 'Be honest. You must feel it too, this growing bond between us. There are days when I simply cannot wait to get home and come to the allotment to see you, George. When Clara is having one of her bad days and everything is grey, you make the sun come out and I love you for it, I honestly do.'

I stared at him across the table. The words I needed would not come, not an unusual situation for me. In the end I shook my head, stuttering, 'Please go.'

He retreated from the shed without another word. I watched him striding away through the rain until he was out of view. I stood in the doorway, anxious, utterly bewildered and without the slightest clue as to what I should do next. I can't describe exactly how I felt at that moment. Empty is probably the best I can do, or perhaps hollow would sum it up better, anyway, it was awful. Shocked and shaky, I went back inside and closed the door behind me. I slipped the latch and locked it because I needed to think with no interruptions.

I sat for the longest time. I kept on wondering, over and over about why it had happened. When occasional intimacy occurred with Eileen it had physically been pleasant, at least for me, but I cannot say it moved the world. That might have been different if one of us didn't consider sex to be a bit of a household chore, like the ironing or scrubbing the front step, you know, just a tiresome thing that needs to be got through, when you would rather be doing something more interesting.

Nobody was encouraged to examine their sexual preferences in my young days. If you were lucky, you got to know the birds and the bees on a very functional level. As a teenager, I'd once had an excruciating 10-minute conversation with my widowed clergyman father on the subject. The thought of it still makes me go cold and that was only about what they used to call *the solitary vice.* Homosexuality and being kissed by your best friend in a garden shed was not a subject that we'd ever covered. I am pretty sure I would have remembered it if we had. The thought that there might be any alternative was not something I'd ever really had much time to ponder. I had hardly discovered sex before I'd been given a ready-made family and whisked off to the desert as cannon fodder for whoever fancied taking a pot shot at me.

I was in a proper old pickle about things and no mistake. I didn't want to lose Henry as a friend. The thought that he might not be in my life made me utterly miserable. I replayed that kiss in my head about a hundred times, like a newsreel at the cinema, and I asked myself a load of searching questions. Could I have given Henry the wrong impression? Did I accidentally do something to encourage him? In the end I came to the only conclusion that made sense.

In my young days, lads got up to all sorts of mischief. It was called sowing your wild oats. You would probably have been forgiven for a youthful indiscretion or two, but the one thing you dare not be, was homosexual. Even if you were a queer, you kept it hidden, deep inside yourself, because the price of discovery was to lose everything including your liberty.

Henry was absolutely right, there was definitely something there. I had been noticing it for weeks, a feeling way beyond friendship, and it was growing. It was bloody terrifying and yet strangely wonderful all at the same time. I had also been having plenty of 'those' sorts of dreams about him, along with many other thoughts of that nature that I had pushed to the back of my mind in shame. I couldn't deny it any longer. I knew for sure that the kiss, however brief, was probably the most exciting moment in my life.

Seeing Henry for a tea at the allotment, or to work on the plants, made me extraordinarily happy. If I got into a bit of a stuttering muddle about things, Henry just smiled and said, 'Breathe, George, then try it again, but slower this time.'

He never laughed or got impatient with me, and he gave me so much confidence. I kept asking myself what it would be like if Henry was no longer there. Deep down, I was absolutely sure it would be unbearable.

I admitted to myself that I wanted him and what is more, I wanted him to want me back. Oh my goodness, how I wanted that to happen. The idea of being with him made me breathless in a way I thought just happened in books, for silly teenaged girls and hopeful middle-aged ladies to enjoy.

I wanted to rush out of the shed and go and find him to say I was sorry. Then I wanted to drag him off somewhere quiet for way more than just one kiss. I was ashamed to admit to myself that I had only the most basic idea about what two men who desired each other would do when they were alone together, but I could take a jolly good guess - and I wanted to find out.

I assumed that my hidden feelings were a middle-aged crisis thing. I half hoped they would fade away and die if I ignored them, probably because I did not have the courage to face how I felt. For the first time, I faced up to the fact that I was most definitely having homosexual feelings and was apparently well on my way to becoming someone who preferred to have a choice; or perhaps it was always there but I needed to meet the right person for me to realise it. We had a chap in the army who fancied both men and women. He used to joke about it in private and say that it "doubled his chances of a date on a Saturday night".

Admitting to myself that I found Henry very attractive was an incredible relief. When he'd kissed me, deep in that chamber of horrors where your darkest thoughts reside, I'd wanted him to. Oh, I'd pushed him away and told him he was being ridiculous, but it was me that was being ridiculous, not him. Someone had opened the door to the dungeon and all the shadowy thoughts that I had locked away with my guilt and fear came marching up the stairs and out into the light. They were free and I wanted them to stay that way.

In the Sunday newspapers of the time, queer men were always portrayed as perverts, unmanly limp-wristed fellows who were a blot on our society. All I can say is that there was nothing in the least perverted about that kiss. My wrists were no limper than they had been that morning, and as far as I knew the sun hadn't exploded, and the ten plagues of Egypt had not descended upon Radcliffe Road. If Henry had walked through the door of the shed at that moment, I would have been very willing and happy to repeat the experience of kissing him, and a whole lot more if I had my way.

I kept thinking of the things he did which amused me. Then I had to say, 'For goodness' sake, George Potter, you are a middle-aged husband and father, stop mooning about like some silly schoolboy.' But it was no good. I couldn't stop it, and what is more, I didn't want to.

There were so many emotions all mixed up together. I wanted to cry and laugh at the same time. I had no idea how it would end, but I knew I wanted to find out, so I went off to find him. Of course, he was hiding, which was awful, and the situation became considerably worse from that point on. He was embarrassed and avoiding me like the plague. Then Eileen got wind that something was up between us.

She asked me one evening while she was washing up, 'What on earth has happened, George? You two are usually as thick as thieves, now he's gone AWOL. Did you boys have some sort of a bust up?'

She eyed me suspiciously over the dishcloth as she scrubbed mince off a saucepan and held it up for inspection. Putting down my paper, I replied that we were indeed having a slight tiff over what we should be using to treat the fungus on the roses, and that Henry was sulking because he was in the wrong.

Eileen snorted back. 'Oh, for goodness' sake, George. Can't you two boys play nicely? There isn't a single one of you that isn't five years old underneath.' Then she went back to scrubbing the pots.

I wanted to clear the air, but Henry refused to speak to me. In the end, I left him a note on the table at the shed asking him to meet me on Saturday afternoon to talk things through, and he scribbled a curt line on the end of it saying he would be there.

He was waiting in his usual spot at the table by the gardening magazines. When I saw him through the shed window looking all lost and fearful, I knew the battle was over.

I wanted to rush in and give him a great big hug. He knew it too - I could see it in his face when I got to the doorway. I shut the door and slipped the latch behind me as he started to speak, filling the yawning awkwardness between us.

'I can't help it, George. Jesus knows I have tried, but it does no good. Every time I see you, I want you. Not just like that. I could get that anywhere if I hung around in the right places, or paid for it I suppose. I am not explaining myself very well, but I know that I want all of you, every single bit.'

He was looking down at the floor between his feet, as if he couldn't quite trust himself to say anything to my face. I wanted him to look up and see my face, and to know that I wanted him too, but he continued his conversation with the floorboards.

'There has always been this empty space inside, a hollow piece of me. I knew it was there, but for obvious reasons I locked it away. When I was young, the thought that I might be a queer completely terrified me. I beat every impulse down and I got myself married off as soon as I could. Did you know we were only 18? My father said we were far too young, but we went ahead anyway.

'I was a good caring husband to Clara, at least I always tried to be. We had a happy marriage and a good sex life until she got ill, but I don't want to pretend anymore. You handed me the key to myself. I opened the door and now it won't close again, mainly because I don't want it to, George.'

He went quiet for a bit, then he looked up and said with a smile, 'I love you and there isn't a damned thing I can do about it.' Then he sighed, such a weary defeated sound. 'I'm tired, George. Tired of hiding, and I don't want to fight anymore against something that seems to me to be absolutely natural and right.'

Still standing, I watched as a tear rolled down his face, and I gave in absolutely and completely. I wanted to tell him how I felt, but of course the words wouldn't come out. Oh, my goodness that was a moment, breathless and world changing. A West End stage could not have surpassed the dramatic tension between two middle-aged men in cardigans standing in a garden shed, lost among the flowerpots and the muddy Wellington boots.

Sometimes actions speak louder than words. In my case they had to. I pulled down the blind then I went to him, willingly and without the slightest fear for the disgrace that lay ahead for both of us. I could feel him physically shaking and I realised that Henry was every bit as scared and excited as I was.

He said something to me in German. Later, he told me it meant '*Oh you are a funny little thing*'. He stroked my face and he called me Georgie for the first time. I liked it. Our lips stayed locked together and nobody said sorry for anything. Nat King Cole was singing softly on the wireless and I could hear the rain leathering it down on the tin roof, but the sound was nothing compared to my beating heart.

For me, it was like the world had suddenly clicked into place. Everything felt absolutely right. Like two halves of a broken cup, we fitted together perfectly, and we could not stop. It's so very hard to describe, as if everything in my life up to this point had been from a duller, greyer world and now the sun had come out, or a light switch had been pulled. We were completely overwhelmed by the power of what we were feeling for each other. Both of us knew that things could not go any further. We daren't even think about that. Admitting our feelings was more than enough.

It was a long, and I have to say extremely passionate, kiss, and it truly meant the world to us. We cast aside pretence and gave in to all the feelings we had been holding back. We were married men, solid citizens and fathers and we knew that we were risking everything, but at that moment it didn't seem to matter. What else can I say about it, except that something that felt so very right could not have been so very wrong. We needed each other and a team of wild horses could not have dragged us apart. Neither of us was exactly proud of the fact that we were cheating on our wives, or at least wanting to. The situation had us more than a bit confused, but it was something we were going to have to work out for ourselves. I never thought a wild love affair could happen to someone like me, not in a million years. Affairs happened to film stars and people like Charlie who had a certain cheeky charisma, a fat wallet and a sharp suit. He also had all the patter needed to charm some unsuspecting young woman into his bed, which he did frequently according to Beryl.

Meek little chaps like me, did not have affairs. We made good fathers, we taught our children how to ride their bikes, we mowed the lawn and turned out at football and rugby matches cheering from the sidelines in all weathers, when we would much rather have been inside with a cup of tea and the paper. Not anyone's idea of a secret lover. And yet somehow it happened to me.

Mind you, when I was 14 a rather good-looking kitchen maid at school had kissed me. It had been during a cricket match and we'd both been in the long grass behind the pavilion. I had sneaked away for a nice quiet read in the sun, and she was on her tea break smoking a cigarette. I remember walking away with regret, because I was up to bat and they were calling my name. I was all shaky with the excitement of forbidden fruit. It didn't stay a secret for long because one of the other lads had seen us and raced back to tell the others that George Potter was in the long grass with Hilda. I was a rather surprising school Casanova for about a week, and I began to feel quite the man of the world. With the wisdom of age, I wonder if she did it for a bet?

As it turned out, the lovely Hilda was pretty high on several teenage fantasy lists. At an all-boys boarding school, a kiss from a pretty girl of around your own age was a rare prize. Most of our female teachers had whiskers and faces like spoiled vinegar. That shy 14-year-old boy was long gone, but it was the same feeling when Henry eventually left me at the shed. I was on top of the world, more than a bit aroused, and utterly confused, all at the same time. He didn't want to leave me, and I didn't want him to go, but he had to get back to Clara, and Eileen would have been wondering where on earth I had got to. That other world, the grey and ordinary one beyond the door of the shed, was calling us and no matter how hard we tried to block it out, we had to listen to it.

We agreed that I would wait at least 10 minutes before I followed him home, so I was left alone with my thoughts and a glass of cold water. I sat worrying, picking fluff off the sleeve of my cardigan, acutely aware that this was not some romance from one of the daft stories Eileen liked to read. In a book, if it all went wrong you could turn the pages until you got to the happy ending. In real life, I had no idea how I was going to get through the next evening, let alone a love affair.

I imagined the conversation over my Saturday egg and chips. *'Hello, dear, the spuds are still doing well, oh and by the way I think I am in love with our next-door neighbour. He kissed me today and I rather liked it. Pass the mustard will you, old thing.'*

Well, I did go home, and I got one of Eileen's looks - one of her special squinty ones that made you feel like an absolute worm. I was sure she could read my mind. She was washing potatoes under the garden tap, in the place where she used to keep the mangle and do all the washing before we got the twin tub. It was very handy for messy jobs because it had a drain. Anyway, I could tell I was in for it because I had been an age at the allotment.

Clara waved over the fence, and Eileen went to talk to her. Then Henry appeared and we ended up chatting like neighbours do. Silly, ordinary things, about the new bin man who constantly dropped things on the step, mostly. We had to stand there with our wives and make small talk when barely half an hour before we had been all over each other in the shed. Then we said goodbye and we went indoors for dinner. It was the most normal, yet the most horrible conversation of my entire life. I was absolutely sure that Eileen knew exactly what had been going on. Of course she didn't, it was just guilt kicking in, but I felt completely wretched and an absolute beast.

When Henry closed his kitchen door, he gave me such a hot look of longing that it made me blush all over. If we are being completely candid, I had to take a few deep breaths and have a stern mental word with '*George Junior*' down below, to tell him to calm down and to behave himself in company. At the same time, Eileen was nagging me with, 'Buck up, George, stir your stumps and stop daydreaming—the table needs laying', or something similar. As you can imagine, I wasn't really listening.

I'd got my first taste of what the future held. Damned to be an eternal ping-pong ball, forever bouncing between my wife and family and the man I knew I loved. We had started something very much deeper than either of us could have imagined, but the way ahead seemed paved with thorns, not roses.

I got myself fully under control because Eileen's nagging could do that to a man; at full speed she was like a dose of bromide. I closed the door and went to do her bidding. I managed to get through my first evening as a fledgling philandering husband. Eileen served up sausage and mash instead of the usual - neither of us spoke much.

She noticed I wasn't eating, and she grumbled, 'What's up with you? It's one of your favourites. I thought you might like a bit of a change.'

I mumbled back, 'I'm not awfully hungry.'

She growled, 'I do hope you and Henry haven't been gorging yourselves on biscuits while you have been at the allotment, George. You know I don't like you filling up and then not eating. It is such a waste of the good food that I have cooked you. The problem with you, George Potter, is that you are spoilt. Any other man might appreciate my efforts. Still, I am glad to see that you and Henry are pals again.'

I lied and said, 'I have a slight headache, dear, not feeling quite tickety-boo this evening.'

I could hardly tell her that I was bloody petrified of giving myself away. My Eileen was a master at spotting a guilty face. I sometimes thought she could smell it out, like a ferret or a bloodhound in curlers. Once she found a juicy nugget, she would not let you go until you gave in and confessed.

I went to bed early just to be alone with my thoughts, but I couldn't sleep, replaying the scene in the shed over and over again, feeling the excitement of being wanted by someone and the pleasure of wanting them back. I had my urges, the same as any other man, and we all need a bit of 'how's your father' now and again, but this was different. That brief liaison had us within seconds of ripping each other's clothes off. It was raw and powerful, but it was also very loving. A garden shed was hardly the setting for romance, but it could have been Paris for all we cared.

Henry had told me once he had a favourite uncle who the whole family knew was homosexual. His father's brother, Friedrich, was a bit naughty and he loved to have a good time. He was a regular at the Eldorado, probably the most famous queer bar in Berlin, before the war. Friedrich would tell Henry stories about the colourful nightlife and how it was a place where people were free to be themselves, which Henry found very compelling as a young man.

I recalled the touch of Henry's hand in mine and the smell of his aftershave as he held me close. I had rediscovered that forbidden fruit, and the taste was divine.

I woke up in a complete state. Eileen was snoring like a water buffalo next door. My mind was panicking about what I should do. The soppier sort of poet and writers of ladies' romances always say that to love is to suffer. I used to think this was complete tosh, now I thought they might have a point, because it was agony. When I did sleep, I had horrible dreams about confessing to Eileen that I was leaving her for someone else. I know this was rather jumping the gun, but my poor old subconscious didn't *know that. It was all messed up and wracked with guilt.*

We were sitting at the breakfast table in the dream, and she barked, 'Out with it, George Potter,' as she always did. Like a Sergeant Major to a new recruit who had gone AWOL.

I got all stuttery and nothing would come out right. Finally, I muttered, 'I am leaving you for someone else, Eileen.'

And she snapped back, 'Don't be so stupid. Who on earth would have you, George?'

It was all very stilted, like an old radio play or something, then it got really mad. Eric, our dog - technically he was Eileen's pug not mine - ratted on me to my wife and barked that he had seen me holding hands with Henry from next door and that in his frank opinion we were a couple of fairies. How offensive! I never did trust that wretched dog. I told Eric to keep his snout shut and I confessed to Eileen that I was running off with Henry. By then Eileen appeared to have turned into my old school headmaster. I was a salt cellar, so she wasn't listening anyway.

Breakfast next morning was truly awful. Eileen was being nice to me. By that I mean more than her usual practical indifference. There was bacon and eggs cooked just how I liked them, with fried bread. I sat there eating it, although I was so tired I really didn't want anything but a cup of tea. I had spent half the night trying to sort out the war that was going on in my head. Like a character from one of the ridiculous stories that Eileen loved to read, I felt 10 feet tall, as well as being as miserable as sin over one guilty kiss.

The next few days were a box of chocolates with no card. The sweet crunchy ones and those awful sickly orange creams that tasted like soap. If I saw Henry through the kitchen window walking up the garden, I wanted to go to him. If he saw me, he smiled and waved, and I smiled back like good neighbours do. It was maddening being so close and yet so far apart.

We burned to be together again, but it was not to be. Clara was ill with some bug and Henry couldn't leave her, so we had to be patient. I know how this sounds - terribly calculating, selfish and awful. Waiting for an opportunity to cheat on our wives. We had already done that mentally, so doing it physically was the next step. I did not want to hurt Eileen any more than Henry wanted to hurt Clara, but the pull we felt to be together was totally irresistible.

When love walks in the door, good sense flies out of the window, so they say, and that is where we found ourselves. We could not take any risks, because we knew full well that discovery would mean ruin for all of us.

Chapter 6

There followed six wonderfully frustrating weeks of joy and sadness, or honey and lemons, my dad called them - lose one to taste the other. My mother always said that life was the bee's sting and the butterfly's wing. She was a farmer's daughter, so it was probably a country saying from somewhere or other, who knows.

Eileen, dressed in her flowered housecoat and curlers, was already out washing the front step when I left for work one Monday morning. She stopped to take a pull on her cigarette as I waved goodbye, and she waved back. The wave meant nothing. Like most things in our marriage, it was just something that we had got used to doing and couldn't be bothered to stop. Any new habits required effort and neither of us had the energy, or indeed the enthusiasm to do that. We went along in our groove and kept the pain away with regular doses of boredom and familiarity.

I sat on the bus, a million miles away from the busy world outside. I would have missed my stop except for the fact that my friend, Ronnie Brown from accounts, was sitting a few rows behind me. He worked on the floor above and I had known him for years.

He tapped me on the shoulder and breezed, 'Buck up, George.'

And I realised that I had been daydreaming for most of the journey. We walked the rest of the way together. Ron was always a bit of a cheeky chappie, and he liked a chat.

'Penny for your thoughts, old lad. You look like you are on another planet this morning, mate,' he chirped.

I shrugged to indicate that it was nothing. We talked for a bit. I tried to be interested in his tales of the company amateur dramatic club's production of Gilbert and Sullivan's the Mikado. He was always trying to get me to join. That constant mixture of backslapping and backstabbing would never have been my thing and, anyway, I sing like a tuneless bullfrog.

Now and again, Eileen provided food for rehearsals and on one occasion a splendid cake for opening night, when their own bakers let them down at the last minute. We always got tickets, because you were expected to go, and there would have been frowns on the top floor if you didn't, but in reality, they were a willing but generally lousy troupe of talentless hams.

There were various company social activities that we were encouraged to support - I say '*encouraged*', but it was expected. Occasionally I turned out for the work's cricket team if they were short. I was never much of a batsman, but I could bowl a bit in my younger days. I can say with quiet pride that many a young clerk was taken off guard by the strength of a Potter delivery.

I thought to myself that Ronnie would probably have a fit if he knew about the current drama in my own life. It certainly outshone their onstage efforts. I imagined the look on Ronnie's face if I told him that yesterday Henry and I had managed a splendidly furtive half hour or so in the shed, holding hands under the table and listening to Gardeners' Question Time on the wireless. We were perfectly and blissfully content in each other's company. It beat the spots off the stupid Mikado, I can tell you. I tipped my hat to Ronnie and went off to the third floor, where I spent my days. I looked for all the world like any other drone on the way to the office, but inside I was singing with secret joy.

We learned to take our opportunities where we found them, but this was as far as things had gone - not for lack of trying. Our affair continued. Don't laugh, but Henry courted me in a rather gentle, old-fashioned sort of a way. He often left me little presents on the table in the shed. Once, there was a blue origami frog made from writing paper. It jumped when you pushed the back. Henry was very good with things like that. He told me his father had showed him how to make them when he'd been a small boy and had the measles. He wanted me to feel special and to show me how much he cared. I was thinking of writing him a poem to show him that I also cared about him, but I didn't want to make it all mushy.

When you are forced to be apart most of the time, it is easy to let doubts get in and pray on your mind. I think it was his way of saying, '*I am yours and you are mine, no matter how much the world feels like it is against us we have each other*'. It was by necessity a secret and, as yet, unconsummated love. We couldn't express how we felt about each other physically. That little shed was our whole world for the foreseeable future. We both hoped that one day we would find a way to be together elsewhere.

Neither of us was the devious type. Perhaps I should have asked my brother-in-law, Charlie, for some tips on conducting an intrigue. He spent more time going over the side than he did sitting in the damned boat. Beryl reckoned all men were like randy dogs sniffing around a lamp post and that given the slightest opportunity to stray, they would do it. Sad to say, and I would never have put myself in Charlie's league, she probably had a point, at least with some of us.

I came home from work one afternoon, ready to change and head for the allotment. When I walked into our kitchen, I found Eileen hard at work with her mouth full of pins, and Clara standing on the kitchen table, wearing nothing but her underthings. I apologised profusely and retreated back up the hall, my face white-hot with embarrassment. Although it was more than fifty years ago, I can still hear them laughing and Clara saying, '*Oh, poor old George!*'

They were making an outfit for Claudie's graduation ceremony. Clara was looking forward to the occasion enormously and it gave her a lift and something positive to focus on. Eileen told me it was a very smart suit in navy blue and that Clara would have '*toning accessories in shades of caramel and cream, with a rather chic little fascinator*', whatever the hell that was. Henry thought the fascinator might be one of those silly feathered hats they wore, that sort of perched on the head like a tiny chicken, but neither of us had any real clue. The complications of ladies' millinery affairs were way beyond the pair of us.

Henry had a new bow tie and shirt for the occasion. They wanted to make her as proud of them as they were of her, not that Claudie would have minded what they wore. She just wanted them with her on her special day. They bought Claudie pearls as a graduation present. Clara always did have exceptionally good taste.

I remember that Eileen and I were invited out for dinner that evening - not something that happened often. We went round to Eileen's friend, Vera. The memory still makes me shudder. She was a pretty good cook, although not in Eileen's league. The thing that made me shudder, was knowing we would have to have her back to ours for supper because it was '*polite*'. I do not like being rude about a lady, but she was a horrible old hag who'd always had a bit of a thing for me and what is more, she'd got drunk and pounced on me once when we'd had our little do for the Coronation in 1953.

It had been upstairs in the bedroom where we'd been putting the coats, and I'd only just escaped with my virtue intact. I had to lock myself in the bathroom to escape, and I could hear her outside prowling up and down like some hideous bear in a ginger wig. She was horrible sober so you can imagine how hateful the gossipy old witch was plastered.

I survived a very long night at Vera's, but I almost died from boredom en route. At one point, when she was describing yet another recipe for soup I nodded off and Eileen walloped me on the ankles to bring me back to life. Damn her, she had a powerful swing with that handbag.

In the early autumn of 1961, I found myself home alone and eating an illicit bacon sarnie at the allotment. Eileen disapproved of me taking breakfast with me, so I usually had to eat it indoors when I was keen to be off and doing.

Eileen had gone off to Beryl and Charlie's for the weekend, because they were having some sort of a posh do for Beryl's birthday and she was doing the catering and making a cake. Henry and Clara were also away, for Claudie's graduation in Scotland. I will admit I was rather enjoying it - the pressure was off on both sides. No wife, no would-be lover, no dog. Living a double life was exhausting, not to say frustrating, and at times utterly heart-breaking. I was going to do a bit of a weed and a tidy up and then take myself off for a treat; a swim and a massage.

The swimming baths were Victorian. A bit shabby, but rather wonderful - all high ceilings and decorated tiles. They still had a punishingly icy plunge pool and a steam room, one of few left. I was going to indulge myself, wrapped in a towel, to steam away my troubles for an hour or so. I'd persuaded Eileen to come with me once, in our younger days. She quite enjoyed it, but she totally refused to try the lovely warm ornamental foot bath with its ridiculous Majolica cherubs and fancy taps, saying, '*You never knew whose cheesy old trotters have been in there first!*'.

Some men get up to mischief when they are left to their own devices, even if it is only eating fish and chips in the front room, with their feet up on the sofa, watching the telly and drinking beer from a can or bottle. For me, a massage was my secret vice, because I had zero chance of it being anything else at that moment. The masseuse was Dilys, who was fantastically vicious. She was a talented Welsh lady, with knuckles like a gorilla, and I am sad to report that the rest of her rather followed suit. It took nerves of steel to survive the pummelling of the Swansea Cruncher. I had heard rumours that she offered 'other' massage services for a comparatively modest fee. Good grief, the woman had hands like a brickie's navvy. The thought of ever letting her near one's tender portions was enough to make me wince.

Eileen returned with leftovers from the party, which was apparently a rather dull affair. Beryl and Charlie's friends and people from the bank mostly. She suspected that most of the guests thought she was the hired help instead of Beryl's sister and, to be fair, they didn't look anything like each other, so it was a forgivable mistake.

Henry and Clara came back from Scotland. They'd really enjoyed their trip to see Claudie. Henry reckoned it bucked Clara up no end and she seemed very much more cheerful, which was encouraging. He clung to any sign that she might be on the way to being well again.

Henry told me he'd missed me every day he'd been away and that, much as he loved Claudie, he couldn't wait to get home, where he knew I would be waiting for him in the shed. I'd missed him too - far more than I can say. Things became very much more intense from here. A few days apart had crystalised how we felt about each other. It wasn't a few stolen moments in the shed any longer; it was love, the real thing. No turning back, no changing our minds, we were head over heels and in it for the duration.

Henry was always a thoughtful man of hidden passion. I knew he wanted more from me, and I was happy to give myself to him, but we could not book into a hotel for the night and call ourselves Mr and Mr Smith. We were rapidly learning that for men such as us there was not much choice. We became hunted creatures, always hiding in the shadows and fearful of coming out into the light. Our relationship became one of snatched fragments of joy. Now and again, I would visit Henry at the shop and we would share our lunch in his office, but his assistant was always there so we were never really alone, which was maddening.

I have always tried to see the best in people, but I did not like Derek, the lad who worked for Henry. There was something very sneaky and underhand about him. He was creepy. He watched everything we did, and he was always hanging around in the doorway, listening to our conversations. I thought Henry was way too trusting, but it wasn't my shop, and it certainly wasn't my place to interfere.

We carried on like this for several months, seeing each other when we could and growing steadily more frustrated. One afternoon, when I was at the shed waiting for Henry to arrive, I heard a polite tap on the door. It was a small boy with a message from Eileen telling me to come home immediately. I tipped the child sixpence and beetled off back to Radcliffe Road.

Chapter 7

The sky fell in that awful day. I had half a thought in the back of my head as I rushed home, that our Sally might have turned up on the doorstep, but alas it was not to be.

Clara Muller had been hit by a train. Barefoot and without her glasses, she'd walked to the edge of the platform and had kept going, right in front of the cross-town express, which did not stop at our station. It stopped that day, I can tell you. The driver, poor man, ended up in hospital where he promptly had a heart attack from the shock and stress. I don't suppose Clara was thinking about him when she did it.

When I got back home, there was a police car outside our house and many a neighbours' curtains were twitching, wondering what was going on. Henry, completely dazed, was sitting in our front room with Eileen. It was patently obvious that he was not firing on all cylinders - who would be? I saw it many times during the war. There was much to be shocked about. Your brain defaults to survival mode. Something up there goes, *'Right, we can't cope with this so let's put it away on a shelf until we can deal with it. Maybe a bit at a time, old lad.'*

Eileen was truly magnificent with him. Calm, practical and totally in control as usual. I watched her from the doorway as she sat quietly holding Henry's hand in hers. When he surfaced, she spoke to him, otherwise she was silent, providing quiet support. She was very good at that sort of thing, and she never was a panicker.

When Henry saw me, something clicked inside his head. Anguished, he exclaimed, 'Oh God, now I have to let my

Claudie know, poor *liebchen*. I don't want the police doing it, but how can I tell her about this terrible thing that her mother has done?'

Eileen, always at her best in a crisis, replied, 'Now don't you worry about any of that, Henry, you just sit here with George for a bit, and I will phone Claudie. Do you have her number?'

Henry patted his pockets. 'Oh no of course I don't have it, Clara kept it for me in her address book in her handbag.' His face crumpled and he started to sob. 'She was always worried I would lose it because I am such a scatterbrain.' His face crumpled as he continued, 'I used to listen to Claudie on the phone and then repeat it back to Clara, so she could lip read, you know...' He trailed off, lost among the wreckage of his once happy family.

My heart went out to him. Sitting on the sofa in their neat front room with its polished wooden fruit, and shelves of German books, I noticed Clara's workbox with a pair of Henry's socks hanging over the handle; a needle sticking out of a half-darned patch. I could imagine her only the evening before, working away while she waited for him to come home from the allotment, with no idea that he was in the shed with me, the door firmly locked behind us. Guilt weighed upon my shoulders, a heavy collar that I fully deserved to wear. Poor Henry. For him it was going to be so much worse. I put an arm around his shoulders. Eileen gave me a nod of approval as she mouthed, *'Keep him in here'* before shutting the door.

Clara's bag was sitting in the hall by the umbrella stand. The police had brought it with them for identification. Not to put too fine a point on it, there wasn't any other way it could be done.

I have never felt so damned useless in my life as I did at that moment. I am not entirely sure Henry knew I was in the room most of the time. Weirdly calm is how I would put it. Waiting for the shelling to start.

I would have taken him in my arms to hug him, and damn the law, but he didn't seem ready for that, so I held his hand like he was a child who was a bit fretful. He was lost and I didn't know how to reach him. The look in his eyes was heart-breaking. I could almost see that clever brain of his battling to make sense of it all and failing over and over again to come to terms with the enormity of what had just happened.

Eileen called me out to the hall. I doubt if Henry even knew I had gone.

She was sitting on the stairs, her eyes full of tears as she looked up and spoke. 'I found the number, George, but Claudie wasn't in. I also found this.' She twitched a bit of writing paper between her fingers. 'It was tucked into the address book. The police must have missed it. I guess she reasoned that Henry would make the call and find it.'

Neat as a pin, Clara had written, *I know this will cause you much hurt. Sorry my darlings, but it will fade in time. My own pain is endless.*

It was clear that their recent visit to Claudie had been a time for Clara to say goodbye. Perhaps she was happier because she had made up her mind and put her house in order, as it were. She was always an orderly sort of person, at least on the outside. Inside might have been a different matter entirely.

The police sent someone round to Claudie's flat to tell her the news and she travelled down from Scotland by train. Terry took Henry's car and picked her up from the station in town.

A sad ending to a life, a marriage and a loving bond between mother and daughter.

Grief makes you remember all the other times you lost someone. I remember losing my own mother when I was nine, and my father while I was away fighting. With Mum, we all knew it was coming. There had been nurses and the doctor coming into the house for weeks and vague little chats about Mummy going to sleep soon and the importance of being a good, brave boy.

She had been fading for months. Throughout the spring and into the early summer she got thinner and thinner, then towards the end, she spent a lot of time asleep in a chair in the garden.

I was at school when my grandfather fetched me from my class. It was unheard of for anyone to be collected from school. Our village was rural and tiny. There were few cars back in 1927, so you just ran home to get your tea because you were starving.

We went into the vicarage, and he led me up the stairs. I remember hesitating outside the door, and he bent down and whispered, 'I don't want to do it either, Georgie, because she is my little girl, but we will do this together for her, OK?'

We went in, and I saw my gran sitting in the corner, furiously knitting away. With the wisdom of age, I can see that it was the only thing keeping her sane and holding the tears back. I do remember that it was a dark red jumper that Mum had started for me for the winter. I don't think I ever got it. Gran probably put it into the dustbin. I would have done. My poor, tired father was sitting by the bed holding Mum's hand. She was hazy and doped up on morphine. I gave her a kiss, and she ruffled my hair with a bit of help. After a few minutes I was taken away by one of my uncles. We went for a kick-about in the garden.

I don't remember too much more about that afternoon except the window in the bedroom being flung open. When I was a good deal older, I found out that when someone dies you are supposed to open a window to let the soul fly away. It was a lovely day, and I am always comforted by the thought of Mum free from pain and enjoying the flowers.

On the day of the funeral, my gran insisted I wore a suit, shirt and tie out of respect. I wanted to wear a rather jazzy blue fair isle sleeveless pullover that Mum had knitted me and I expect I created a bit of a fuss.

Dad told her wearily, 'I don't mind if he wears pyjamas, Elsie, if it helps him get through the day.'

I saw Mum off wearing the snazzy jumper she had made me. I have always retained a fondness for sleeveless knitwear.

After the funeral, I spent my summer holidays at the farm with my grandparents. Dad was grief stricken, depressed and questioning why on earth a merciful God would do such a horrible thing to one of his humble and loyal servants and to his small son.

He was a gentle man, very kind and giving with a winning smile that hid a wicked sense of humour. We Potter boys began a new life, and we stumbled on together with the help of a housekeeper.

My father lived for another 13 years until the fateful day a wall fell on him. He never remarried or, as far as I knew, found anyone else.

We got through Clara's funeral. It was more of a memorial service really. It had to be. Henry tried to hold himself together, but the cracks were appearing. Claudie kept herself busy running the shop, and Terry and Eileen gave her a hand when they could.

Sometimes having something to do is the best medicine there is and so much better than a ton of pills. Problems come at night, when you have no distractions and you have to face the darkness alone.

Claudie went back to Scotland. She gave up her flat and began the business of packing up her life. Henry was left to himself. Funerals are a bit like weddings in that way. The ceremony and ritual consume everything for a while, but the day after it is over, normal life begins to take over as it has to.

Kind neighbours left Henry casseroles on the doorstep. They wanted no thanks; it was enough to feel that they were helping. Henry washed the bowls up and pretended he had eaten the food, but the majority of it went into the bin. He told me he had no appetite because every time he looked at the cooker it made him cry because there was a Clara shaped hole in front of it.

Eileen put an end to Henry's 'wallowing', as she called it. I thought she was being a mite brutal, but she told me he had to begin the journey and start to rebuild his life. Indulgence, it seems, wasn't going to help him out at all.

She decided that the best way she could assist Henry was to teach him to cook. To get that fertile mind of his working on a new project and give him something else to think about besides himself.

My wife was a very clever woman. Sometimes she was far too tough on herself and on the people around her, but she understood how they ticked.

She started him off with a boiled egg and moved on to more complicated things like soups and stews. They got along surprisingly well.

Eileen told me one Saturday morning when we were having elevenses and a break from housework, 'He's a good pupil, George, not like some others I could mention. He listens and he is very keen to learn.' She smiled. 'But I do see what you mean about his boundless enthusiasm. It's a bit exhausting, isn't it?'

I nodded in agreement. Curious, I asked Eileen why she thought they had bonded?

Sitting in her usual spot at our kitchen table, ciggie in one hand and a cuppa in the other, she said, 'I think my mum did herself in, George. It wasn't the sort of thing you told a child back then, but it was hinted at by the nuns. It was a sin, you see. We were taught that only God can give you life and only He can take it away. You get no say in the matter. For years I felt abandoned and cast aside by my mother, although I hardly knew her. I only came to terms with it after I had my own children to love.'

She took a puff from her cigarette, then continued, 'People who end it all think they are leaving their problems behind, George, and in a sense they are right. It's all over for them. What they leave for the rest of us is a load of unanswered questions. Henry is going through the worst imaginable pain.' She tapped her head. 'And that's because it's all in here. All those "what ifs" and "why didn'ts", they nag away at you. At least if you know a painful thing, you can deal with it. The not knowing cripples you from the inside.'

She sighed and poured herself another cup. 'The mind is an endless source of dark thoughts, George. Henry is asking himself the same things I used to torture myself with, the main one being "why?". Alternating between deep sorrow and being bloody furious with the deceased for ducking out of life and for causing so much pain.'

I patted her hand because I knew she'd found opening up difficult. I said, 'You've been a titan of strength, old girl, thank you for looking after him.'

She shushed me and got on with her hoovering. It had been a rare moment of connection.

Henry appeared, on the surface, to be coping. Goodness knows what was really going on in that head of his. I could not begin to imagine the grief, along with the exhaustion and anger, that was boiling away inside him.

The wall he had been building crumbled away one morning when he did not appear for his cookery lesson. Eileen sent me out looking for him. We were both extremely worried because you never know what a grieving person might do. It is a state of mind that can lead you down many unhappy paths.

I found Henry in the shed curled up on the floor and sobbing. I experienced genuine panic because I had no idea of how to deal with a fully grown man who was howling like a toddler and in obvious distress. I half wished that Eileen was there to tell me what to do. As I have already said, she was absolutely marvellous in those sorts of situations and definitely someone you would want on your team in a crisis.

I loved Henry, I really did, and I knew that he loved me, but apart from a bit of hand holding and one or two long kisses, we had not been physically intimate with each other. Firstly, through lack of opportunity and then the tragedy with Clara, which had thrown everything and everyone up into the air.

I locked the door on the shed and pulled down the blind. All I could think of was to lay down beside him on the rug and take him into my arms. Sometimes all you can be is a shoulder to cry on. He shed some of the pain that had been building since Clara had died. When he was done and had no more tears to give, I carried on holding him. I couldn't take away his grief, it was his to carry for life. All I could do was to walk beside him and steady him if he needed me.

We stayed on the floor for an hour or more. Henry was exhausted so we lay not speaking, with me stroking his hair like he was a child. When we did get up, we were covered in cobwebs and fallen leaves trodden in from the allotment outside.

Henry took my hand and murmured, 'Thank you, George,' then he left without another word. I suspect he was a bit embarrassed although he had no need to be.

As I stood in the doorway and watched him walk away, I heard Reg Braithwaite braying, 'What's up with old Fritzy today? Extra sauerkraut for breakfast, I suppose.'

Then he laughed like a donkey, until one of my plot-holder neighbours snapped, 'For fuck's sake, Reg, have a heart will you. The man's wife just chucked herself under a train!'

I locked the shed door and went home. There were times when I could cheerfully have punched Reg Braithwaite right in the teeth.

Henry took himself off to visit his older sister in Germany. He told nobody he was going, not even Claudie. He was the middle of three children, with sister Anna, four years his senior, and Erna, two years younger. He liked Anna and got on well with her. Erna had married a Nazi sympathiser, and Henry had told me the family would never speak to her again.

He was gone for over a month. Apart from a tear-stained note left for Claudie on the kitchen table, he made no contact, no word about how he was doing. He wrote that he needed to go back to where he and Clara had met, and to remember their early days for a while, before he could '*put her into his pocket*'. I think he meant he would always carry her with him, and he knew she was there, but he wouldn't have to look at her all the time.

Henry had no idea that Anna had phoned to tell Claudie he was safe. Apparently, he turned up on her doorstep with no warning, carrying nothing but the clothes he stood up in and a bunch of wilting flowers. At times of extreme stress, you might not remember to bring clean underpants or an extra shirt, but daft stuff, like buying tulips for your sister because she likes them, remains firmly stuck in your head. Perhaps uncomplicated ordinary things are a bit of a comfort in a time of crisis. He promptly had a full meltdown, and a doctor had to be called.

With care and the loving attentions of his big sister, he started to recover, or at least begin his way back into life again. After what seemed like the longest time, he phoned to say he was coming home, and Claudie passed the message on to us. I could not wait to see him. My hours at work seemed endless and I rushed home as quickly as I could, hoping he would be there. He didn't come around to say hello to us or appear at the shed, although I waited there for hours. The last thing I wanted to do was to crowd him, just knowing he was next door had to be enough.

He had been home for a couple of days before I caught sight of him. He turned up at the shed, briefly. When I went to lock the door so we could be alone, he said somewhat coldly, 'Don't bother, George, I'm not staying, and I have a lot to do at the shop. I came to apologise for leading you on. It was a mistake, I see that now. We were both looking for male companionship and things got a bit out of hand, didn't they?'

He looked down to his feet. 'Clara needed me, George. I let her down, because I could think of nothing but being with you. I still want to be friends, but that's all. I'm sorry, but this is the way it has to be.'

The shockwave from the bomb he had just dropped damned near threw me off my feet. It was the biggest load of old rot I had ever heard. Male companionship, my foot. I was genuinely stunned. I could feel the door shutting on the happy world we had discovered. I wanted to say *'punishing yourself won't bring Clara back'* but I knew it would probably make him angry, so I nodded and walked away, leaving him standing in the shed for a change. He called after me that he was sorry, I ignored him and kept going until he was out of earshot.

I went for a long, cold walk and ended up in some grimy café, drinking tea out of a chipped mug and watching the world through steamy windows where the water ran to inky puddles on the sill. It was most definitely not one of the hip coffee bars full of young people that our Terry, and Henry's Claudie, seemed to go to all the time.

I suppose I could have gone to a pub and got myself plastered, but I never found one. The woman behind the café counter was missing several teeth but she was cheerful enough. She refilled my tea and then she gave me a look and said, 'Never mind, dearie, it might not happen.'

I gave her a gloomy look and said, 'It already has.'

She put a couple of biscuits onto my saucer and winked at me. I stayed until she got a broom out and started to put chairs up onto the tables.

It was pouring with rain and the reflections from the shopfront lights blended into roadside puddles like a French painting. Oddly pretty if I hadn't been so utterly miserable. As I turned for home, an odd thought hit me. There are times in your life when you feel alone and divorced from all those around you, floating in your own misery. Some people can talk to God. I have always envied them their certainty of a constant companion. I was the son of a vicar, but I had stopped believing in the Almighty a long time ago. Shocking, I know, but there you are. My dear mother died before she was 30, my lovely father was violently killed, and my tiny daughter died in my arms.

I don't put my trust in any deity. I think we make our own way in this world and sometimes things happen that are tragic and there is simply nobody to blame. Sad, but in my opinion it is true. God, if he existed, would not be interested in me anyway. I am a nasty little sinner who still does not feel the slightest bit like repenting to earn his good favour. OK, I was sorry for the infidelity, or at least the thought of infidelity, because I never wanted to hurt people, even if they didn't know they were being hurt. The rest I would do all over again in a heartbeat, because you can't help who you fall in love with, can you? It could be the woman on the fish counter in Sainsbury's or next door's cat. When it happens to you there is not a thing you can do about it, unless it is the cat, then you seriously need to seek urgent medical attention from a head shrinker.

I went home to Eileen and slipped below the waves of a grey world that smelled of polish and pine disinfectant. I ignored her moaning about my tardiness and took myself upstairs for a soak in a warm bath, because it was the only place I knew that she couldn't get at me. I didn't want a row, and she might have got a bit more than she bargained for if she had started one.

I lay there for ages, refilling the hot water when it went cold. Then I got out, dried off and took myself to bed. Madame trotted up later. She paused outside the door, obviously deciding if she should come in or not. She thought better of it, and I heard her use the loo and go to her own room. When she started to snore, I turned over and tried to sleep. Eventually a bleak exhaustion overtook me, and I didn't have to think about any of it for a few hours.

Surely 'heartbreak', which I always considered a trashy, lazy word, is for the young and romantically inclined. I was neither of these things, but I think I could have been romantic if I had been given half a chance. Henry no longer wanted me, or at least he thought he didn't, and that hurt. How cruel to find love and have it drift away like a sandal on the next tide, just out of reach, the pair no longer whole or indeed useful to anyone except a man with one leg.

Henry moved out of next door and took to living over the bookshop, while he tried to figure out what he was going to do with his life. I imagined he would sell up and start afresh somewhere, away from all his memories and from me. It stunk!

Chapter 8

1962 was a year filled with goodbyes. Our Terry went into the army for two years. He had to do his National Service. The requirement for it had stopped, but people who deferred, still had to go and do their bit for Queen and country, not quite sure why. He was among the last of the lads to go. I gave him the advice my own father had given to me. 'Don't cheek your sergeant, keep your kit clean and lay it out neatly before you go out on the beer, and look after your feet.'

Eileen and I watched him from the front garden as he went up Radcliffe Road to catch his train. I couldn't help remembering what it had been like for me going off to war. I'd spent a couple of days leave with my dad at the vicarage before I'd been shipped out. He'd been overjoyed to see me looking so well.

When I left to join the army, I was a skinny 22-year-old, painfully shy and as wet as a thunderstorm sandwich. Barely six months later, I was a married man in uniform; a trained soldier, with a wife and a child and another on the way. I had bulked up because of all the physical training they put us through, and in the best shape of my life. My goodness, what a whirlwind those months were. I don't think I stopped spinning until 1945. It was only later, I realised what a hole I had drilled myself into.

When it was time for me to leave, Dad got tearful and told me he was proud of me, then he gave me a great big hug and whispered, 'Come home safe, son. I simply could not bear to lose you as well as your mother, you know.' Then he smiled and said, 'Off you go then, boy.'

There was always a bit of a gap in his teeth where he'd fallen off a bicycle when he was 12 and the front ones never went back straight. When I was a small boy, he used to make me laugh by producing a sixpence through them. I thought he was magic, and I always got to keep the sixpence.

I asked him to keep an eye on Eileen and Sally for me, and the new baby when he or she arrived. Then I saluted and marched off up the road to catch my bus. Neither of us had the faintest idea that I would survive with barely a scratch and he would be dead before the year was out.

After six long months, things at Radcliffe Road were pretty much the same.

Henry had settled himself at the bookshop flat. He told Eileen that he felt less lonely in a smaller place, which was peachy for him. My feelings didn't get a look in and I missed him. He stopped coming to the allotment, but I kept his plants watered out of kindness to them. I resigned myself to the fact that whatever we had shared was gone. It hurt me, but I had come around to the idea that it was for the best.

Not being near him was painful enough; him not wanting to be near me was damned near crippling. I soldiered on because I had no choice, and I hoped that in time I might find a way to live with it and accept it as my one great adventure in love. Pretty laughable and a bit pathetic really, a middle-aged man mooning away in his garden shed and pining over the love of his life.

Things were pretty cruddy, and the Henry thing was killing me inside. Then they got a whole lot worse. First,

I saw a man come round to put up a 'for sale' board in Henry's front garden. The love of my life was buggering off to pastures new and leaving me behind like I'd never existed. I could not help thinking, *So long and thanks for nothing, Heinrich.*

Then, as if that were not enough of a slap around the chops, Henry's new best pal, Eileen, informed me that we had been invited to dinner at the bookshop flat on Saturday evening. Oh, that one caused me deep joy, I can tell you. He wanted to tell us all about his plans to move to the coast and start again.

Eileen had accepted for both of us, without so much as asking me if I wanted to go. No chance of me saying I was washing my hair or clipping my toenails then. She was anxious to see how her protégé was getting along with his cooking, so, basically, I was a done turkey.

He was looking forward to catching up because he was still kidding himself that we were just mates, with all the awkward 'you know what' business in the shed forgotten, like an embarrassing relative after the wedding. Pathetic. Now I had to go and eat dinner with him and make small talk, like nothing had ever happened between us. I was hoping that Henry would get chatting to Eileen about pastry or the riveting subject of Pyrex baking dishes, and I would be all but forgotten.

It didn't turn out like that at all. No recipes or kitchen implements were examined or exchanged. Eileen didn't come with me; she went to Beryl's instead. It was all very sudden. I was told it was an emergency, a woman's complaint. I didn't see why it had to be wrapped up in a mystery. We all have bits and pieces down below and sometimes they go wrong and that is that. As it happens, I already knew what was causing her problems because Charlie had told me years ago, when he'd had one too many brandies.

A botched backstreet abortion when she'd been 16 had left Beryl with all sorts of damage, so they never had any kids. It was also the reason Eileen went off the deep end and had that massive blow up with our Sally, and we all know how that one had turned out.

Eileen rushed off to be with her sister at the hospital. They needled each other all the time, but when the chips were really down, you could not get a cigarette paper between the two of them.

Eileen phoned Henry and told him I would be coming on my own for dinner. When I got back from the allotment after tucking the seedlings in for the night, Eileen explained with a casual, 'You can still go, George, he's looking forward to seeing you. Anyway, I said you would meet him in the pub, so you have to turn up.'

I wasn't asked for my opinion on the matter. Like a lamb to the slaughter, I followed her instructions and went off to meet my doom.

Henry's new local was near my office. Eileen and Eric caught the train, and I walked the rest of the way. It was raining and the bar was packed. I looked around for Henry, but I couldn't see through the crowd. There was a tug at my sleeve. It was Ronnie Brown sitting with a crowd of people from accounts celebrating somebody's birthday.

He teased me in his cheery chirpy way, 'Why, George Potter, you rascal. Don't let the lovely Eileen catch you in here, old chap.'

Everybody laughed, and I had to join in and pretend that I found it funny too. They were all quite merry and they asked me to join them for a drink, but I told them I was meeting a friend and left them to it.

I found Henry in a corner reading the paper. We left as soon as he had finished his pint.

'I'm disappointed that Eileen couldn't make it,' he said, putting on his coat. 'Dinner is in the oven, and we can have a good old catch up over a beer, just us boys. How about that then?'

I genuinely think he had convinced himself nothing ever happened between us. It is amazing how some people can do that, slap on the blinkers and forget anything that makes them the slightest bit uncomfortable.

The bookshop flat wasn't large - an estate agent would have called it bijou. I would have said it was 'cosy' and Eileen would probably have said 'pokey'.

There was a barely adequate coal fire and a kitchenette, as well as a dining area. I could immediately see that it needed a damned good sort out, some new carpet instead of yellowing lino and a coat of paint throughout, because it was terribly scuffed and scruffy looking and frankly quite unloved, just like me.

Henry was cheery and overly chatty. He served us up a decent steak and kidney pie. He'd got the recipe from Eileen, of course. Everything was more than a tiny bit edgy and awkward, from my side at least, because I didn't want to be there. He found us two large bottles of beer. We talked about the plants, discussed the damned nuclear bomb business at some length and then the chess set appeared. I started to relax and to enjoy his company again, like we always had done when we'd been friends and not potential lovers. Henry was always less shy when we were alone - and he was funny.

I knew in my head that this was going to be the final time that we would be together. Apart from everything else, he was full of talk about his plans to move to the coast and to start afresh. In one way, I wanted to savour the feeling of being there with him, because it was going to last me the rest of my life, and in another I was actually quite relieved that the torture would soon be over. We watched a bit of telly, and I helped him to wash up and put everything away neatly because, typically for Henry, the kitchen was a bomb site.

About half 10, I yawned and said, 'It's been lovely seeing you, old chap, but I need to go. I have to catch my bus.'

Henry shrugged. 'I can drop you off in the van, if you want to stay a bit longer,' he suggested. 'It isn't as if Eileen will be there waiting to tell you off. Go on, why not have another beer? We'll make a night of it.'

Being together, like we used to be, was wonderful, but it made everything so much harder to deal with. I threw caution to the wind, and I found the courage to say, 'No, Henry, I'm going home.'

He was hurt, but I continued, 'Our affair, or whatever it was we had, may be over, but I can't switch off my emotions just to suit you. Do you have the slightest idea of the agony you have put me through over the past six months? You walked away, but what about my feelings? I think it is better that we get this said, then you can move away and we can both forget it ever happened.'

He gave me a withering look, his face tight with anger, but he kept his mouth shut.

After putting on my jacket, I said my final piece, the words coming out of nowhere, 'I love you, Henry, you know I do. Nothing is going to change that for me and being friends is not enough. All that stuff about it being a mistake because we were lonely is utter crap and you damned well know it. My goodness, if it isn't crap, you made a wonderful job of faking desire, several times if I recall it all correctly. Now I'm going to get my bus. I will pack up your gardening bits and leave them in the shed for you to collect when it is convenient. I don't want to see you there again, but you can take any flowers you want. They might cheer this depressing dump up a bit.'

I was bloody annoyed. Anger came pouring out of me in a great wave and I knew I had to leave. I wanted to run, as far and as fast as I could, away from the shabby little room that smelled of cabbage, and away from Henry. I got as far as turning the door handle when Henry spoke.

'Oh, who am I kidding? I have been an idiot, haven't I, George? A complete and total fucking idiot.'

I was shocked to hear him use the 'F' word, because he knew I didn't like it. Swearing wasn't something he did unless he was furious with himself.

'Why?' I asked, hoping the answer would be quick, so I could go out into the cold and the dark, where I could disappear and he couldn't see my face. I knew it wasn't manly to cry but I couldn't help it. I was a ridiculous mess, a middle-aged man in a cardigan blubbing like a child over an affair that had never really got going. I was embarrassed as much as anything else, and I needed to go somewhere quiet to sort myself out.

He gave me a look and sighed. 'You know damned well why. I have missed you so much and I'm very sorry for hurting you. All I seem to do is to hurt people these days, including myself.'

He put out his hand, saying, 'Georgie, please don't go.'

Something about him calling me Georgie made me very angry indeed. I turned and replied firmly, 'Oh, like that, is it? Now that you have stopped pretending, you want me back again, do you? Well, I'm not on a piece of elastic, Henry. You can't take me out of the box to amuse you when you want to play and then tidy me away again when I'm inconvenient.'

I took in a breath then continued, 'I am genuinely and truly sorry for what happened to Clara, and I know you feel horribly guilty, so do I. Maybe one of us should have spotted that Clara was very near the edge, but we didn't and there is nothing any of us can do about that now because she is gone.'

'Clara would have done it anyway,' I said, pulling up the zipper on my jacket. 'One day, whether you had met me or not, she would have taken that step off the platform or off a building or under a bus, because she wanted to do it. It was nothing to do with us. It was always about her and the pain that living caused her every single day of her life. Now let me go.' I thumped my fist on the door. 'You can get on with feeling sorry for yourself, you stupid, pig-headed German idiot.'

He swore, under his breath and spat out, 'So you turned out to be a coward after all, George. Go on then, trot meekly back to Eileen and your miserable little life.'

I stuttered back in astonishment, 'Misery with Eileen is nothing compared to what you have put me through. If anyone is a coward, it is you, Heinrich Muller. At least I was prepared to fight for the chance to love you, no matter how long it took, and it wasn't me running away, was it? You are beyond ridiculous, you deluded fool.'

His eyes blazed in temper, and I was expecting an earful, or for him to order me from the premises, but he sagged visibly, like the fight had gone out of him.

He nodded and mumbled, 'Yes, I am a coward and a ridiculously foolish one at that. Please stay, I need you, but until this moment I didn't know how to say it.'

I stared daggers at him, my own temper properly up, then I surprised myself by going to him. He hugged me close with the flickering yellow bulb from the streetlamp outside, shining down on us through the skylight. I put my head on his shoulder, feeling dizzy and confused but sublimely happy.

He stroked my hair and whispered, 'Do you want to go to bed, Georgie?'

I could only manage to get out one word and it was, 'Yes.'

We made things up as we went along, learning what pleased us and letting Mother Nature tell us what to do, which I have to say she did extremely well. I have never felt anything like it. Sexual pleasure had always been a secretive, closed off thing for me, something shameful. To be perfectly honest, Eileen always wanted to get her 'wifely duties', as she called them, over and done with as soon as possible so that she could have a cigarette and go to sleep. I always got the feeling she would charge me rent if I didn't get a move on.

It had been more than a good while since we'd been intimate in that way. In our younger days, I'd rather stupidly suggested that we made an effort to spice things up a bit for both of us, but she'd told me not to be disgusting, and that I was lucky I was getting any at all, let alone going in for mucky stuff like the French people do. It had pretty much killed off any thoughts of that nature I might have had. From then on, I'd put all my efforts into gardening instead, until Henry had come along, of course.

I enjoyed every single second of our forbidden mutual pleasure, and I didn't care a fig, because I knew I was loved. I felt powerful and alive, and I never wanted the feeling to end. We trusted and we loved as equals, both mentally and physically.

I will say, with complete honesty, that we would not have broken any records for the longevity of our lovemaking. When two people who desire each other have been denied the opportunity of any physical love, the culmination of all their pent-up feelings will be swift - the first time around anyway.

Twenty minutes later, content and happy, we lay together in the dark still wearing our vests, two middle-aged men in love. We held each other and then we agreed that the vests could probably go, in the name of romance. I was somewhat breathless and pink, but I managed to stammer out in amazement, 'Bloody hell!'

Henry, still puffing, asked, 'Any complaints?'

I replied, 'Absolutely not. My goodness, Mr Muller, what on earth have you done to me? I am a wreck.' And I was, a truly satisfied man.

Henry's hair was a mess, and he had this huge, stupid grin plastered right across his face, which was damned near adorable. A tear rolled down his cheek as he pulled me into his arms and whispered, 'How on earth am I supposed to let you go home now, Georgie? You have my heart, always. No matter what happens, you know that, don't you?'

I kissed him and said, 'I love you, you idiot. Don't you ever run off and leave me again.'

I had never fully experienced what people call the 'afterglow' before. In Eileen's world, no such thing existed. With her it was a case of '*OK you have had your fun, now bog off back to your own room and don't come bothering me for a good long while, because you have had your ration for this quarter, little man*'.

That sweet sensation of lying in somebody else's arms, relaxed and warm and tired, loved and totally at ease. We did a lot of talking and an awful lot more loving. Finally, we slept together, naked and peaceful, and we forgot all about the harsh world outside, a world which could not and would not accept us.

I woke up on Sunday morning with Henry beside me in the half-light through thin brown curtains. He was still out cold, so I curled myself around him. Pulling the blankets over us, I listened to the slow sound of him breathing and the occasional contented snore.

Unlike me, Henry, as I soon found out, slept like the dead. Seriously, he slept like a church front door, heavy and generally pretty noisy. I envied him a bit. I could hear the milkman rattling bottles and in the distance a bus changed gear as it readied itself to climb the hill. Most days I was a passenger on it, just another drone en route to the office, nobody special. But this day I was different. I was a man apart from the crowd. Someone loved me and that made me a king.

We were safe in our own world where nobody could get at us. I had a chance to think dreamily about the night before. Until that night, I had never knowingly broken the law. And it had been worth every single second. They could have jailed me, and I would willingly have done my time in prison, for the chance to come out and do it all over again.

Henry was always a shy, gentle lover, as much concerned with my pleasure as his own. We matched each other perfectly. When he touched me, I did not want him to stop, and I could not keep my own hands off him. His body was a foreign country. New smells, new tastes, new sensations, a feast for a man who had spent so much of his life in famine as far as affection was concerned.

I was intrigued by new sources of pleasure I'd never known, yet they existed on my own body too; how strange. Henry felt bulky, not at all fat but much bigger built than me. He was lean and hard from carrying books, not soft like Eileen (whenever she let me get near enough to find out). Instead of breasts, there was a hairy chest quite unlike my own. Oh, how I loved running my fingers through his brown curls.

The odour of sleep had settled upon his slumbering form. A not unpleasant mixture of aftershave and beer, blended with sweat and the smell of sex. It was everywhere, on the sheets and in the air, in his hair and in my own. I could not help but find it erotic, evidence of our love for each other and proof that it had not been just a wonderful dream. It makes me blush all over to describe how brazen I was with him, and just how much I enjoyed it.

I felt no need to apologise for my actions, because there was nothing to apologise for. Oh, the law could think what it liked, if our few stolen hours had taught me anything, it was that love was all that counted. It seemed to me that the legislation was very much concerned with sex and with the physical act between two men. It made no mention of the genuine love that was behind it.

There were no barriers, just skin on warm skin. I wanted us to stay like that. Him sleeping, me awake and dreaming. Henry was very broad across the shoulders, and he had freckles, which was a surprise. Who knows what anyone hides under their clothes? I have a tattoo, a tiny star on my shoulder. Most of my platoon got them when we were in the desert. Some shop in a filthy back street. I am amazed that we didn't all catch something nasty.

I rolled over, happy to snooze until he surfaced, but he was half awake and he curled himself around me in return. We lay, not speaking much, content to be together until a voice murmured, 'I love you. Now do go to sleep, Georgie.'

I closed my eyes in wonder, that someone would ever say that to funny, stuttering me.

I dozed again, satisfied with the world. I woke to the smell of toast and bacon frying. Henry was cooking us breakfast. It was chilly because the fire had gone out, so he was wearing his shirt and his socks. I could see him from the bedroom doorway. He was humming away to himself, like he hadn't any care in the world. It was fascinating to see him totally unaware that he was being watched.

'Pom pom pom,' he went. It sounded like Gilbert and Sullivan, but it could have been Bing Crosby for all I knew.

I got up and went to him, dragging one of the coarse blankets from the bed with me. I wrapped it around us, and he turned and kissed me with real passion. We both needed a shave. One stubbly chin against another; it was an odd feeling, like we would end up hooked together. I wouldn't have minded if the world had ended right there and then; we could have faced eternity as long as we were together.

You need to see someone asleep or first thing in the morning to know them. Henry was a bit creased, and his hair was looking slightly mad. I touched one of the curls that he usually kept flattened down. Such an intimate thing to do to someone else, it feels like you are claiming them as your own. Apart from your barber, or your mother, who else would you let close enough to do that? It is a lover's privilege.

Both of us knew our time was limited so we made the most of it. Just him and me in our rooftop hideaway. We sat under the covers eating bacon sandwiches and munching toast. I had a tea but Henry, being German, loved a strong morning coffee. The room was chilly and there were no carpets, so I had my cardigan on in bed and not much else.

Henry laughed at me, saying, 'You look awfully silly.'

He disappeared for a minute and came back wearing nothing but his woolly gardening hat, a bow tie, blue socks and a great big smile, which gave me the giggles because he looked ridiculous, especially with his 'mad conductor' hair sticking out everywhere.

'Ta-dah,' he sang, doing a sort of tap dance across the floor.

I could not have loved him more. He was showing me the inner Henry, the one that other people didn't get to see. Life under the Nazis had taught him to be very guarded, but he was letting me in. When someone trusts you that much it is simply intoxicating.

With a cry of '*Geronimo*' he launched himself onto the rickety bed, which creaked like it might collapse at any moment, and we made love again. A joyous rolling romp under the covers. Until that moment, I'd had no idea that sex could be anything approaching fun.

We spent the rest of the day together, either in bed or sitting in front of the fire reading the papers. Henry lent me a shirt, which came down past my knees.

I had no idea when Eileen would be back, I was certain she would be gone for a while because Beryl was in a pretty bad way. I stayed Sunday night too and on Monday Henry had a go at ironing my clothes for me while I had a shave and took a quick shower - the flat was nowhere big enough for a bath.

'Here,' he said, proffering his efforts. 'I'm not very handy with the iron yet. Will it do? I also made you a packed lunch, Georgie, a cheese and pickle sandwich and an apple.'

Everything was ridiculously domestic, and I loved it. As I left, I noticed Henry had a queue forming outside his shop, wondering why he hadn't opened up on time. I knew exactly why, and I couldn't wipe the smile off my face.

I slunk into work straight from Henry's, like a much younger man who had been living it up all weekend. It was all rather thrilling.

My colleagues just saw good old George a bit late for work and looking unkempt, because his wife was visiting her sister and he was doing his own ironing. They had no idea that my weekend had been filled with a passion so intense that we'd had to drag ourselves out of bed and away from each other.

Mark Windlesham, my boss, remarked, 'It's not like you to be late, George.' Then he winked and said, 'Don't make a habit of it, old lad.'

He was always a good sort. I liked him a lot, although he was rather too keen on the gee-gees for my liking. Rumour had it he spent his lunch hours in the bookies placing bets.

Eileen sent a telegram to the office to say that Beryl was pretty bad, and she thought she might be away for a good few more days. By the end of that week, Henry and I knew for certain that we wanted to be with each other for the rest of our lives.

Eileen arrived home from Beryl's quite cheery because her sister was on the mend. Her good mood didn't last and before long we were back to normal.

She grilled me with, 'Why didn't you answer the phone when I called home? I rang you several times and you never picked up once, George. I'm not made of telegram money, you know.'

I shrugged, feeling like a complete worm and I answered, 'Probably down at the allotment, dear. There is a lot to do at the moment, now Henry isn't there to share the load.'

Eric gave me a cool look. At least I think it was a look. The ridiculous dog was cross-eyed so you never could tell, but I wouldn't have put it past him!

We ate dinner in virtual silence, with Eric sniffing around my feet for scraps, which he was not allowed because he was a greedy little so and so. Everyone slipped back into the grooves of domestic boredom we had worn over many years. Except, of course, I was a totally different George to the one she had left behind. I'd cheated on her a rather surprising number of times during the week she'd been away, and I had found the person I was always meant to be.

I didn't want to hurt her. I wondered if it would have been worse if I had spent my time with another woman instead of a man. I think my conscience knew the answer to that one. Cheating is cheating when you come down to it, whoever you are doing it with.

I realised the irony of the situation I found myself in. I had a wife that didn't really want me, except for convention, and a next-door neighbour who wanted me as much as I wanted him, but it was that same convention that determined we couldn't be together.

Henry came back home, and he got a new tenant for the flat. Creepy Derek, the assistant, moved in upstairs. He had fallen out with his mother, who was a war widow, over her new boyfriend.

He had nowhere else to go to that he could afford, so Henry said he could use the flat, but just until he found somewhere else. So, we were back to furtive kisses in the shed and the odd passionate moment when Eileen's back was turned.

I remember getting quite shirty with Eileen because, quite frankly, I wasn't getting any. She kept asking me if I needed something to sort out my bowels, because I was being bad tempered. Bran Flakes appeared on the breakfast table. I always loathed Bran Flakes, which didn't help one little bit.

One lunchtime when I called round to Henry's shop, Creepy Derek was out on some errands. Henry had sent him to the stationers where there was a shop girl named Brenda that he fancied and endlessly tried to chat up.

As soon as Creepy was out of the door, Henry locked it and pulled down the blind, then he dragged me into the office to have his evil way with me against the filing cabinet, which was absolute heaven.

When we emerged smirking and I had left via the delivery yard, Henry found a furious Derek standing on the shop doorstep in the rain, because the stationers had been shut for early closing. *Serves him right, the little sneak.*

When I was working in the garden before dinner, we stopped and chatted politely across the fence for a few minutes like neighbours do. Just about how the roses were doing, pretty tame stuff considering the two of us had spent lunchtime in each other's arms, and I don't mean doing the fox-trot!

Chapter 9

Our affair continued whenever we got the opportunity, usually when Eileen was at her sister's. To the rest of the world, we were best friends sharing an allotment plot; they had no idea that our relationship was flowering too.

Reg Braithwaite, our fearless leader (he thought), joined the Civil Defence Corps and became obsessed with hunting down the red menace. He saw Communists everywhere! He was also very much down on Asians and queers, but Communists were currently in his sights.

Most people thought he was a bit loopy and ignored him, or told him to go cool his head under the tap, or worse, but Reg was relentless in rooting out what he thought were 'reds under the vegetable beds'. What he expected to find the Lord only knows, but he said extreme vigilance was called for, in case we were infiltrated by bugged potatoes or something I expect; the man's paranoia knew no bounds.

There were several humorous suggestions from the plot holders about what he might have been looking for, possibly Commie Carrots or Pinko Parsnips. Henry suggested Bolshie Beets.

Reg wanted us to mount nightly patrols to stop the Communists from running riot during the darkened hours. Nobody signed up, but the thought of doing it crossed my mind. Not because I wanted to help him in his lunatic scheme you understand; it's just that he would have had to be nice to me all night, which would have annoyed him.

That bit of lunacy was the beginning of a weird few days.

I got promoted at work. Eileen said it was long overdue and that I should have pushed myself forward years ago instead of waiting to fill a 'dead man's shoes', as the saying goes. Actually, it was not a dead man's shoes I was filling. It was a pair of prison issue boots. Mark Windlesham, the manager of the drawing office and my boss, left us under somewhat of a cloud. There had been some discrepancies noted in the fees we had been charging for our external work and the amount coming in.

Mark was called up to the top floor, where two gentlemen in raincoats that Joe, our doorman, said were '*Rozzers*' (I assume by this that he meant the law) cuffed him and took him away smartish. Shortly after this, yours truly was also given a call to the top floor, meaning everyone thought I had also dipped my fingers into the pot, and I was getting my collar felt by the '*Old Bill*'.

The managing director, Edward Seymour, a Canadian, was on the panel. He was always a pompous ass, and he never remembered my first name.

'Bit of a tricky situation, Potter,' he purred. 'Windlesham has been caught red handed fiddling the accounts, the monumental idiot.'

He asked me a few questions (I found out later that he knew all the answers anyway). He looked into my file and snorted, 'I am rather surprised to see that you went to a decent school. What did your father do for a living? Tradesman of some sort, something like that eh?'

I replied meekly, 'My father was a clergyman, Mr Seymour. He was killed in an air raid in 1940.'

It brought to mind the letter Eileen had written to tell me that Terry had been born and that my dear gentle, absent-minded father had been violently dispatched from the world by a German bomb. It was the most joyous, and the saddest message of my entire life and I memorised every single word of it. I went through it in my head while Eddie prattled on and on, and on!

Dear George,

I have good news and bad news.

I will start with the good. Please find enclosed two photographs. One of our new son, Terence George Andrew Potter. I hope you will approve of the name. I had to call him something, and Terry seems to suit him nicely.

He came into the world a few days ago, a little early but weighing in at a respectable 7lb 4oz. Sally is very excited to be a big sister. I think he looks a bit like you, without the hair and the teeth of course.

The second photograph, as you can see, is of your father holding Terry. He was very excited to be a grandad, and he told me he had all sorts of plans for things that they could do together when Terry was bigger, and the war was over. I was happy for him because I know how much he misses you.

That is the good news but now you must prepare yourself for a nasty shock. Your father came up from the country to see the baby after Beryl sent a telegram. He kindly brought me eggs, butter and fresh milk for Sally. We have terrible trouble getting these things now. The ration is very mean, because it has to go around a lot of people. He also brought apples and some honey that one of his parishioners had given him.

I am sorry to have to tell you that he was caught in the bombing on his way home. Being a stranger in town, he didn't know where the shelters were and, as far as I can tell, he died when a wall fell on him. They informed me because they found our address in his pocket. You said he was terrible with directions. I suspect he wrote the street name down so he could ask someone if he got lost. With no road signs, getting around has become a nightmare.

He was cheerful when he waved us goodbye and headed for the station. He told me that he liked the name Terence and that it probably comes from Terruncius, which was a small Roman coin rather like a farthing.

He was a good, kind man and I am very sorry to bring you such terrible news about him. I thought you would want to know about the baby, and of course I needed to write about your dad.

They asked me where he was to be buried. As you are away fighting, I had to make the decision. This war forces many unwanted decisions on us, doesn't it? He will be buried in his own churchyard next to your mother. I am sure that this was what both of you would have wanted.

We won't be able to attend the funeral, but if things calm down a bit and the children are OK, I will try to make the journey to your father's church to take some flowers for the grave. In this flat there is no room to grow anything beyond a pot plant, which you know is something I cannot seem to do, but perhaps when you come home from the war we can find somewhere with a garden to grow a few flowers and for the children to play. They might help, but I suspect they will get in the way. We could even get an allotment. How about that?

You could grow all our veggies, and I can get back to cooking. Rationing is a challenge, not a joy!

I will have to stop writing now because your son is calling me. Yelling fit to bust, he is. He has a very good pair of lungs on him and a jolly good appetite.

Keep safe, George. Sally has drawn you a picture of the baby with the crayons your father brought her as a present. They used to be yours. Do you remember keeping them in a bashed-up cocoa tin with Georgie written on the lid? He also brought a couple of your toy cars for Terry and a wooden cow on wheels, the one your grandfather carved for you.

He'd stuffed everything into his old knapsack from the first war. It was so full I am surprised that he could carry it with his bad arm. He told me he was jolly glad to have a sit down and a nice cup of tea. He politely brought his own leaves with him, as I would have expected him to do.

Once again, George, I am truly sorry.

Yours, Eileen and Sally and baby Terry of course x

When I came back into focus, Seymour was still rattling on. He hummed a bit as he whipped through the pages of my file.

'Did your bit for King and country I see, well done. Married with two children, and what do they all do, Potter?'

I replied, 'Eileen is a housewife and my boy, Terry, is in the army.' Then I lied and told him that Sally worked in advertising.

He nodded and mumbled, 'Excellent, Potter. Rather surprisingly, you seem to be exactly what we are looking for. Do you think you are up to the challenge, old chap? In short, old boy, we need someone of the right sort to keep the ship afloat while we get to the bottom of the mess Windlesham has made. We know you to be a reliable fellow. If you make a success of it, we can see about giving you the job permanently in a few months.'

I couldn't understand what my father's job or the school I went to had to do with me keeping my paws off the company funds, but I went along with it and assured him that I was up to the job.

So '*good old George*' was expected to save the day, probably because I was considered far too dull to pinch anything from the petty cash. There was a pretty good raise, my own office and even a car. I'd learned to drive before I'd gone into the Forces, so that was no problem.

Joan, who was my friend and my spy in the boardroom told me all about the conversation they'd had before they'd called me in.

'How about George Potter?' one of them had suggested.

Most of them went, 'Who?'

'You know, George with the stutter, a hand-knitted pullover and glasses.'

'Oh yes, that George, always brings a packed lunch to the canteen. Bit henpecked, apparently. Funny chap, but he's not at all daft.'

Someone else piped up, 'Yes, him. Oh, and by the way, the fragrant Mrs Potter may be a bit of an old dragon, but she can bloody cook. Have you seen him? He eats like a tiny king out of that lunchbox. I sat next to him once and I asked him what was in the pasty he was eating. So he shrugged and said '*devilled crab*', then he gave me half because he couldn't eat it all anyway. It was amazing. His wife's sister lives at the coast, and they had just visited and brought a couple of fresh crabs as a present for Mrs P. Every Christmas the lovely Eileen makes a huge cake, and a ton of sausage rolls for the office. The queue is out of the door.'

'But is he any good at his job? I mean, he isn't really our sort, is he? Windlesham may have been light fingered, but at least he went to a decent public school, knew the right knife and fork to use, that sort of thing.'

'So did George, I believe. Take a look in his file if you don't believe me, it's all in there. His father was a vicar, I think. George told me he was killed in an air raid. He was going to train as an architect, but the war mucked that up. He's your man alright. He's quiet and unassuming, but he knows his stuff and he will gently move you round to his point of view if he thinks he's onto something.'

'Yes, George Potter is your man alright. Let's call him in!'

Eileen was absolutely thrilled. It was one to drop on Beryl, who always lorded it over us, and Vera B had told the entire world by nightfall. I was very sad for Mark, who had only had one leg since the war and would have found it difficult to get another job.

It was a crazy thing to do. I couldn't understand why he would have considered it, unless he was desperate. He could be a little patronising sometimes, but I was used to that. Generally, he was fair and a very good man to work for. I missed him.

To round off that weird week, we went to Beryl and Charlie's for a three-day session of family torture. Not exactly my venue of choice. Their leather sofa squeaked in a most distressing, lower gastro-intestinal manner and everything else was household perfection, not a tasteless ornament out of place or a speck of dust anywhere, and it made me nervous. Eileen kept our place clean and neat as a pin, but she was not a Nazi about it, and we didn't really do knick-knacks.

Beryl and Charlie had a lovely house in Hastings with two lavs, a padded drinks bar in the living room, and an unbelievably hideous plastic ice bucket in the shape of a gold pineapple. They even had an extra phone upstairs. This phone was a lurid pink affair. Eileen thought it looked like it came from a 'knocking shop', and a cheap one at that.

Because they never had a family and Charlie earned good money, they indulged themselves with great abandon, hence the rows about money and the thumping.

I missed Henry, but we both had to continue with our other lives no matter how we felt about each other. I did try sneaking out a couple of times to call him from a phone box, but he wasn't in, which made me feel even more miserable because I wondered what he was getting up to without me. Charlie kept giving me odd looks and winking, which was horrible.

When the girls were off making tea in the kitchen and we were alone in the lounge, he leaned over and whispered, 'If you are going to call your fancy piece, George, do it from the box on the seafront, old man, because you can see right into the one on our road from the living room window.'

He chuckled in a truly disgusting way and nudged me with his elbow saying, 'Well, well, you are a dark little horse, aren't you? I never thought you would have had it in you. A word to the wise, though, your Eileen isn't my Beryl, she's much smarter. If you are going to play the game, you had better learn the rules and not get found out, because your Eileen won't just screech like an old hen, she's going to bloody well kill you.'

I went red up to the ears, panicked and lied that I was phoning the bookies to place a couple of bets, because Eileen didn't approve of me gambling.

He winked and said, 'Oh of course you were, George.' Then he went back to his paper.

Behind her back, Eileen called Beryl 'Charlie's Aunt' like the old play, because she was a fair bit older than Charlie. Beryl referred to Eileen as 'George's Dragon.' Who would ever have believed they were sisters.

Charlie was funny in a laddish sort of way, and more than a trifle naughty. Of course, I didn't approve of him knocking Beryl about. Eileen reckoned he was too flash for her taste, and she was right, he was flash. He wore very sharp suits, which were always beautifully cut, but there was still a bit of the spiv about him.

In a rare glimpse of humour, Eileen suggested that somewhere in the attic he probably had a suitcase full of nylons left over from the war. I couldn't help but agree.

Charlie's father was a greengrocer who had made his money supplying the troops in WWI. He'd sent Charlie away to school to turn him into a gentleman. He had a good brain and a good job, but he was still an East-End barrow boy underneath!

We were generally the poor relations, but on that visit, we had the work's car to show off. The Memsahib had indicated that the doors of 'Chez Eileen' might be thrown open for a spot of 'how's your father', if it all went to plan.

It had been years, but Eileen always did use sex as a reward, like throwing the dog a biscuit if it had behaved. Frankly, the offer of a quick marital bounce did not interest me at all and as far as I was concerned, she could have kept her curlers in and the door closed.

The threat of impending *'maritals'* when we got home caused me to lose sleep. It felt like I would be cheating on Henry if I had to sleep with my wife. It was all rather stressful and confusing. I was never cut out for skulduggery.

I am a simple man, and I used to be an honest one, at least I'd always tried to be, but I had crawled down into the sewers like Charlie and the rest. Nobody had dragged me; I'd made my own way into the dirt. Principles fly out of the window when love walks in the door.

If I told her *'no, thanks'* she would have smelt a rat, and that of course would be me!

I needn't have worried. Charlie had a spanking new Jag delivered while we were there and he told us he had bought Beryl a rather smart red mini to drive around in because she had recently passed her test. I think it was compensation for his last visit over the side. Our sensible grey family bus didn't cut it, and we looked exactly like what we were, dull and suburban. Eileen was absolutely fuming, so the offer of marital relations was taken off the table, thank God.

Their house had a sea view, from the toilet window. Not exactly on the beach, but close enough. We went out for a meal, to a place Charlie knew. Compared to Eileen's food, it was distinctly average. Beryl upset her by saying, 'We thought it would be a treat for you, dear. Makes a nice change from all that home-made food.'

Charlie winced, and I headed for the gents before Krakatoa exploded. They were such a funny pair. Put them together for more than a few hours and they fought like cats in a sack. *'More needles than a dodgy Christmas tree,'* as Charlie put it. Yet they could not do without each other.

Their time in the orphanage had taught them that they only had each other to lean on, not that either of them would ever admit that. Eileen had grown a suit of armour to keep the hurt away. A sensible and practical outfit that she showed to the world. It had a big, red label that read, *'Don't come any nearer because I can see right through you, and I am nobody's fool, so don't try anything'.*

Beryl's armour came in a jar. Her 'war paint', as Charlie called it. She'd learned early on that men responded to a pretty face. She was always immaculately overdressed, and she made her way in the world with a bucket of perfume, extremely high heels and a regular appointment at the beauty parlour. As she'd grown older, the make-up had become thicker and the clothes a lot more colourful, but the heels stayed the same.

At the time, leopard skin was her current fad. Not the real thing, of course, Charlie wouldn't have shelled out for that, but she had made an attempt at something approaching a big cat. She had a fake leopard skin coat that Eileen called the 'pub carpet'.

Chalk and cheese they were, but when you got beneath the armour, they were exactly the same. Brittle and damaged beyond repair, forever showing the world that it could not hurt them, which was rubbish. I would have dearly liked to know who had done this to two little girls. Then I would have shaken them until their fillings dropped out.

Chapter 10

My goodness, winter 1963 turned out to be a bugger, even beating 1947 and that one had been a complete pig.

It started at Christmas with snow and freezing temperatures, then it carried on throughout the new year and kept going. We got to the beginning of March before we had a day without frost. The entire country lay in thrall to this icy beast, and the papers, when we got them, were full of stories about people and poor defenceless animals who had died in the grip of a winter like no other we had known.

Isn't it funny how people come together in a crisis? All the men of Radcliffe Road, me included, were out clearing paths and putting down cinders, so that the old people in the street wouldn't slip over. The first time we did it, we had a sort of community snowball fight afterwards, which was fun.

Eileen, true to practical form, bless her, dusted off the WI tea urn that we kept in the cupboard under the stairs. She wheeled it out into the road, filled with cocoa. The other ladies of Radcliffe Road all contributed something too - buns and bacon sarnies, mostly. Even snotty Muriel Wellington at number eight. Eileen had always said Muriel thought she was above the rest of us. Well actually the phrase 'all fur coat and no knickers' came out. John Wellington, who was a teacher, helped me to dig out the phone box in case anyone needed it in an emergency.

I never loved Eileen, and she never loved me, although we did care about each other. We knew full well how the situation stood in that regard, but seeing her standing behind the tea urn in her stout winter boots with their sensible heels, a scarf around her head and an old green coat she only wore for sluicing out the bins, I was overtaken with admiration for my wife. She would have made a magnificent general. Muriel Wellington might have looked like a film star in her posh coat and her pearls, but my Eileen, handing out the cocoa and efficiently feeding an army of chilly, red-nosed workers, was a queen.

Terry was home and helping out; so was Claudie. We all pitched in until our fingers were numb, and everyone agreed that we had done a good job. The chances were that we would all go back into our burrows until the next crisis, or a Jubilee or Coronation, or something, but it was a jolly good feeling while it lasted.

On the way indoors, Henry slipped and fell, landing in a pile of cleared snow. He wasn't hurt. He just lay there laughing like a drain. Terry and I helped him up, and I felt him squeeze my hand slightly. Nothing anyone else would notice, but it happened.

I thought he looked lovely wearing Clara's knitted gardening hat, all pink from the cold, happy because snow reminded him of Germany before the war had taken everything away.

I wanted to give him a hug but, as usual, I couldn't, so he let go of my hand and we all trooped back indoors behind Eileen and the cocoa trolley.

When I went to light the allotment lamps that evening, I found two tiny snowmen on the shed windowsill, each of them was no more than six inches high. They had twigs for arms, and they were holding hands.

Henry sometimes surprised me. He never made grand gestures, well we couldn't really, could we, but behind every surprising thing he did there was love, and to me that was worth so much more.

The snow didn't stay fun for long. It became a never-ending pain in the rear end with frozen fingers and frozen pipes. When it was bad, I tried walking to work, but it took hours and when you got there, you had to turn around and come home again before dark. The buses managed to keep going when the roads were cleared, but, of course, they were rammed tight with people. They crawled along, leaving many standing in queues by the roadside.

At times, travel became impossible, but we found a solution which seemed to work. A few times when I couldn't get home, I stayed at the bookshop flat with Henry, who couldn't get home either. Creepy Derek, the assistant, was long gone by this point, dismissed for being insolent and rude to the customers, so we had the place to ourselves.

It was a short walk to my office in the morning, and I could open up and check for mail or any telephone messages. I even started putting on a large pot of coffee and some cocoa for the others when they trailed in, soaking and cold.

I used the shop telephone to check that Eileen was OK and then I spent some cosy evenings with Henry. He had purchased a decent TV for the flat and had it all done up ready for a new tenant. We spent our evenings like any other couple, eating dinner, washing up and watching television. For once, we had a legitimate excuse to be together in plain sight.

Just to get up and put the kettle on while the other one had a shave was a real delight. I liked to imagine that one day every morning would be similar. I got quite depressed thinking that it might never happen.

After my appointment as manager was confirmed, and believe me they made me wait for it, I made a few bold decisions - most unlike me. I got a decent pay rise, and I thought a few luxuries for the home were in order. We purchased a rather smart radiogram in walnut veneer that had a socket for headphones. I could listen to Wagner as loud as I liked and nobody complained.

I asked Eileen if she would like a new kitchen and an automatic washing machine instead of the twin tub, something she could show off to the neighbours and to Beryl if she wanted to, not that she would.

I trusted that she would do her sums and stick to any budget we made. It was entirely her project from design to installation. Some women would think that the offer of a new kitchen was a male insult, but for Eileen it was a dream come true. She chose a solid wooden one, which could be repainted as fashion changed, and not some flashy trash that would fall apart in no time.

I cannot kid myself that there was not a huge amount of guilt behind this but, to be fair, she had made do with an out-of-date kitchen for a long time with hardly a grumble, so it was the least I could do for her.

She could have had a fur coat instead, but apart from the fact that she thought fur should stay firmly on the animal it came from, I knew she would have chosen the kitchen every time.

We were not the only ones with home improvements in mind. Muriel and John, across the road, also had a new kitchen to show off. Eileen was keen to see what could be done with the space, because their house was a mirror image of ours. In due course, we got invited round to theirs for *'brunch'*, as Muriel Wellington called it. To me, it sounded for all the world like elevenses that had got too big for its boots. Half the street went to see the new kitchen dinette that she wanted to show off. They'd knocked through into the dining room, which must have cost them a fair bit.

According to Muriel W, dining rooms were old fashioned and 'so 1950s' because the modern hostess conversed with guests whilst preparing a meal. Eileen snorted and said she couldn't think of anything worse than having people interfering when you were trying to cook, not that we entertained much anyway. She was as curious as I was to see this wonder, so we went.

My God, it was a sight to behold. Mustard-coloured cabinets, which Muriel told us were in a trendy shade called Mango, and a lime-green floor in wipe-clean vinyl tiles. The work surfaces were made of something called Formica and they were pretend wood. In fact, nothing in this technicolour monster was real - it was all false, a bit like Muriel Wellington.

Eileen was polite and she made all the right noises to Muriel. When we left, she laughed like a drain and said, 'Blimey, she must need sunglasses to cook the dinner, George.'

Eileen's new kitchen was the one highlight in a terrible year. For a while, we were all at sixes and sevens with stuff everywhere and a camping stove and the fridge installed in the dining room. Henry helped us out as much as he could and we endured multiple visits from Muriel, who was nosy, and from Beryl, who was quite frankly a complete bitch about the whole thing. She had also seen the Wellington's kitchen, and she loved it because it was 'trendy'. She made it quite clear that she thought our kitchen was horribly dull and she insisted on making unhelpful suggestions with regard to décor, until Eileen lost it with her and told her not to come again until it was finished.

Eileen was in her element. Totally preoccupied and happy as a clam making her own decisions and liaising with the workmen. She completely failed to notice that my own life was falling apart.

It started one Saturday morning. I got a letter that was pushed under the door of the allotment shed. I thought it was from a member of the committee, as they often did this if they wanted Eileen to do a cake and I was not around. I was expecting something like, *'Plain sponge please George, for the meeting on the 24th'*.

Instead, it read, *'You filthy little queer. I have been watching you and I know exactly what you have been doing with the German. You disgust me'.*

I sat on my chair in the shed, trembling like a leaf. In fact, if I am being brutally honest, I threw up in the sink! I was still shaking an hour later when Henry turned up. I handed him the paper and he sat down opposite me, pale and shocked.

After a minute, I ventured, 'I don't know how this has happened. We are always so careful. Perhaps they will go away if we ignore it?'

Henry shook his head and replied, 'No, this is just the beginning. Soon they will be asking for money, and we will pay, and then more money and more. These people are leeches, George. They will not give up until they have squeezed us for everything we have. They feed and grow fat on our fear.'

'What do we do?' I asked, not that I was expecting him to give me a solution.

Henry shrugged. 'Wait for the second letter and see how much they want, I suppose. I have heard of these things happening before. What choice do we have?'

We were both miserable. Of course, I had read in the Sunday papers about men being threatened. An actor, from a famous theatrical family, had recently been up in court for importuning in a gentleman's public lavatory and it was all over the news. He was recently widowed, and I guess he was feeling lonely. It was a bad law that gave every blackmailer an opportunity and made every homosexual into a potential victim. Many men such as ourselves, who lived an outwardly married existence, had secret lives because of feelings that we could not deny. We were persecuted by everyone just for being ourselves.

The thought of disgrace haunted us constantly. Some poor men had been driven to suicide by these vultures. We waited for the next note to turn up, and it did. It was sent to Henry at the bookshop.

This time it called him a filthy Nazi queer, and it contained a threat to break all his shop windows and to write to the police and to his family to tell them about his homosexuality. It was all rather odd, though, because no money was mentioned.

Henry had a theory. 'I don't think this is about money, Georgie,' he said one evening, when Eileen was at Beryl's and we were lying in his bed.

'It's about power. This person is sick. He or she knows and now they want to play cat and mouse with us. They are getting their jollies from scaring us witless and it is working.'

I couldn't help but agree with him.

We lived in constant fear for spending a few nights in each other's arms. Then, just as we thought whoever it was had forgotten about us, or got bored, another letter arrived, through the letterbox, at home no less. Thank God, Eileen was preoccupied with choosing kitchen door handles or something, so I collected the mail. I recognised the typed envelope immediately and took it off to the loo to read it in private.

Same disgusting threats and no demand for money, only this time it was worse, so much worse. There was a grainy photograph of the two of us. It must have been taken with a long lens through Henry's kitchen window at the flat. I was washing up, wearing his dressing gown and he was shirtless with his arms around me, mucking about with the dish mop and pretending to help. Nothing too graphic, but it was more than enough. There were icicles on the windowsill, so it must have been taken during one of the times we'd got stuck and I stayed at the flat. I remained terrified, sweating and shaking in that bathroom for almost an hour. I only came out because I didn't want Eileen to think I had the back-door trots and start asking awkward questions. As for the photo, I flushed it right back into the sewer it had come from.

I lost weight because of the stress and my stutter got much worse. Henry was withdrawn and reflective. We were trapped rats waiting for the cat to pounce and we only had each other. I mean, who else could we tell?

Outwardly, we had to maintain the façade of our other lives and the strain began to show. Both of us became obsessed with the notion that we were being watched, and we were wary of being alone together for more than five minutes. Henry insisted on keeping the shed door propped open when both of us were in there, which was draughty and cold, as well as daft.

I started to have bad dreams. Not exactly nightmares, but very unpleasant and disturbing. Thank God Eileen and I had separate rooms, because I might have been talking in my sleep. Usually, the dreams involved me being led away by the police in front of a jeering crowd of football fans. Henry was there, dressed for the allotment in his gardening hat and Wellingtons, and not much else. He was always holding Eric on his lead. I was only wearing my vest and no drawers. I am sure Professor Freud would have had a few things to say about that little lot.

Festering away in my mind was the constant nagging worry that the police would come for us and it would be in all the papers. I would lose my job and the respect of my family. When I spoke to Henry about my fears, he said he knew exactly how I was feeling because he had been there already. Then he sighed and mumbled, 'Try being German, George. It isn't just a few friends and neighbours; the whole bloody world hates us just for being Krauts.'

Anxiety was driving a wedge between us, and I couldn't help but think that somebody out there was laughing his or her socks off! I am relieved to say that three months passed, and we did not get another letter. We hoped that whoever it was had found a richer vein of gold to squeeze.

We were not totally convinced that everything was absolutely hunky dory, but we could at least sleep at night.

It made me realise just how vulnerable we were. Our blackmailer might well have grown bored with us, but how long would it be before the next one came along?

Chapter 11

1964 came in with my birthday, as it always does. As I was a bit early, I have always presumed myself to be the result of a liaison between my parents during the spring of 1917.

How my parents met, is a funny story. In late 1916, my father was a young army chaplain just out of the seminary and doing visits to wounded soldiers before he did his turn at the front. He went to a farm where a man (my uncle) was recovering. Dad arrived at the gate to hear a cry and a lot of extremely bad language coming from the pigsty. He rushed to help and found my mother completely covered in pig muck and slops. The sow had got a bit greedy and knocked her flying.

When he hauled her up, she laughed, and he told me that was the moment he fell in love with her. Dad was five feet five on a good day and very slight, just like me, although I was a fair bit taller in my prime. Mum, as her father used to put it, was a big, healthy girl, tall and strapping with curly yellow hair and a pink complexion.

They walked out together for a while as one did in those days, then my father was sent as chaplain to the front. He got shot through the elbow and that ended his military career pronto, because his left arm was smashed to splinters and never much use after that. Somewhere along the line, their walking out had become a little bit of staying in, because he arrived home to find out that I was most definitely on the way. He proposed to my mother immediately then he went to face my grandfather and his shotgun.

Grandpa gave him a bit of a look up and down, then his ruddy farmer's face broke into a pumpkin grin as he roared with laughter and said, 'And you, a man of the cloth and all that! Well, we was all young once. Better get them banns read double quick then, Mr Potter, before the bishop finds out, or can we call you Andy seeing as you is going to be family?'

They were married by special licence and, in due course, I arrived - early and unexpected on a truly filthy winter morning. Dad told me that my gran and the midwife brought me into the world while he and my grandfather played cards all night. At 3am on New Year's Day, I announced my presence by yelling the place down. My grandfather rolled his eyes in the direction of the bedroom above.

He finished the Scotch he was drinking and put out his hand saying, 'Congratulations, Andy, and that, if I am not very much mistaken, is a boy.'

Dad asked him how he knew, and he shrugged and told him he had been father to four boys, and they'd always sounded completely peed off and totally outraged when they'd arrived, whereas my mother, his only daughter, had come into the world with hardly a sound. Dad guessed he was joking but, of course, he was right. Four pounds ten ounces, I was. A funny-looking thing with great big eyes and as bald as a goblin, apparently. They all joked about sending me back in exchange for a prettier one, but in the end, they decided to keep me and love me anyway.

The reason I am going over all this is that in 1964, Eileen and I became grandparents.

Terry had come out of the army. He'd found his own place in town, got himself a half-decent job and started on his career. We saw little of him as he was building his new life, but he always phoned on a Sunday afternoon and, now and again, he would appear for a jolly good feed and to get some washing done.

One Saturday morning, he turned up looking a bit sheepish and said he had brought his intended to visit. We were delighted and he went to fetch her from the car. That boy of ours certainly knew how to keep a secret. You could have knocked us down with a feather when Henry's Claudie walked through the door.

Eileen gave them both a questioning look before eyeing Claudie, as she said with a raised eyebrow, 'Anything else you two want to tell us?'

Terry sighed. 'I knew there would be no getting around you, Mum. How do you fancy becoming a granny in October?'

They had already been to the town hall to arrange a wedding for the earliest possible date.

We called Henry in from next door. He was as surprised as we were because they had kept things very quiet. Everyone stood around drinking sherry and feeling a bit awkward. In the end, we did what most families do when an unexpected baby is on the way, we pulled together and made the best of things.

Eileen decided that she was going to be Nana Eileen, no matter what the baby thought about the matter. Beryl didn't seem terribly keen on being a great aunt because it made her sound old, but she was pleased for her sister and not being at all bitchy about things, which was a welcome change.

Henry also made his choice. Opa is German for Grandpa, so that left me to make up my own mind. I rather fancied being Poppa, as Opa and Poppa kind of went together.

Eileen suggested that 'Poppa Potter was a bit of a mouthful for me to manage, let alone a small child.'

I replied that, 'It was my choice and Poppa it was going to be.'

They had a short registry office wedding. Eileen bought a new hat, and Henry was a proud father as he walked Claudie down whatever they have that passes for an aisle in these places. He was not Claudie's biological parent any more than I was Sally's, but we were the only dads they had ever known and, as far as we were concerned, they were our daughters. I had hoped to be walking Sally down the aisle one day but, alas, it was not to be.

Shortly after this, when they had gone off on their honeymoon, I was taken ill. All I can remember is waking up feeling absolutely lousy and calling for Eileen. She took one look at me and bolted to phone for the ambulance. Something I picked up from a scratch at the allotment they think. I was completely out of it for a few days. It was a hazy time of shivering cold and burning hot, sometimes at the same time, with various people coming to stick things in me only to disappear again with a cargo of precious Potter fluids on board.

Once, I woke up at some ungodly hour to find Henry sitting in a chair by the bed. He was reading under one of those tall, angle poise lamps and didn't notice me at first. I coughed and he looked up and smiled. I reached for his hand, and he touched my fingers.

I had a bit of trouble talking so he put a finger to his lips and told me, 'Go to sleep, Georgie,' which was a comfort.

I found out later that he was there under false pretences. When people are very ill and have their own room, close family can visit at any time, but only relatives. Eileen, bless her, invented me an adopted German refugee brother so that Henry could visit too. Apparently, they never checked.

When I started to feel a bit better, I had lots of visitors, and I was thoroughly spoiled. Eileen brought me clean pyjamas every day, and lemon and barley water to aid my recovery. Beryl and Charlie came. He recounted some filthy jokes, and Beryl swanned around looking at my chart and tutting. She'd been a nurses' aid during the war, so she thought she knew a bit about medicine, prompting Eileen to mutter darkly about,

'People who think they are bloody Florence Nightingale.'

Henry told me a funny little story. He'd been in the post office looking at the get-well cards. Vera Bulstrode had been chatting to one of her cronies and he'd heard her say,

'There's a rather nice Jag parked up in Radcliffe Road.'

'I wonder whose fancy man that is?'

Vera snorted, 'Oh, outside Eileen Potter's, you mean? That will be her brother-in-law, dear. You know, Flash-Harry from Hastings. He's married to that brassy sister of hers. Lady Muck that one, always giving herself airs and graces, but in my opinion she's no better than she ought to be.'

She dropped her voice. 'A bit of a T.A.R.T by the looks of it. Probably come to visit poor old George. He was took proper bad and Eileen had to call out the ambulance. It's touch and go, I heard.'

Vera always loved to make a proper old drama out of everything, probably because she had nothing interesting happening in her own life. Henry coughed and told them I was doing absolutely fine, and they shut up, but it did make me smile to think of Beryl described as a T.A.R.T because, well, she was a bit!

While I was recovering and looking forward to going home and getting on with the preparations for our new arrival, a truly awful thing happened. My old pal Ronnie Brown died. Eileen brought me the evening paper so I could read about it for myself. Poor old Ron, he'd been knocked down late one night when he was coming home from rehearsals. Apparently, he'd stepped off the kerb without looking and a vehicle had hit him. The driver hadn't stopped, and it had been too dark for the only witness to see very much. He was known to get a bit absent minded when he was in the middle of a big production so he might well have been concentrating on something else.

He had no family, so the firm paid for everything, which was very good of them. The funeral was well attended and a few of his musical am-dram mates shouldered the coffin. He went out of the church with Ethel Merman belting out *'There's No Business Like Show Business'* and for once he was the star of the show. Oh, how he would have loved it!

I was allowed home and eventually I got back to work. Life has a way of smoothing itself out; births and deaths are the bumps and dips that we go through but generally life carries on, until it doesn't.

I got back into the world of baby prep, and we went halves with Henry on a decent Silver Cross pram, which was, in fact, delivered to my work because of some mix up. I only gave them my work address and phone number in case they needed to contact me over any problems, not for them to dump it in reception and scarper, which was exactly what they did.

It was huge and expensive looking with shiny blue and cream coachwork, impossible to hide. Whichever variety Potter junior turned out to be, he or she would be travelling around in style.

Oh, how the staff in my office teased me when the doorman wheeled it in. I had to tell them that I was going to be a grandfather. I didn't really share many details of my private life at work, apart from what was growing on the allotment. None of anyone else's business as far as I could see.

At lunchtime, I wheeled the damned thing down the front steps and over to Henry's shop and he brought it home in the van. We kept it in the cupboard under the stairs until it was needed, because everyone knows it is bad luck for the parents to take receipt before the child arrives.

Eileen and I knew the pain of losing a baby shortly after birth. Neither of us was superstitious, but we weren't going to be taking any chances.

Baby Helena Clara put in an appearance early one morning. The call came around breakfast time and we were all thrilled skinny. Young Miss Potter had taken her time getting here. She was two weeks' late, which had put us all on edge. Eileen had told me that babies were rarely punctual, especially first ones.

Claudie had an easy time of it and the baby was a bonny 8lb. Terry was there when it happened, as that was the new way of doing things. Eileen did not think this was a very good idea, as according to her, men only got in the way. When she'd had Terry, she'd just got on with it with a midwife, while Beryl had looked after Sally. She mentioned her first husband, a thing she rarely did, and she snorted that when Sally was born, Arthur was exactly where he should have been, in the pub.

Typical Henry, he was excited and making all sorts of grand plans. I loved his enthusiasm, but sometimes you needed to pull on the reins a bit to slow him down. I suggested we plant young Helena a dwarf plum tree in a pot so she could help him pick the fruits when she got bigger. This satisfied him for a moment, but I knew he would soon be galloping off again and coming up with fresh ideas.

Eileen suggested, 'Get him to make her a dolls' house, George. Filling it with handmade furniture should keep him busy. I will make all the curtains and carpets and stuff, and you can make her a garden with pretend plants and pots that she can play with when she is older. Maybe you could make a wooden greenhouse. What do you think?'

I thought it was a splendid idea. She was always so sensible about these things. Helena was, at this point, only three days old, so we had plenty of time to get it ready.

Eileen stayed at Terry's for a couple of days to do some cooking for their freezer, to keep the new parents going for a bit when the baby came home. I spent the time with Henry, which was wonderful, but deep down both of us knew full well that the sharing of a grandchild meant we were unlikely to ever go off to be together. Baby Helena was the tie that bound us and the one that would probably keep us apart.

By the time the baby reached six months, she had blossomed into a blonde and bonny little charmer, who captured her poppa's heart. I was absolutely besotted. I think she knew it and I was willingly wrapped around her tiny finger. Her Opa Henry was not very far behind.

Eileen called us a pair of daft old beggars when we vied with each other to get Helena to laugh. The rest of the time, Helena was her Nana's darling, and we didn't get a look in unless Eileen was busy. The baby also had a full wardrobe of beautifully smocked dresses with matching cardigans.

We minded her for the day while Terry and Claudie were out looking at houses. Their tiny flat was beginning to resemble a branch of Mothercare.

Much against her better judgement, Nana Eileen let the pair of us take Helena to the park. She seemed a bit distracted that day and she told us she had some paperwork that she needed to get on with. The baby was fretful because she was teething and letting us know how she felt about the situation.

So, we set off into the spring sunshine with instructions to give Helena some fresh air, hopefully until she fell asleep. It was a lovely stroll. All leafy greens and snowdrops. Any opportunity for us to spend quality time together was a real pleasure. Even something as simple as a walk around the pond felt like a treat. We sat on a bench for a bit and chatted happily while Helena snoozed. I was nattering on about how

I couldn't wait for her to be big enough to feed the ducks, although I suspected that she would eat a fair bit of the bread.

Henry patted my hand and said, 'Don't be in such a hurry, Georgie. Enjoy every moment, because it doesn't last long with babies, they change so much in the first few years.'

He was talking from the experience I lacked, because it had all been taken away from me by Hitler and the war. It made me a bit sad, but I kept it to myself because Henry didn't need to be hit over the head with it.

A man ran past us and bumped the pram with his arm. Henry shouted, 'Oi! Watch out there, you arse.'

The runner stopped. It was bloody Edward Seymour, my big boss. Someone did tell me he had moved into one of the posh villas that surrounded the park. Helena started to grizzle, and I rocked the pram to soothe her.

Seymour gave Henry an odd look - it was the German accent that had done it, no doubt. Then he saw me.

'Potter!' he exclaimed, as if he hadn't spoken to me only the morning before.

He peered into the pram. I am not quite sure what he expected to find in there. The hanging gardens of Babylon perhaps, or a chimpanzee in a bonnet, but he found Helena. I was frantically trying to get her off to sleep again, before she woke up properly and screamed the park down.

He looked at me and asked, 'Is it your baby, Potter? A bit old for all that sort of thing, aren't you?'

I replied somewhat coldly, 'Helena is our granddaughter. I'm babysitting her because my wife is busy.'

I saw no reason to give him any more information than that. 'It' indeed; she was dressed from top to toe in pink.

'How very domestic,' he sniped, as if it were a crime to be a family man.

He looked over at Henry, obviously expecting an introduction to this German who had shouted at him so rudely. I sighed and gave in explaining, 'This is my neighbour and very good friend Mr Muller, who is Helena's other grandfather.'

Nobody extended a hand in greeting and at no point did he apologise for waking the baby. Thank goodness he hadn't noticed Henry holding my hand under a folded copy of *The Times*. Then he went. Henry called him a very rude name in German under his breath, and I called him one in plain old Anglo Saxon.

We both wanted a coffee, and Helena seemed to have settled again, so we headed for the café that was near the old bandstand. Judy, the woman who ran it, was a friend of Eileen's.

So, there we were, baby Helena's opa and me, her poppa, sitting in the sunshine with the pram and madam, contented and happy, tucked into her carriage.

We shared a piece of tart and let the world pass by for 10 minutes or so until there were signs from the pram that our tiny kraken might be waking up. Henry peered in for a look and made a face. It was obvious even from where I was sitting that a change was in order.

He picked the baby up as if she might explode and went to hand her over. I shrugged and told him, 'Don't look at me, I have no idea of how to change a child. Mine was well beyond the nappy stage long before I got to meet him, remember. Can't you do it?'

Henry shook his head. 'Clara dealt with all the necessaries where Claudie was concerned, George. I know there are pins involved somewhere, oh and something to do with a kite possibly, but apart from that, I'm stumped.'

We couldn't take her home with a full load on board, so to speak, so we were in a bit of a fix and no mistake. Eileen's friend, Judy, came to the rescue. I liked Judy, a kind and helpful soul. She was an American who had come to Britain before the war; she'd liked it and stayed.

We both turned to look because she was laughing fit to bust, then she smiled and said, 'Oh for goodness' sake, give her to me, Henry. She's a baby, not a bomb. Come along, sweetheart, we'll soon put you to rights, won't we?' She cooed at Helena, then back at us. 'I've had four of my own, so I've seen more bums than the Whitechapel Workhouse.'

Henry and I handed over the bag of supplies and we were both breathing a sigh of relief when a voice rang out, 'I don't know what you two are looking so smug about. It's lesson time, gents. I cannot believe Eileen would let you two out without proper instructions, so come on, because we have work to do.'

She meant it too. By the time we left the park, we were both fully clued up on nappies, liners, pins, powder, and plastic pants. She promised not to rat on us to the Mrs, and we beetled off home in case young Helena was harbouring any other surprises.

When we got back, Eileen had a surprise for me. She'd been a bit jittery all week because she'd been plucking up the courage to tell me she had got herself a job.

'It's three days a week, as a trainee receptionist down at the new doctors' surgery. You don't mind do you, George?'

'I think it's a brilliant idea, love,' I said, taking her hand. 'It's about time you gave that clever brain something else to do but housework and looking after me. Go out and show the world what you can do.'

Privately, I mused to myself that any malingering patients would have to look to it; she would soon have everything ship shape and in apple pie order. There would be no getting around her.

She raised an eyebrow, a sure sign that something was going on inside that head of hers. I think she had been expecting trouble, and she said with a certain amount of relief, 'Well you do surprise me, George, and thank you for the encouragement. Some of my bridge-playing ladies have thought about giving work a try because their children have gone and they are a bit bored with hoovering, but their husbands won't hear of it. Don't you feel threatened?'

'Not a bit,' I told her. 'You go for it, old girl. The only thing I absolutely insist upon is that you keep your wages in your own bank account. You will still have your housekeeping and access to the joint account, but whatever you get paid, you keep, OK? Because, by golly, you have earned it over the years!'

Eileen smiled and I'm sure I saw a tiny tear. 'You are a wonder sometimes, George. Who would have thought you could be ever so modern and open minded. But, then again, perhaps we all underestimate you, don't we, dear.'

We left it there, as I wandered off up the hall with its neatly polished lino and brass umbrella stand, to find my paper before the dog got to it. I remember thinking that we were both embracing changes to our middle-aged lives, the difference being that I could tell no one about Henry.

As Eileen needed a smart new wardrobe for her job, Claudie offered to take her shopping on Saturday afternoon and to help her choose some new clothes in the sales. I was happy to pay for everything, and I hoped she thought I was being supportive.

Terry and I watched the football. Helena and Henry snoozed through most of it, while the Potter ladies shopped till they dropped. The girls came back from their trip with armfuls of bags and Eileen had a smart new hairdo.

She looked lovely and the shorter hair took years off her. She usually went to Madam Enid in the parade at the end of the road, but even Eileen admitted that they were very set in their ways style-wise. Claudie had persuaded her to try somewhere a little more trendy. Despite a few protests, she'd given in and had let them restyle her. Eileen was all bubbly and excited when she told me that Claudie had taken her for lunch and a frothy coffee in some hip place that she knew.

After everyone had gone, Eileen showed me what she had bought. Some dresses that were above the knee, but not too short, and long, brown boots. She even modelled one outfit, a crimplene pinafore dress in navy blue with a matching spotted blouse.

'What do you think?' she asked. 'Not too young and trendy for me, is it?"

I whirled my finger around. 'Not a bit. Give us a twirl then.'

'Don't be daft,' she scolded, but she did it anyway.

She was very happy, like the young girl she had never been allowed to be. I had a gift for her. With assistance from Claudie, I had purchased a new handbag, which I'd been assured was just right for the working woman.

'This is for you. I hope you like it? I kept the receipt if you want to change it.'

Tearful, she opened the wrapping and gasped, 'Oh it's beautiful, George, it must have cost you a fortune.' After dabbing her eyes with her hankie, she gave me a peck on the cheek and called me '*a daft old beggar*'. Then she went off to phone Beryl.

True to form, Beryl was the nasty old fly in Eileen's ointment. I think she was jealous. Some people can't stand it when other people grow. I got the full rundown when Eileen came back. She mimicked her sister's whiny voice beautifully.

'I can't understand why on earth you would want to go out to work, Lena dear, not when you can do what you like on his money anyway. It doesn't make sense.' (Lena was the baby name she'd used before she could say Eileen properly, and she knew full well that Eileen hated it).

Eileen had tried to explain about exercising her brain, but Beryl didn't get it. Apparently, she'd got quite bitchy when Eileen had described her clothes and the new bag and hairdo. She said it sounded very 'last year' but the pinafore dress would be just right for the larger bust and the fuller figure.

Eileen told me she stopped listening after that, but it made her quite nervy. I could honestly have wrung Beryl's scraggy neck.

Watching Eileen go up the road on her first day was a bit like sending her off to school. (Once again, many thanks Adolf for robbing me of the real thing with both my children). I don't mean to be patronising. Eileen was more than capable of dealing with the world of work. It was lovely seeing her grow as a person. She deserved to find out who she was, earn her own money and make her own choices. Above all, I think she needed to feel valued for herself, not as someone's wife or mum, but as Eileen.

She settled into her new job and within a fortnight they told her they would definitely be keeping her on. It was an exciting time for her, and I had never seen her more confident. I took instruction and got to be rather nifty with the washing-up and dusting.

A few weeks later, it was our silver wedding anniversary. Twenty-five years of being shackled together. Outwardly, we appeared the same as most other couples at this stage of life. We lived together, we'd brought up a family and now we had a grandchild - all very normal on the surface, except of course it wasn't.

I asked Eileen if she would like a party, as that was what people were expecting. She sighed and touched my hand in an odd gesture of solidarity, then she winked and said, 'Oh stuff their bloody expectations, George. We both know this marriage is a bit of a knackered old war horse, although we do seem to be getting on a bit better lately, don't we?'

She was right. Since baby Helena had come along, and Eileen had started work, things were easier between us. We were more relaxed with each other, and we had stopped pretending that our marriage had ever worked on an emotional level, so we were both a lot happier.

When we came home from work, we both had interesting things to talk about. I respected her point of view on things, and she respected mine. We still argued, but not as much as we used to.

We went out to dinner, to a posh French restaurant she had always wanted to try. We drank champagne, ate snails and clinked our glasses. Eileen made a toast to us not actually killing each other and we had a splendid time with a bit of dancing afterwards. She could cut a rug with the best of them.

I bought her a fancy new mixer, which she had been lusting after for ages, and somehow, she managed to obtain gold dust - two tickets for the Chelsea Flower Show later in the year. She suggested I go with Henry as she thought he would enjoy it twice as much as she would.

When we came home from the meal, we were both a bit squiffy. She stopped on the landing and asked, 'Do you fancy coming in for the night?'

I shook my head and said, 'It's OK. I think we both know that side of our life is over. We've had a splendid evening, and I wouldn't want to spoil it.'

She gave me a kiss on my cheek, and said, 'Thank you.'

Then we went our separate ways and off to bed.

My old friend, guilt, made his scheduled appearance. Like an ugly mole on my backside, he was always there, just out of sight.

Eileen knew that Henry's friendship was very important to me, like her newly gained independence was to her. Neither of us had got the life we'd expected to have, but most people don't. We learn to live with what we get, or we spend our whole lives looking for it. A thought which inspired a short poem.

> *A mournful longing feeling,*
> *so sweet and yet so sad.*
> *Wistful for a something*
> *you probably never had.*

As a young man, I'd had simple but very definite plans for my future. Become an architect, establish a practice and one day build my own home not too far away from my dad. How did I know a world war would blow everything to smithereens?

I suppose life, when you come down to it, is really about managing expectations, and that is what Eileen and I did. A line had been drawn with an honest hand. I hoped it marked the start of friendship and the beginning of a new era of understanding for both of us.

Chapter 12

In 1966, World Cup fever infected Radcliffe Road, and pretty much everywhere else as far as I could see! We Potters gathered together in our front room for the final. Claudie was heavily pregnant with number two and the baby was a few days late, so this added to the overall tension.

Eileen provided refreshments and beer. She even had one herself, out of the bottle no less. She had become very much more relaxed about a lot of things, and she regularly joined the rest of the surgery girls on their monthly night out.

Henry was a bit torn. In the end, he decided to support Germany. When Geoff Hurst scored that final goal, we all went a bit nuts, well most of us did. Terry did a victory lap of the garden with Helena on his shoulders.

Eileen was dancing around the living room with Eric who was yapping fit to bust, while Claudie and I were cheering like crazy. Poor old Henry, I did feel for him, but he was pretty gracious in defeat. He had another beer and made the best of it. Of course, it had to happen. Claudie's waters broke in the excitement, and they went off to the maternity hospital quick smart while we looked after Helena.

Terry joked, 'If it's a boy, I want to name him after the whole squad.'

Claudie gave him a look and replied, 'No child of mine is going to be named "*Nobby*". It's Nicola for a girl and Nicolas for a boy, remember, but you can choose a couple of middle names from the squad, if you like.'

She must have given way a bit because Martin Geoffrey George Potter arrived later in the evening. Terry swore the George was after me, but we both knew it was after George Cohen.

Martin was a very contented baby, who ate like a horse and quickly got to be quite a porker. Eileen thought he might end up being a rugby player. Terry laughed and said perhaps sumo wrestler would be more accurate!

****

Ghosts of the past are generally painful ones. Just when we think we have put them peacefully to rest in our heads, they pop up again to remind us of things we thought were long dead and buried.

It was a Wednesday afternoon, and I had to go over to Sputnik on the other side of town. Some wag had named it that because it was one of our satellite offices - boom, boom!

My meeting finished later than expected and as it wasn't worth going back to work, I decided to do a bit of shopping for Eileen's birthday. There was a particular brand of perfume that she liked, and you could only get it in the larger stores.

I always tried to make the day a bit special. The family were coming over for tea at the weekend and Henry had promised to make her a cake. She always enjoyed her day, but deep down, a card from Sally to say she was well and happy was the only gift that she wanted and none of us could wrap that up for her.

Anyway, I was coming out of the shop, parcel in hand, when a familiar voice called out, 'Hello, George.'

I turned to see none other than Mark Windlesham, my old boss, behind me. He was looking a bit thinner but otherwise pretty good. I was delighted to see him. I shook his hand and asked brightly, 'Fancy a coffee? I know an Italian place around the corner where we can catch up if you have the time.'

He looked at his watch and said, 'Oh why not. I've got ages to wait before I get my train.' He hesitated then mumbled, 'Are you quite comfortable having coffee with a jailbird, George? A lot of people wouldn't be you know.'

'Don't be daft,' I exclaimed. 'If anyone else has a problem, then that is their loss, and I'm dying to know how you are getting on.'

The place was almost empty because it was still early. We sat at a corner table surrounded by vines of plastic grapes and got ourselves comfy with our drinks. He thought I was looking well, which I was to be honest. Of course, I was a bit embarrassed to admit that I was given his job after he went to jail, but he already knew, and he was pleased that it was me.

Unusually chatty, I related the story about Seymour running into Helena's pram in the park. He always thought Eddie Seymour was a complete arse as well.

After a bit of catching up, he got serious and he started telling me about his time in prison. 'It was sheer bloody hell, George. There wasn't a week when I didn't end up with a thumping of some sort, or worse. Posh boys like me don't do well inside. We are easy meat for felons and screws alike.'

I asked him straight out, 'Why on earth did you do it, Mark?'

He lit a cigarette with shaking hands as he told me. 'I'm not a bad person, George, or a dishonest one really. I was desperate and I couldn't see any other way out of my situation'.

I let him talk because it was blindingly obvious that he needed to tell someone.

He took a deep breath. 'I was being blackmailed, you see, because, my dear old friend, now please don't be shocked... I'm queer, George. One of those chaps who preys on my sort found out about me and they started sending me letters. Just nasty, vicious threatening notes at first. Then, of course, they appeared in the flesh and demanded money, more and more of it, until I didn't know where to turn. So I took it from work and that was that, goodbye career, goodbye reputation and goodbye self-respect.'

I fell silent for a long moment. Something was rattling around in my brain and knitting itself together like a pair of socks that matched. 'These letters, did they always start the same way?' I asked.

Mark nodded. 'Yes, they always began with something like "You filthy little queer", but how on earth did you know that, George?'

My eyebrow raised as his mouth dropped.

He gasped. 'Bloody hell! He didn't get to you as well? I would never have taken you for one of the gang, George.'

I answered him with a wink. 'It isn't that much of an exclusive club, Mark, anyone can join if they want to.'

He choked on his drink, spraying the table and me. A slow smile crossed his face as he raised an eyebrow and exclaimed, 'Good God, all those years and I never had a clue. I always thought you were a fine, upstanding husband and father.'

Flushing pink, I answered, 'I am, or at least I have always tried to be, Mark.'

He bent his head closer to mine and whispered, 'Go on then, spill the beans, you intriguing little horse.'

Sighing I shrugged as I dropped my own voice. 'Pretty simple really,' I told him. 'I fell in love, Mark, head over heels for the man next door. He's a widower. We know we can't be together, but we see each other when we can, and we hope that one day things will change for us.'

Mark reached out and briefly touched my hand with his fingers saying, 'Wow, get you, all lit up from inside when you talk about him. Things are changing, George old lad, just keep loving each other and you never know. Now how about a proper drink, because I think we need one, and I'm buying.'

We had a glass of red wine and ordered a round of their rather good open sandwiches, then I nipped off to the payphone and told Eileen not to do dinner. She had only just got in from the surgery. She was tired and happy not to cook, so I was in her good books.

When I got back, Mark asked, 'How long were you paying him? The blackmailer I mean.'

I shook my head and said, 'We never paid a single penny, because the letters just stopped after a few months.'

Mark gave me a funny old look, then he lit up again and breathed out a plume of blue smoke. It made me want one too.

'Of course, the letters stopped, George. Don't you know why?'

'Maybe he got bored with small fry like us and found himself a couple of wealthier pigeons to pluck,' I suggested.

Mark leaned forward and said, 'Oh no, my old friend, that really isn't it.' He finished his wine and then he said, 'It was Ronnie, George, Mr Chirpy, dear old tone-deaf Ron from accounts. Your mate from the bus, that's who was blackmailing you - vicious sod!'

It was my turn to be astonished. Stunned into silence that star-struck, tuneless Ron, the man I had shared a regular bus journey to work with for 15 years, was capable of blackmailing me, or anyone else for that matter. I simply couldn't believe it.

Mark sighed. 'I know, hard to take in isn't it, George? The vindictive weasel bled me white for a couple of years. When he sensed I had nothing left to give and I was about to turn on him, he shopped me to the management. Ronnie had a big problem, George. He was completely addicted to playing the horses. I know everyone thought it was me who loved the gee-gees, because I was always in the bookies, but it was him. He forced me to put his stupid bets on for him, and he owed an awful lot of money to some rather unpleasant people.'

I listened wide-eyed, amazed that I could be so wrong about someone I'd thought I'd known. I'm sure that many of us would be surprised if we could see into the heads of the people around us.

Mark continued lighting up again, then he offered me a cigarette, which I took. 'It was part of his job to process our departmental accounts, so it was easy enough for him to turn a blind eye to the shortages, George, until I told him I wouldn't play ball, then it was, "*Oh dear, I appear to have found a financial discrepancy, Mr Seymour, and let's drop Mark right down the hole*".'

Still a bit confused, I asked, 'So why didn't he demand money from me then, Mark? We just got a few threatening letters and a photograph. No money was even mentioned.'

Mark took a pull on his cigarette, and growled, 'Oh, he would have made you pay in the end, George, but he was clever and he liked to play mind games. In another month or two, he would have sidled over to one of you after work, or some other place, and started to put the pressure on. He liked to ramp up the fear first. Give it six months to make you feel like everything had gone away and then pull the rug out from under you. I guess it made his victims more compliant, and he probably enjoyed the drama of it all. You know what he was like.'

It was true. Ronnie always did love a drama, both on stage, and off it, it seemed.

Mark smiled. 'You really have been very lucky, George. Ronnie died before he could start to turn the screw on you.' He raised his two middle fingers in a gesture of defiance. 'And here's hoping they make that hellfire he is burning in, extremely hot!'

I am not a vindictive man, but deep down there was a part of me that wanted Ronnie Brown to be burning too.

We finished up and made ready to leave because Mark had to catch his train. As we parted, he shook my hand, and we wished each other well. He had a good position in a department store up north somewhere and a steady relationship. He was obviously fragile but happy, which was very good to hear.

Getting a decent job had been hard for him after he'd come out of jail. He'd been living in some miserable bail hostel in a large northern town. He'd grown so desperate for work that he'd been considering putting an end to his troubles and to hell with it all, when an interview had come up via the labour exchange, where he had signed on for the dole.

The department store manager had taken one look at him - all mismatched shabby suit and public-school accent - and had asked him plainly, 'Been inside, old man?'

Mark had nodded, expecting to be shown the door, but the manager had offered him a cigarette and asked him if he was likely to do whatever it was again. Of course, Mark said no, and the man asked if it was thieving. Mark had ended up telling him the whole story about being blackmailed. He figured that if he was going to top himself anyway, he had nothing much to lose.

He got the job, and the manager told him that if he kept his nose clean for a year and nothing went missing from the tills, he would see if he could find a job more suited to a man of his education. He also said that the store payroll was full of 'ribbon queens', as he colourfully called the homosexuals who worked for him, and that Mark would probably find that he fitted in quite nicely. He'd made his way up the ladder to chief buyer for menswear, a role that he thoroughly enjoyed.

As he was turning to go, he asked me the name of my friend and I said, 'Henry, his name is Henry.'

He winked and said, 'Look after each other then, George, and one day you will be together.'

Then speaking more to himself than anyone else, he added, 'And to think Eddie Seymour used to call you a boring little man. What an idiot.' He limped away into the rain, and I went to the car park and home to Eileen and Henry.

Chapter 13

When Eileen went to her sister's for the weekend, as she did every few weeks, she left Eric behind with me, because the journey to Hastings was getting a bit much for the old boy; also Beryl disliked him, for leaving his fur on the furniture and for making her pristine house smell all '*doggy*'.

I was in charge of Eileen's treasure, with strict instructions on the feeding of his particular fancies. Unfortunately, however, he popped his puggy clogs on the Sunday morning. He was curled up quite peacefully with a belly full of minced steak. I had to steel myself to tell my Mrs that her baby had departed this life at the grand old age of 13.

I felt horribly guilty because I'd spent the night at Henry's, and I'd taken Eric with me. It was there that he breathed his last, under the radiator in the hall. Henry got up to make us both a drink and noticed a distinct lack of morning yap from the little fellow. He was always a great yapper.

Henry came back into the bedroom and said, 'Georgie, I think the dog is dead.'

I will not repeat what I said to him.

We had to relocate the deceased and his basket respectfully over the fence and back to his usual spot under our kitchen table. It was horrible, like those old body snatchers Burke and Hare. Thank goodness nobody saw us in the grey dawn light. I cannot begin to imagine what the

164

milkman would have thought. I mean what do you say, '*two extra pints and ignore the dead dog please*'?

Henry felt as bad as I did and he didn't like Eric much, after the late lamented had nipped him on the finger once or twice. Eileen knew it was on the cards, but she really loved that dog and it was going to be a proper wrench.

We laid Eric under a blanket in the garden shed and went back to Henry's for a while. When I got home, the phone was ringing. It was Charlie. He snapped, 'Where the hell have you been, George? I have called you twice already.'

'Burying the dog,' I lied, before I asked him. 'What's up?' Well, I could hardly say I was tucked up all warm and cosy in my lover's bed.

'It's Eileen, old chap, you need to go to her,' he said, his voice softened a bit. 'She collapsed, just as she was about to leave our place in the Jag. You need to prepare yourself for bad news, mate, she's had a stroke.'

****

It had felled her on the doorstep, and it toppled all of us to be honest. When the strongest tree in the forest falls, it is the rest who get battered by the storm.

Terry and I sat with her for days, in a stark hospital room with harsh overhead lighting, and blinds at the windows. One of them was broken, and we both itched to fix it. The room smelled of disinfectant, spilled meals and lost hopes.

She knew we were there, I'm sure of it, but she was terribly confused. Sometimes she tried to speak but it wouldn't come out right. Seeing her struggle was horrible because she had always been such a dreadnought - a strong and trusty battleship ready to take on all comers.

Work were pretty decent. They gave me as much time off as I needed but I was back at the office within a fortnight because, quite honestly, we needed the money. I had no idea of what the future might bring, thoughts of bills for specialist care or private nurses kept me awake at night. I found sleep impossible, most of the time anyway, until the doctor gave me some pills to knock me out.

The reason for my insomnia was blindingly obvious. It was good old-fashioned guilt. There is nothing like a guilty conscience for keeping you awake at night, and I should know. For the rest of my life, I knew I would feel ashamed because I hadn't been there. There was nothing I could have done, but that made little difference.

Eileen had received an awful lot of kicks in her life and she'd conquered them all. She was a good person who deserved so much better than a crappy childhood, a missing daughter and a faithless bastard of a husband.

Things had to change between me and Henry. I tried to talk to him but as usual the damned words wouldn't come out. Taking my hand as we sat in the shed, he said,

'It's OK, I know, Georgie. You love me but you can't carry on seeing me while Eileen is so ill. That is it, isn't it?'

I nodded, miserable and, as usual, torn between the two of them.

He smiled and continued, 'Of course you can't, sweetheart, you are far too honourable for that. Well then, we will just have to be loving friends for a while won't we, because you above all people need to do the right thing.'

He understood full well that I wasn't the sort of man who could ever think about carrying on with our affair while my wife was so ill. I will fully admit that I was a philandering bastard, the sort who had been cheating on his wife for years, and I was a steaming hypocrite too, but not the totally heartless kind. At least I hope I wasn't.

Henry was the most wonderful source of comfort to me over the coming weeks. We discussed the situation many times and he understood the guilt I was feeling.

'You do know I will never be able to leave her, don't you?' I said, as we washed up after he had cooked me dinner one night.

He finished the pan he was scrubbing viciously over the kitchen sink, then he turned and said, 'Of course you can't. Do you think I would ever have been able to leave Clara? We make our beds with the sheets we are given, George. You and I, we know how we feel about each other, but sometimes love is a mountain. Maybe it's the climb that makes the view worthwhile.'

It took a while, but Eileen made good progress, with support. She was indomitable, and slowly the titan that was Eileen started to emerge from the fog. Bit by bit, we got most of her back again, at least mentally, although physically it was a different story. Henry was very good, bringing books from the shop and reading to her at the hospital. He even made her a book stand so she could try reading on her own.

She was transferred to a physical therapy centre, which helped her enormously. I tried to keep things ticking over at home and I was frantically busy getting things ready for her return. For weeks, there were workmen in the house.

They turned the dining room into a downstairs bedroom and created an adapted bathroom. All the doors were widened to allow for wheelchair access. It was messy, expensive and chaotic, but we got there in the end. I became used to coming home from work to paint tins in the hall and plumbing equipment all over the place.

Henry kept me fed and watered - and sane. I do not know what I would have done without him when I had no water or electricity. Through it all, he lifted, supported and loved me, patiently and without any fuss. In the eye of a storm, you fail to see what else is going on around you. The fact that the laws on homosexuality had just changed did not go unnoticed, but I was too damned busy to think about what this might mean for me.

Men over the age of 21 were allowed to be together without fear of arrest, if they stuck to certain rules, like people on parole. I suppose it *was* a sort of parole. We were on trial to see if we could behave like civilised members of society. How patronising and sad, but it was a start, not that it made much difference to me because I wasn't going to leave Eileen anyway.

I saved a cartoon, just to mark the occasion. It was from Private Eye Magazine, which I always enjoyed reading, and it was drawn by William Rushton. He always made me laugh, with his grotesque figures, all with huge noses or piggy little eyes, staring out of a face that often looked like a boiled plum pudding. It depicted two rotund rather elderly gentlemen sitting up in a brass bed in the street. A policeman was bending over them saying:

'Adults you are...consenting you may be...but I would question the privacy of Lowndes Square!'

It cheered me right up because Rushton had a lovely way of popping the bubble of pomposity and letting all the hot air out.

Eileen came home for a weekend, just to see how she got on. She cried when she saw the changes to the house, and, as she wheeled herself into her newly painted bedroom, she muttered, 'All ready for the cripple then, I see.'

What could I possibly say in return? There were changes that we all needed to accept, but it was hard for her to do that because she had lost such a lot, including her much treasured independence.

Henry jollied her up a bit with his idea for the kitchen table. He removed the original legs and made four shorter ones, so she could still make biscuits with the grandchildren. His father and grandfather had been carpenters, and he knew his way around a toolbox.

Eventually, Eileen came home for good, but things were bumpy to say the least. We had both grown used to our new ways of living and it took us some time to adjust. Some days she was really good, others not so great. There were times when we had a small triumph and others where it all went wrong and she was hell to live with.

A thing you learn when you are a carer is that it leaves you no time for yourself.

One Saturday morning, when I needed a haircut and a change of library books, Henry offered to sit with Eileen to keep her company, although she made it extremely clear that she did not need a babysitter. He told me to take my time and get a coffee or sit in the park and relax for a while, because I looked exhausted and it was obvious I needed a break. He was right. I was running on empty, and I had been for quite some time. It was too cold for sitting outside, but I sat in a café with my new book and people-watched for a while.

When I got home, I heard noises coming from the kitchen, which looked like the Somme. They were both covered in flour and there were eggs everywhere. Henry had suggested that making a cake for me to have with my tea might be a nice way to say thank you, but Eileen had decided to be difficult, and she'd told him she needed no help because she wasn't a child. Then she'd thrown an egg at him in frustration. Exasperated, he'd thrown one right back at her. She'd lobbed a handful of flour and so on, as you can imagine.

After a few tears, they both ended up laughing fit to bust. Luckily, I had brought a cake back with me. Of course, we had to clear up the kitchen first. Eileen cleaned her share. I think it did her a power of good to let go and feel normal again. I decided it was high time we stopped babying her and let her work things out for herself, and that was the way we continued.

As 1967 turned into 1968, I had my 50th birthday. It was a quiet celebration for such a big milestone. There were the usual family gatherings and a cake, with the promise of a treat when the weather was better. As a New Year's Day baby, I am well used to delayed presents. It goes with the territory, along with never having anywhere open on your birthday and celebratory phone calls from relatives and friends who always sounded hungover.

I eventually got my present and, oh my goodness, it was needed. Apparently, the whole family were worried about me. Terry thought I was working myself into a breakdown. I was absolutely exhausted, that is true, working all day and coming home to look after Eileen at night.

I had a long weekend away - Friday night to Tuesday. Henry's friend owned a pretty beamed cottage in the country. We went down there to do some walking and for me to unwind a bit. I always found hiking relaxing and it was great to spend some quality time with him, knowing all was taken care of at home.

We arrived in high spirits. I put our walking things in the quarry-tiled hallway and started to unload the car. It was Henry's job to make the beds and mine to sort out downstairs and to put the shopping away.

Henry, direct as usual, called down from the top of the stairs, 'Just asking, do you still want separate rooms then? Say if you don't think you are ready. No pressure, birthday boy.'

I quipped back, 'I'm looking forward to unwrapping my presents and one of them is you, so don't bother with the other bed, because I won't be using it.'

It had been almost a year since I'd been in somebody's arms, or anyone's bed besides my own. You can get quite used to a situation until someone offers you a much more agreeable alternative, then it is all you can think about. I could not wait for bedtime, which looked like it was going to be about 6.30, if I had my way.

Henry had gone all out for my belated birthday meal. Candles, wine, Nat King Cole on the record player and a splendid beef wellington he had brought with him. We were both excited and looking forward to a romantic meal, followed by what I very much hoped would not be a good night's sleep.

Of course, things didn't quite go as might have been expected. I dozed off on the sofa in front of the news while Henry was cooking. I was out like a light for more than 12 hours until I surfaced covered with a blanket, all groggy and confused, with a mouth that felt, and indeed tasted, like I had been chewing the doormat.

Henry was nowhere to be seen. He'd left me a note saying he had walked into the village to get breakfast in case I ever surfaced. He drew a little stick man of me with a load of Zs coming out of its mouth.

I seized the opportunity for a bath and a shave because, blimey, it was needed, and I had definite plans for Henry when he got back.

I had just got into the tub when Henry's face popped round the bathroom door with a cheery, 'Avon calling—are you home?'

I waved from the bath, and he knelt down beside it. He nibbled on my ear and kissed the star on my shoulder. He had a bit of a thing about my tattoo.

I asked why he liked it so much and he murmured through his kisses, 'It's a jolly good place to start on the roadmap of George.'

It was a large, old bath with room for two, so I asked, 'Well, are you getting in then? I could use some company in here.'

Henry laughed and said, 'Try and stop me! You look amazing covered in bubbles.'

So, we took our first bath together in that lovely bathroom with its huge taps and whitewashed wooden floor.

Henry suggested, 'This is fun. Why don't we bring the chess set next time and set it up on the bath bridge?'

I joked back, 'You take such a long time to make a move, we will both be prunes before we have finished a game.'

He threw the sponge at me and said, 'I can think of a much better game to play.'

I don't think I need to draw another couple of stick men to explain what happened when we got out. Oh, my goodness, how I had missed being in his arms, and he showed me, in no uncertain terms, exactly how much he had missed me.

We hiked and went to the pub for lunch. In the afternoons and evenings, we came home and shut the front door on the outside world. I felt 10 years younger just for being with Henry again. So, the affair was very much back on, not that it had ever really stopped. It just changed for a bit.

****

After our blissful weekend away, everything went downhill again. We went through a truly horrible time. For some reason, Eileen seemed to be everywhere. She started popping up at the allotment, telling us how a bit of gardening was helping her fitness and mental wellbeing and, horror of horrors, threatening to dust the shed.

Henry and I got few moments alone together and it was torture. Both of us were miserable, not to say extremely frustrated, because we needed each other, both physically and mentally. We were forced into extreme measures, just to get a bit of private time together. I pretended I had to go to the dentist once and took a long lunch hour. It was half day closing so the shop was shut, and Henry was waiting for me upstairs in the flat.

He was supposed to be cooking us lunch, but of course we ended up in bed. It was wonderful to be alone with him for a while, but I had to keep one eye on the clock because I couldn't risk being away for too long, in case questions were asked. When it was time to leave, I was putting on my shirt and Henry, who was still under the covers, muttered, 'Is that all I am to you now, a quick jump in the hay and back to work? It's been years. Is it going to be like this forever, George?'

I had no answer for him. After all, I was the one who was *'having my cake and eating it'*. My day-to-day needs, meals cooked, socks washed etc., were catered for by Eileen, and my emotional and sexual ones fulfilled by Henry. I was not doing right by either of them, I knew that. I could not leave Eileen, yet I would rather die than give up Henry.

Being patient was not in his nature. Sometimes the weight of it dragged him down. He was a widower, a free man. He could have found someone else to love, someone he could have built a life with, instead of this endless hiding and hoping. Hell, I began to think I should just end it and let him go. Be lonely to the end of my days but grateful that I'd once been loved.

I told him, 'I hate this as much as you do.' It made everything feel grubby and deceitful.

Henry, blunt as usual, pointed out that we were masters at being deceitful and that he was my de facto '*bit on the side*'. I finished dressing and left without so much as a goodbye kiss.

I returned to work and busied myself in my office, angry and hurt but knowing that he was, of course, absolutely right. There had been times when I'd felt it would be fairer and much easier for me to do a Sally and walk out on both him and Eileen, so they could get on with their lives. Later at the shed, when mercifully Eileen was out at her WI meeting, Henry turned up looking utterly miserable. I hoped we weren't going to have another row, but he said earnestly, 'I'm sorry for being such a pig. I was feeling mean because I didn't want you to go. I am as trapped as you are, George.' He sighed. 'And, yes, I could go off and find myself someone else, someone who is free, but I don't want to. Sometimes I watch you running between the two of us, tearing yourself apart, because you are a good person placed in an impossible situation. You want to do right by everyone, but you end up pleasing nobody and you hate it.'

He put out his hand. 'I gave myself a proper old talking to this afternoon when you had gone, George, and I am sorry. We can weather this storm like all the others we have known. One day, I am sure it will happen, but until it does, I am happy to wait. Now come here and let me hug you while we have the chance. *Unser tag wird kommen* - our day will come.'

I was hoping that whatever bee Eileen currently had nesting in her bonnet would fly off and settle elsewhere before long. I wondered vaguely if she was just enjoying the feeling of being well again. She seemed distracted, which meant there was something definitely going on. I hoped she would speak to me about it, but you never could tell with her. I knew full well that she was, and always remained, an enigma, wrapped in a mystery, locked inside fort Eileen, which had walls 10 feet thick.

A few months later, our Sally turned 30. Strange to think of her all grown up and living an independent life somewhere. Eileen refused to mark the occasion. As usual, she dealt with the pain (or did not deal with it) by pulling up the drawbridge and completely refusing to accept delivery. Some damaged people do that. It is a skill they learn when they are young, and it never leaves them. The bruises remain, but they are on the inside and not for anyone else to see.

We had to accept that we would probably never see Sally again, after all, it had been more than 10 years since she'd walked out on us. Nevertheless, a little flicker of hope remained that she would arrive on the doorstep with a couple of kiddies in tow and all would be well. Of course, the reverse was also true. The police might turn up to give us some awful news. Who knew, and it was killing us—the fact that we didn't know what, if indeed anything, could be around the next corner. No news is good news, goes the well-worn phrase. Anyone who has lost someone, and I do mean lost as in they don't know where the person has put themselves, will tell you that is rubbish. Healing cannot begin until you have closure, as the Americans say, as without it, the box remains painfully open.

Just as Helena started school, we got a surprise bonus, a third grandchild. Claudie and Terry had thought they had completed their family, but nature seemingly had other ideas.

Baby Jamie arrived in 1969. He was an adventurous soul, and everyone had their hands full keeping him out of trouble. From the moment he could crawl, he was off and exploring. He even managed to take a tumble down our front steps when someone (Eileen, not me) left the front door open. Lucky for him, he escaped with not much more than a graze on the chin, but Claudie purchased a pair of strong reins the very next day, because believe you me, this child was an infant Houdini.

In July of that year, we had the moon landing. What a moment that was, although I couldn't help thinking that perhaps we should have attended to our own planet and all its problems before we tried our luck elsewhere. The moon always seemed so serene and far away. It felt remote and mysterious, the realm of something vast and eternal, not for us mere mortals. We conquered her in the end, because mankind does not like to play second fiddle to anyone.

It made you wonder what they would do with the moon, now they had it. Probably nothing, just file it away under, *'one up for the Yanks, and stuff you, Comrade'*, I expected.

It was odd to think of someone up there taking a stroll or maybe eating dinner. I wondered if they were looking down on us and thinking about the millions of people on earth, when they were a population of just a few souls. It must have been strange to be Mr Armstrong. I would have loved to know if he felt lonely or scared to be stepping out into the unknown. Nobody else can or ever will be the first to do what he did.

It set me in an odd, dreamy mood. I mused about how many people had looked up at the moon over thousands and thousands of years and wondered what it was like up there. Only Neil Armstrong knew the story. I suspected he would be telling it for the rest of his life.

Chapter 14

Life continued unabated for this resident of Radcliffe Road. The Potter family continued to bloom just as well as the plants on the allotment. The grandchildren were growing fast. Helena had taken up ballet, gymnastics and piano, and Martin started playing football. Both of them looked like they were going to be among life's enthusiastic joiners. They loved being with others, and they were forever being driven off to parties and clubs by their poor exhausted parents.

Eileen made Helena a beautiful bag for her ballet pumps. Pink satin, it was, with a white silk ribbon. She wanted our granddaughter to have lovely things and to be like all the other little girls. I know that her own scars ran deep, and it was very important to her that Helena never felt like she didn't fit in, or was ashamed because she was not good enough.

Henry finished the dolls' house. It was beautiful and Helena loved it, or at least she did love it until Martin and Jamie discovered that the detachable roof made a splendid slide, then World War Three broke out.

I did my grandfatherly bit by teaching young Jamie to swim. We went to the pool on Saturday mornings, when Helena and Martin were at their clubs. Eileen came along to help with changing and encouragement, then we all had a cheese toastie and a jam doughnut in the café before we handed him back. Terry and Claudie did their best, but they couldn't be in three places at once, and it meant they could do their weekly shop and fit in a child-free half hour for a coffee together before pick-up time. I am writing about the swimming because it dovetails very nicely into what I have to tell next.

Eileen had a bit of a win on the pools. It wasn't a fortune, but a tidy little sum all the same. She was thrilled.

I asked her, 'OK, Mrs Money-Bags, what are you going to do with it all?'

She gave me a beaming grin and said, 'All our lives, we have been thrifty and sensible. Let's buy a colour TV and blow the rest on a trip to the sun.'

So we did. It was all very exotic. Two weeks in Majorca on one of the new package deals. A Potter family holiday, with added Muller.

Beryl stuck her oar in over the phone and said, 'But it sounds so terribly common, Lena, couldn't you do a bit better, dear? Being herded around like so many sheep with all the other bargain-seeking plebs sounds ghastly. Motoring off to a hired French villa in the Jag is so much more *refained*,' as she pronounced it.

Eileen told her to, 'Have a word, and get over yourself, Beryl Martin.'

She also gave her two fingers while she was holding the receiver and a cigarette with the other hand. I had to stifle a belly laugh because Beryl had incredible hearing. She was like a jungle panther searching for prey. Socially, it must have come in handy when a new source of gossip was required.

We didn't care what Beryl thought anyway, because we were all excited. The kids had never been abroad and neither had Eileen. The last time I had been anywhere foreign, people were shooting at me, so I can't say it was relaxing.

We'd always managed to have some sort of a break when our kids were young. It hadn't been easy just after the war, but we'd managed it just the same. Eileen and I never liked boarding houses because they always felt just a tiny bit creepy, full of ridiculous rules and run like a seaside prison, as if you were being punished for wanting to enjoy yourself and paying for the privilege.

We'd taken them to a holiday camp once, when Sally had been a teenager and Terry a youngster. It had been one of those rare times when the whole family had got along. After she had got over her adolescent disgust at our bourgeois taste, Sally palled up with a group of other young girls and they spent the whole time giggling about boys, when not under the beady eyes of their mothers. Eileen joined in with the spirit of things and entered the 'make a bonnet' competition and I won the archery contest, which meant free ice cream for the kids all week. They teased me about it being a lucky shot and Eileen explained, quite proudly, that I had won a silver cup for archery at my posh boarding school, so not to scoff. That stopped them in their tracks and unleashed a load of questions about midnight feasts and all that rubbish. As they seemed interested in my past, I told them that I had lived in New York for a while when I was very young and that I had quite an accent when we came back, earning me the family nickname Yankie for a while. I still had the accent when I started at the village school, but it had faded by the time I was about seven. They were impressed, and for a moment I had a tiny sprinkling of film-star glamour, instead of being boring old Dad.

Our Majorcan adventure seemed to take ages to come round, but all of a sudden it landed upon us in a flurry of suitcases and early morning taxis to the airport. Eileen was understandably nervous, but she didn't get too worked up about the flight. She sat in the middle between me and Terry as we took off and we held her hands. She rather enjoyed it, apart from the airline food, which was pretty horrible, so I will give her that one.

She had never flown before and she had been worrying that we wouldn't get fed on board, so despite our best assurances she'd brought some cheese and pickle sandwiches, just in case. They actually came in pretty handy, when the kids took one look at whatever swill they served up in that little plastic box and completely refused to touch it.

We had a really good time. Because of Eileen's wheelchair, they gave us a room on the ground floor, which led right onto the pool. There was a cabaret show every evening, except Sunday. It seemed to consist of rather a lot of Spanish dancing with added hoofing provided by the entertainment staff (I mean 'hoofing' in the sense of all the grace of a pantomime cow galloping about).

One morning, Claudie and Eileen took themselves off on a coach trip to local markets to look at the lace work and Majorcan goods. We men were left in charge of the children, which sounded very much better than enforced touring of tablecloths and doilies. We spent the time in the pool. Henry and I went for ice cream, and everyone had a splendid time. The youngsters went to their children's club after lunch. It lasted until five, so the adults got a break too.

I found out something I'd never known before on this trip. Henry could not swim. He stood in the water to play ball with the rest of us, and he confessed to me that he could not swim a stroke. In my younger days, I'd been a strong swimmer, mainly because my father as the vicar had been pretty chummy with the local big-wigs via the parish council, especially our local Lord of the Manor, a man we'd called Goff. He was very kind to Dad, especially after he was widowed so young. Years later, I found out they had gone to the same school, Winchester, but decades apart. I was often asked over to play when his grandson was visiting, because, like me, he was an only child and needed company of his own age.

William and I spent many a happy hour in their pool racing each other and generally messing around while the adults played chess and drank iced gin. He was an easy-going lad with an adventurous spirit, and we kept in touch throughout our teens. His last letter to me was sent from the ship he was serving on. It found me in the desert several well-travelled months later. His vessel was just about to depart, and he had a quiet half hour while everything was being made ready. He sounded depressed and just a bit moody, which was unlike him because he was generally an upbeat sort of a person. I supposed the war was getting him down, as it got to everyone in the end. He wrote fondly of those long-gone halcyon days, not so many years before, when all we'd had to worry about was what Cook would serve us up for tea. Then he compared that lost and privileged world to the restless iron-grey sea that lay before him and wished for a moment that we were boys in the pool again. He finished with the lines, '*If the ocean is my mistress, then she is a nagging witch, and I want no more to do with her*'.

Sorry to say, he drowned when his ship was torpedoed on his next trip out. The grief and the irony still weighs heavy. But, I am wandering again; old men do that.

Jamie seemed to be doing fine. He was happy paddling about after the others, armbands off while we kept an eye on him. So, I thought why not teach Henry.

We started lessons when the pool was quiet. Sometimes early in the morning, we would nip off to grab some sun beds before anyone else got them and we would get in a bit of swimming practice. Hilariously, there were a lot of Germans in the hotel, and they did tend to hog things a bit. Henry got on extremely well for a beginner and he was pootling about with the kids after a few days.

Of course, we found a bit of time for ourselves. When Eileen went for a nap and the rest were busy doing various activities, or just lazing around in the sun, we would slip away to Henry's room, which was not near anyone else's.

Henry, as a single person, had been given a twin-bedded room in a completely different block. It had a distant view of the hills and a closer view of the bins, which was more than a bit rotten. Personally, I think his room was staff accommodation that they had pressed into service to make a bit more cash.

Sometimes we sat on the balcony and had a beer while we played cards; other times, we pushed the beds together and took the opportunity for a relaxing snooze in each other's arms. It was all very gentle and caring, lying naked together in the sultry heat of a Spanish afternoon and listening to the faraway sound of a sluggish ocean rolling in.

'Heaven isn't it,' I whispered to Henry as he lay beside me, but he was fast asleep.

We even managed to have a day out alone, which was a bonus. Terry hired a car for two days. Very brave of him, I thought. He used it the first day and then, unfortunately, some rather gippy tummies started among the youngsters. Rather than leave the car idle we took it out, because Henry and I had been spared the Delhi belly, and Eileen fancied a quiet day on her own, reading under a sun umbrella.

Henry was fine with driving on the wrong side of the road. We set off across the island and into the hills, with a picnic made from some rolls and some cheese and ham that Eileen had smuggled out of the breakfast room in her handbag.

'Here you go,' she said, handing everything over like it was a drugs deal. 'I'm sure you can manage without any butter.'

The butter over there was revolting, like axle grease, so we were more than happy to do without it.

What a magical day. We found a restaurant and had coffee and Spanish pastries for elevenses. In the late afternoon, on the way back, we drove past a lovely quiet beach and stopped off for a swim. Henry had a deep paddle as he was not terribly confident outside the pool. We had a mighty fine time, and the sun was getting low in the sky by the time we took the car back.

I will confess, with a bit of a blush, that it was the first time I ever skinny dipped. We had taken a swim earlier and our things were still wet. There is nothing nastier on the skin than cold, damp swimming trunks, so we threw caution to the wind, as it were.

Henry was not the slightest bit bothered about baring all as long as he could keep his hat on, but you know how it is with Germans. You can take the boy out of Germany, but not the other way around. I am a more modest chap. He just laughed at what he called, '*My adorable English public-school repression*'.

Hidden by the rocks, where we were safe from prying eyes, we stripped off. It was distinctly liberating at 55 years of age to be wallowing in the warm, blue water, naked as the day I was born, and more than a little on the thrilling side.

It was terribly risky, but we were caught up in the moment and we didn't consider much else. I swam off for a bit, and Henry waved at me from the shoreline. When I emerged dripping wet and hauled myself up onto the hot stones to dry off, he grinned and said, 'Get you, George Potter, you sexy beast, all tanned and gorgeous and completely in the buff. Tut tut, what would Reg and our Vera say?'

I told him, 'Nuts to the pair of them,' and then I took him into my arms to show him I meant it. We had a long kiss on a sun-warmed beach towel, which definitely led to more than it should have done. The sheer naughtiness was rather delicious.

I didn't expect to be doing anything like it again anytime soon, more's the pity, but it was rather a badge of honour for a quiet chap like me to realise that he had just done something erotic. Now I think about it, blimey, General Franco could have had us both shot!

We came home tanned and feeling good. In fact, everyone had enjoyed it so much that we started making plans for the next year. The Potters and Mullers would no longer be spending their holidays at the English seaside. Like so many other people, we had discovered the delights of the sun, and we couldn't wait to get back to it.

The chaps at work teased me about how well I looked. I brought them back some weird Spanish sweets and a sort of nougaty thing that looked like it might pull your fillings out. Edward Seymour from the top floor stopped me outside the lift and exclaimed, 'My goodness, Potter, where on earth have you been to get that tan? You didn't get brown like that from working on your allotment, I'll bet.'

I explained that we had been to Majorca, and he sort of snickered as the doors closed, saying, 'You do surprise me, Potter. A wet week in Southend seems more like your style, old chap. We must be paying you too much!'

He truly was a world-class pillock. The cheek of the man. Even mild-mannered people like me got time off for good behaviour. I really wish I had said that to him now, but I would have started to stutter and made a proper idiot of myself, dammit! As I walked away, I remembered the skinny dipping and that sun-warmed beach towel and I thought, *What a ridiculous fool you are, Edward. You don't know the first thing about me or my life*, and I felt much better.

After that first trip away, we made quite a few more. Eileen and I sometimes took a short break together, often

with Henry in tow. The world was opening up and travel
became so much easier.

Terry and Claudie took their kids to Florida one year.
We oldies stayed home, but Eileen and I went to Florence for
a week when Henry was busy at the shop and couldn't come.

I loved the architecture; she enjoyed the art and we both
enjoyed the food. Who knew that proper parmesan cheese
was actually delicious and didn't come in a tub that smelled
of sick, or horrible sweaty feet. We got along pretty well
all in all. Sometimes she did her own thing and visited a
gallery, which left me free to wander the streets looking at
the buildings, and at other times, we did things together, like
people watching and drinking a glass or two; red wine for
her and beer for me.

Henry, I think, was a tiny bit jealous and, of course, I
missed him being there with me. Funny to think that Eileen
and I could ever enjoy each other's company quite so much.

She hit the nail squarely on the head when we talked
about it over a coffee one evening. Her explanation was a
good one.

'I think we felt a bit trapped, George. Rats in the maze
of a closed-down, post-war world. We had limited funds and
felt hemmed in by societal expectation, so we circled the
same few experiences day in, day out, snarling at each other.'

She was right. She'd had no outlet for her undoubted
intelligence in a society that didn't value women and felt that
they should be fully satisfied with domesticity and home
making. In turn, I'd felt under huge pressure to be the
husband she'd wanted me to be, always failing, but

constantly trying to please her, which could not be done because it wasn't me she was frustrated with; it was herself.

Now there was more money around, we were free to explore new parts of our own and each other's personalities.

She had recently completed a Foundation Study Year in Art History with the Open University, and she had been accepted onto the degree course, which was the main reason for our trip. I had no desire to go back to school in any formal way, but I had resumed my poetry writing, and Henry and I were very much looking forward to starting an evening course in organic gardening in the autumn.

We felt that we had more freedom of expression. I think a lot of people started to reject the old ways of doing things, in favour of a less starchy and formal approach. I sometimes wished that I could tell her about my affair with Henry, but deep down I knew it wasn't the right time, and, to be honest, I had begun to wonder if it ever would be.

Chapter 15

The rest of the 1970s proved to be a busy time for our family.

The grandchildren were growing up fast. First Helena then Martin started secondary school, both with partial scholarships for fee-paying establishments, which pleased Eileen because she valued education, and she was near to completing her own OU degree.

I cannot tell you how proud we were because she'd worked like a dog for years to get it. Not so easy when you are pushing 60. Late nights and early mornings were the norm until we clubbed together as a family to buy her a video recorder for her birthday. It cost a mint, but the look on her face was worth every penny. It also meant that she could record her beloved Coronation Street if she was out, and I got to record the football if I was lucky.

She became what she was always meant to be, an independent woman who made her own decisions. I was so damned happy for her I could have burst. After she retired, she taught needlework one afternoon a week at the local college in a class that was designed as physical therapy for people who had suffered a stroke or similar problem. She was exceedingly patient, because she knew full well how frustrating it was when your hands and brain would not obey and do what you wanted them to do.

She also gave an occasional art history class at our local hospice. A room full of terribly sick people would put a lot of us off, because nobody likes to face their own mortality, do they? But not my Mrs. The way she saw it, if you were going to go, then why not have the memory of something beautiful to accompany you in your final weeks.

Beryl, as usual, was the bitchy old fly in Eileen's ointment.

I remember the phone conversation they had when Eileen told her about the hospice class. Eileen often put the phone on speaker so I could sit on the stairs and have a giggle too.

All excited, she told Beryl, 'No I can't come to you that weekend, Ber, remember I told you I am giving a lecture over at the hospice? The last one went down pretty well so they have asked me to do another, which is nice.'

Beryl snorted. 'Oh, Lena, what do you want to go and do all that for? All those sick people won't be interested in a bunch of boring old paintings. Anyway, you might catch something nasty and those places smell.

'Since you got your qualification, you have become terribly la-di-dah, Eileen Potter. No time for anything anymore, not even your own family. Lecture indeed. It's just a little talk and a few slides, so don't go bigging it up into something it isn't!'

Eileen made me a silent gesture, which I assumed meant she would like to ring Beryl's neck.

'Well, Beryl,' she said, 'I'm sorry you think like that, but I am doing the lecture, and you will just have to wait for me to come and hem your bloody curtains. In fact, get someone else to do it.'

Then she slammed the phone down so hard that the cactus we kept on the telephone table in the hall made a bid for freedom and landed hard on her stockinged foot.

'Do you think she has a point, George?' she said, shaking soil off her toes. 'Am I turning into an intellectual snob? Be honest.'

'That's a bit bloody rich coming from Madame Fancy-Pants herself,' I replied, cleaning up with the dustpan and brush. 'We are all really proud of you, love. You fly as high as you like, for as long as you like, and don't let Beryl put you off. You know she's jealous.'

We all knew Beryl envied Eileen's brains and determination, but she would never get out there and give it a try for herself. She had little conversation beyond her latest purchases and the occasional bit of gossip picked up at the hairdressers, which was a sad and limited way to be, if you ask me.

Opportunity had knocked (without Hughie Green) and Eileen picked up the educational ball and ran with it, well wheeled it away anyway.

Several of my own changes happened at work. Sometimes, when you are a manager, you have to put your foot down. It was not my natural way to be, but now and again it did no harm to show you were not a complete pushover.

Some of the young chaps in the drawing office had girlie calendars hanging by their desks. Of course, I wouldn't have allowed anything too revealing and they knew that, but we had two ladies working in our office - one admin and the other a fully qualified draftsperson.

They complained to me that the photos were demeaning to women, and they shouldn't have to look at them. Everything came to a head one Monday morning when, as a protest, our female staff hung up calendars showing body builders, leaving absolutely nothing to the imagination.

I called a staff meeting in my office and said that nobody could put up any image which would be considered insulting. Furthermore, I told them all such material needed to be cleared by me before it went up on the wall, and I meant it. I don't think it did the younger ones any harm at all to realise that soppy old George was not quite the pussy cat they'd thought he was.

More and more women were entering the workplace, and I decided that the lads in my office would show respect. If they wanted to grumble about equality and Women's Lib, they could do it outside work where I didn't have to hear it.

There were some on the top floor who thought my ideas were wacky, especially the ones about equal pay, but even then, I could see the way the future was going.

That evening, I stopped off at the bookshop hoping for a lift home. I got chatting and told Henry all about me and my big stick. He clapped his hands and said, 'Bravo, George', then he spoilt it by saying the thought of me getting all tough was really rather alluring.

I hit him with my rolled-up newspaper, which I don't think was quite what he had in mind!

****

Difficult conversations are always tricky. Nobody likes having them, but sometimes they have to be done. Talking about it reminds me that I'd once had a toe-curling conversation with my widowed clergyman father. It had been horrible for both of us, but he'd done it well and I'd gained a new respect for the old boy (I think he was about 36 at the time).

I was 14, bored and kicking my heels in the last few days before I went back to boarding school after the summer holidays. My father called me downstairs, and I distinctly remember thinking, *oh, what now?* because I was going through a rather difficult phase. We went into his study and shut the door.

He sat on the edge of his desk and said, 'Sit down, because we need a bit of a chat, George.'

It put the fear of God into me to have '*the chat*', whatever it was about.

'Don't worry, you are not in any trouble,' he continued, 'but the subject is rather a tricky one. Mrs Beavis,' (Mrs Beavis was our housekeeper), 'has found an item of, now what shall we call it, '*gentleman's literature*' under your mattress and has asked me to talk to you about it.' He produced a rather dog-eared magazine from under the blotter on his desk.

I truly wished that the floor would have opened up and let me fall in. Poor old Dad; he was on his own and he had to step up to be both parents. I was scarlet and shamefaced, looking at my shoes. He flicked through the pages of the magazine and smiled at one of the rather well-thumbed photographs.

'A fine-looking woman,' he mused, 'but perhaps a mite chilly, considering the lack of clothes and everything, don't you think?'

Oh, dear God, it was awful! If the good Lord had seen fit to strike me down on the spot, I would have been grateful.

My dad sighed and continued, 'I want to talk to you man to man, George, because this shows me that you are very obviously no longer a child. I imagine you got this from your school? From some other boy perhaps? That is exactly what used to happen in my schooldays.'

I stuttered out, 'It's from a friend. He took it from his dad, who is a bishop.'

Dad smiled and said, 'The clergy are people too, George, even bishops! It isn't wrong to do it, son, and I am assuming that we both know what we are talking about here. What they used to call the 'solitary vice'. It won't turn you blind, or mad, or make it drop off or anything, and don't let anybody tell you otherwise. In fact, it is a very good substitute for a chap, until he is ready to try out the real thing in company.'

I was, quite frankly, amazed at his candour. Dad was normally quite shy. Mum, being a farmer's daughter, was very much more up front about these things. He put the magazine down on the desk and gave me a wink. I think he was trying to be a friend as well as a father, but it felt weird.

'I think it's time we made a few changes around here, George. For a start, you will be doing your own cleaning from now on. That will keep Mrs Beavis out of your room and hopefully off both our backs. We know she is inclined to be a bit inquisitive' —both of us knew perfectly well he meant nosy bitch— 'so we will get it fitted with a stout lock, to which only you and I will have the key, OK?'

He looked down at the magazine again. 'And perhaps a lockable desk would also be a good idea. I have asked

Bishop Bob if I can do some repairs and modifications to the vicarage, and he has agreed.

'You know the church won't help with funds anymore, but I think we can manage. Next time you come home from school, we will have knocked through into the box room next to yours to create a bathroom. How does that sound as a Christmas and birthday present?'

I was thrilled. 'It sounds terrific,' I told him, hoping the worst was over.

'There won't be room for a bath, but you are used to showers so that shouldn't be a problem. I was thinking that perhaps we could stretch to a sofa and a larger bed and we could redecorate in a more grown-up style. Maybe get you a gramophone or a wireless up there and make it look like a batchelor flat. How about that? We don't have an awful lot of time so perhaps a trip into town to look at paint is in order. Maybe we could stop off at the gramophone shop? You can look at the records while I get us some iced buns for tea, eh?'

He handed me the magazine and joked, 'You might want to find new lodgings for this buxom young Jezebel and her friends. The top of the wardrobe, where Mrs Beavis can't reach, may do rather nicely.'

Then he left, leaving me absolutely speechless.

He was as good as his word. I got a tiny bathroom and a new grown-up pad to call my own. I saved my allowance and bought a second-hand gramophone and Dad did the rest. It marked a new phase in my life and the beginning of understanding between us. The old childhood rules were relaxed, and we started to value each other in different ways.

There were times when I wanted to be alone and others when I was happy to join him for dinner. He never grumbled if I preferred to take my meal upstairs and mooch around listening to records or the wireless, and he always knocked before he came into my room.

Sorry, I was wandering off again. Anyway, an extraordinary thing happened. George Potter, humble, long-serving slave of the drawing department, got promoted again, which was rather miraculous. They needed a new area manager because Alf Scott, the previous incumbent, dropped dead from a heart attack on the way home from work one evening. All the heads of the drawing offices were invited to come for interview, me included. Eileen was very pleased. As I recall, I got double egg and chips for tea, and on a weeknight instead of a Saturday!

I never thought that I would get it. I managed our office efficiently enough, I think, but nobody, me included, would have put me down as tipped for greatness! Anyway, there I was up on the top floor with my suit neatly pressed, my shoes polished up and my old school tie on, because Eileen had insisted. I must have done something right because they offered it to me by the end of the day. Joan Hallam, the director's secretary, took the minutes. As I have said previously, she was a friend and my spy on the board, and the source of a lot of interesting gossip. We'd met when we'd started work on the same day way back in 1946. Her Colin had gone to the same grammar school as our Terry, and she knew Eileen from the WI.

It had been a unanimous decision, except for Edward Seymour who'd objected on principle, because he didn't like me. The feeling was mutual on that score because, to be crude but frank, he was and always had been an arse.

I got to keep the same office, but I was expected to manage all the satellite offices too and they gave me a new car - a bright red Volkswagen Golf, which was absolutely smashing. I called her Lola, but only in my head. Anywhere else would have been silly.

Henry had told me I would get the job, and he was right. He threw his arms around me and hugged me in delight when I visited him at the shop. Sometimes he would get so over enthusiastic that he forgot himself - the door wasn't even locked!

So, I was a happy man. My spring veggies were doing well, my wife was pleased, and my lover was proud of me. Who could ask for anything more?

One rather splendid afternoon, the rest of the family went to see Helena play the violin in some Christmas concert at the Albert Hall - she was in the school orchestra. There were only three tickets and Eileen wanted to go, leaving Henry and I with the boys. We went to the pictures to see the Star Wars film that everyone was raving about.

I assumed it was some silly children's adventure and prepared to put up with it. Oh, my goodness me - it was brilliant! Surprisingly, it had two of my favourite actors in it; Alec Guinness, who I always admired, and Peter Cushing, playing the baddie. Looking back, I imagined their pension pots were nicely topped up by this extravaganza.

We had tickets for the Odeon Leicester Square, but the queue was still around the block. Coming out, every kid in sight was waving a pretend light sabre, a sort of illuminated sword. We were renamed 'Opa One Kenobi' and 'Chewpoppa' for the afternoon.

Chapter 16

We moved swiftly into the 1980s, and I could see retirement on the horizon. It didn't come galloping over the hill, but I knew it was out there lurking, and I didn't quite know how I was going to feel about it. Unless we are extremely fortunate, most of us spend our adult lives in a familiar working groove, a lot of us wishing that we could pack it all in early and get the boss off our back for good. But bills have to be paid and there are jobs that need to be completed, so we get swept along with the general tide of it all until one day we look down and the water has gone and, bang, we are a washed-up bit of driftwood, expected to fill our empty days with something, but nobody ever tells us exactly what that is.

We Potters spent Christmas Day 1980 apart. It was yet another sign of the grandchildren flexing their wings, and it made us feel old. Helena went skiing with a friend's family, and the boys just wanted to be with their mates.

Eileen and I were actually looking forward to a quiet day, with Henry doing the cooking. Although she would never admit it, Eileen, at 63, was beginning to find catering for a houseful of people quite a strain.

I went for a solitary leg stretch to the allotment after dinner, because I had eaten way too much Christmas dinner and I feared the sprouts were about to make a musical encore. When I got back, Eileen had nodded off on Henry's sofa watching *The Sound of Music*, and Henry was cooking for boxing day when everyone, minus Helena, was coming over.

We had a few private Christmas moments together in his lovely, blue-tiled kitchen, sitting up at the breakfast bar with a beer, while he attended to the roast pork he was cooking. Cold meat, mash and home-made pickles always was one of my favourites.

He made a Victoria sponge for tea and told me I could have the spoon to lick while he had the spatula, a rare treat, and I always loved cake mix.

From under the counter, he produced a sprig of mistletoe, demanding, 'In payment for the spoon, I want a big fat Christmas kiss.' He pointed to his lips. 'Go on then, pucker up and make it a proper old smacker, Georgie, or no cakies,' he teased.

I thought he had gone mad; Eileen was only next door, but she was snoring away like a bull elephant seal, so I thought why not.

Just to be alone with him was Christmas present enough. Silly I know, but sometimes I pretended that we lived together, and every Christmas was like this.

We shut the door and snatched a few stolen moments. I cannot remember when I'd enjoyed a Christmas more. As usual, I had no idea that the wind was getting up and weeds were once more heading into our garden.

****

The economic crisis of the early 80s hit very close to home. I was just about to retire on a fat pension, but Henry still had a business to run, and it wasn't doing well, to the point where he thought he might have to say goodbye to his assistant because there was not enough work for her to do.

Trade was ticking by, but only just. Beside himself with worry, he tried to cut costs wherever he could, and he ended up letting the bookshop flat out again in an attempt to bring in some much-needed cash.

Claudie and Terry were struggling too, because Terry's engineering firm was on the verge of going under. He was working all hours to keep it afloat and drinking way too much into the bargain, which led to a lot of tension in their previously happy marriage.

Eileen and I offered to help out where we could, although they were adamant they would manage somehow. We ended up paying the boys' school fees, which took a bit of pressure off, and Helena found herself a part-time job to supplement her grant for university in September.

This was just the beginning. Oh, those weeds, when they came, grew tall and strong. It was all I could do to hack my way through them to rescue my family.

Henry went off to Newcastle for a couple of weeks, buying books for his shop. He was hoping to use his trade contacts to get some discounted ones because stock was low and suppliers weren't extending credit. He found himself a modest place to stay. A bit different to pigging it up somewhere fancy and treating himself, which was his usual choice.

His boarding house only did breakfast. One windy night when he set out to find himself fish and chips for dinner, he was mugged, jumped on from behind and robbed. They took his wallet and watch before kicking seven bells out of him.

For a while, the authorities had no idea who he was, until his landlady reported him missing when she realised that his belongings were still in his room and he hadn't done a 'moonlight flit' without paying his bill.

The first we knew about it was a phone call from Terry, which came at 5am when neither of us were awake. I sat on the stairs barefoot, with the phone in my hand, unshaven and bleary eyed, without my glasses and wearing nothing but a hastily donned pair of underpants and my pyjama top.

Eileen, with an old shawl slung over her nightie and her teeth out, hovered beside me in her chair, listening in.

Terry was in a complete panic. He had been living on his nerves for months trying to keep his firm afloat, then Claudie caught chicken pox from a child she'd been teaching, and it had turned into a nasty case of shingles, so he had her to look after as well. It was obvious that he couldn't take a lot more.

'Dad, would you go to be with him?' he asked. 'The police told me he's in a pretty bad way and there isn't anyone else.'

Wild horses wouldn't have stopped me from going, and I was off work to do some decorating anyway, so I said, 'Of course I'll go, son. Just let me get a pen and I'll write down the details.'

I wanted to go that very minute. I would have flown there if only I had wings but, as usual, I had to put my everyday face on things.

Eileen made tea and we sat in our kitchen, grey dawn light just filtering through the blinds.

'You OK with me going?' I asked, scratching at my unshaven chin and squinting at the clock.

Eileen stirred the pot and nodded. 'Of course, George. You go to him because he needs you, dear, and you need to be with him. I'll be absolutely fine.'

'That's an odd thing to say,' I queried.

She turned, gave me one of her looks, then she sighed. 'Oh, for goodness' sake, George. I am not entirely stupid. I do know what you mean to each other, you know.'

My jaw dropped—genuinely it did. I am surprised I didn't have carpet burns on my chin, and I could not say a blessed thing.

She lit herself a cigarette and then she continued, 'It was years before the penny dropped about you and Henry, but when it did, everything fitted like a well-made glove.

'It hit me like a thunderbolt. I honestly thought I was being ridiculous and making something out of nothing. The more I observed the pair of you together, it became patently obvious that you two adore each other, and that it was way more than being best pals or trying out a bit of middle-aged gay experimentation.'

She poured two cups of tea. 'I won't say I wasn't angry and very hurt for a long while. After all, you have been cheating on me for decades, George. Who would have thought that would ever happen? When I had mulled it through, I realised, with surprise, that I didn't actually mind too much.

'We get along much better now than we ever did before Henry came into our lives. You are a lot happier and that makes things easier for both of us, so I decided to say nothing.'

She sighed. 'Some women do stay silent, you know, and it appears that I am one of them. It was a bit of a revelation, because I always imagined that I would be the vengeful kind – you know, the wronged woman with a rolling pin in her hand.

'Beryl turns a blind eye all the time to Charlie and his never-ending stream of tarts. I know that this is different. What Charlie does is an insult to all women, to Beryl and to their marriage. He doesn't love the girls he beds, he just treats them as something to be thrown away, like a used tissue when he has finished with it. But you really love Henry, don't you? And Henry loves you. I presume there haven't been any other lovers?'

I shook my head, looking at my toes, because I couldn't quite trust myself to meet her gimlet gaze.

'Glad to hear it.'

She took a puff on her ciggie. 'You are a lucky man. It must be wonderful to have a love like that, George.'

As I lifted my head, she turned away from me so that I couldn't see her face. What could I say to her except, 'I could have loved you, Eileen. I think we would have been much happier if things had been a bit different.'

She nodded. 'I know you tried, George. I did try too, honestly, I did, but the damage was all done to me long ago. I find it hard to let anyone in, except perhaps Terry and the grandkids, because they go home at the end of the day and I get a bit of breathing space.'

She wiped her face with the back of her hand. 'Now look what you have done to me. I am a soppy old cow, don't you dare tell anyone.'

I stuttered out, 'Your secret is safe with me.'

Then I put my arms around her, and we cried together. It was probably the closest we had been in decades, and we both knew it marked the death of our marriage.

'So where do we go from here?' I asked. 'I mean, where do you want this to go, Eileen?'

She shrugged before saying, 'We do need to have a very long chat when you get back, George. You, me, and Henry when he recovers. We need to decide what works best for all of us.'

'I am sure we can come to some arrangement. If you want to leave me, I will accept that, but no divorce. It does seem a bit daft to upset everything when it has all been going along quite nicely and, from what I have read in the papers, life is not an easy one for openly gay men, particularly at the moment. Perhaps we need to talk about this later? It will do us both good to have a bit of time.'

I started to protest but she held up a hand and said, 'Oh don't worry about me. I have decided to go to Terry's for a few days to help out with the cooking, until Claudie is feeling better, and anyway I want to talk to Terry about his drinking. That is going to stop.'

'I spoke to Beryl about it all, you know, years ago. Oh, don't worry, I just said I had suspicions you were having an affair, not who it was with.'

Beryl had apparently snorted, 'So what, Lena? Men are always at it, even your funny little George, dear. If you don't let them get their end away now and again, they go looking for it, like randy dogs around a lamp post. There isn't a single one of them that can be trusted.'

Eileen smiled to me in a friendly way before saying, 'Now do finish your tea then go and pack yourself a bag, George, because you will be catching an early train to Newcastle. There is a tall, rather battered, German who will be overjoyed to see you when he comes round.'

Before we went our separate ways, I asked her how she'd found out. She shrugged and said, 'In 1968, when you came back from that long weekend away with Henry. I was looking through the front room window. You got out of the car, and I saw him brush your hand as you picked up your bag from the boot. I watched your faces as he went indoors and started to shut his front door. Such a look of longing between you. Then you turned and walked up our garden path as if all the world had settled itself on your shoulders, and I knew for certain that the last place you wanted to be was indoors with me.'

Then Eileen touched my hand and wheeled herself out of the door, just like that, without another word. It was fully 15 minutes before I could go anywhere at all. I will admit that I filched one of her ciggies from the packet on the table. My hands were shaking so much I could hardly light the damned thing. Eileen never ceased to amaze me. All those years of hiding and she'd known, and she'd never said a damned thing!

She waved me goodbye as I went up Radcliffe Road, just like every other time she had done during our marriage, but this time it meant something.

I think we turned a respectful corner that day. There was no going back, but perhaps something else had sprouted among the weeds. Exactly what it was, remained to be seen.

****

My goodness it was a long trip, made so much worse by the fact that I had no idea if Henry would still be alive when I got to him.

I sat hunched and cold in a corner seat on the train, with a flask of tea, cake, and some cheese and pickle sandwiches that Eileen had made me.

What a wonder she was. We had just discussed the fact that I been conducting a clandestine affair for over twenty years, and she'd still found it in her heart to make sure I was provided for on the journey to see my ailing lover.

Looking out of a train window on a long journey, you get snippets of other people's lives. Their back gardens and corner shops, parks, churches and football grounds. Sometimes there is scenery and livestock, but mostly it is tiny glimpses into the world of someone you will never know.

It passes by so fast that you tend to forget most of it, but occasional scenes stay with you. In return, I suppose people would have seen an exhausted middle-aged man in a raincoat, drinking tea from an old-fashioned flask that had definitely seen better days, and they would have had absolutely no idea that he was panicked and in the middle of an unfolding crisis.

I spent a lot of time thinking about my conversation with Eileen, what it meant for the future and for Henry and me, if indeed we had a future.

When I got to Newcastle, I found myself a modest hotel and phoned Eileen at Terry's. Thoughtful and practical as always, she had ascertained when I might be able to visit. she also got me some directions to the hospital because I didn't have a clue.

Henry was heavily sedated, quiet and pale in a room on his own. He was a proper mess; eyes welded shut, and, in places, there were more scrapes than skin. I don't think he knew I was there. If he did, he was too ill to let me know.

I sat for a while in one of those ridiculously uncomfortable visitor chairs that they give you to make sure you don't stay too long. All around the bed there were wires and machines that monitored his every function.

I will fully admit that I sobbed into my sleeve. I could only hold his hand very gently, because they had broken some of his fingers to get his rings off, the bastards.

I knew times were tough and they'd wanted the money but why did they have to beat him to a pulp? He had this huge, livid bruise on his forehead exactly the shape of a Dr Marten boot, where some bastard had stamped on him once he was down.

I sat in the sterile room with its white walls and crisp bed linen, feeling utterly demoralised and completely useless. If I could have swapped with him, I would gladly have taken the pain.

I suppose the young nurses who kept bustling in and out viewed me as some tragic old codger in a raincoat, holding hands with his boyfriend. To them, I probably looked a bit pathetic but, I didn't give a rat's.

They wouldn't let me visit for long and, to be honest, there wasn't much point, because he was floating around in some medicated heaven anyway.

When I got back to my hotel room, with Henry's collected suitcase under my arm, I cried buckets until my eyes were sore. A glass of Scotch from the mini bar was sorely needed. I slept with his pyjamas on the pillow next to me for comfort because they smelled of his aftershave.

I tried to see him at the same time of day when he was most awake. Every visit he seemed to be a bit more with it, smiling, well more like wincing really, when he heard my voice. He even managed to squeeze my arm, although you could tell it caused him a great deal of pain to do so. He couldn't talk but at least he knew I was there. I wanted to stay with him until he was better, but I had to get back home because of work.

On my last visit, some young doctor, who appeared to be about 15, asked, 'Are you family then?'

I replied, 'Yes.' And then I got brave and said, 'He is also my partner, if it helps.'

The young man beamed. 'I thought I saw you holding his hand. He's been talking about you in his sleep. You must be Georgie then.'

I blushed and said, 'Yes, I'm George.'

'Well, George, your Henry is a lucky man. If his broken rib had moved a hair lower, we would have lost him. As it is, he's comfortable and I expect we will be able to get him transferred to somewhere nearer to home in a week or so.'

I was so pathetically grateful to hear the news that I could have kissed him, but I shook his hand and left for the station.

****

I returned home to Eileen, which was a mite awkward. Not that she was narky or anything, because she wasn't. If the truth be told, I think we were both trying a bit too hard. We ended up circling each other like a couple of domestic panthers, wary of invading each other's space. I spent a huge amount of time at the allotment, and she buried her head in her sewing, each of us hiding from a painful truth that had to be faced.

It was a tough time for both of us. The borders of our lives had changed, although in reality we had known for many years that the map had been redrawn. Where we were going next was anybody's guess.

One evening, when we were finishing our meal and I was tucking into a lovely bowl of sherry trifle, she looked up and asked, 'Did you know you were gay when you married me, George?'

The question came out of the blue. It was so sudden and unexpected that I almost sprayed the kitchen pink with jelly and custard. I shook my head and stuttered out,

'If you remember, dear, I didn't have much of an idea of what I was at that age. Anyway, there have been a few ladies I have been attracted to, including you of course.'

Seeing as the dialogue door appeared to be open, I asked her, 'Does homosexuality make you at all uncomfortable?'

She waved a hand and said, 'Not at all. I knew lots of queer young men when Beryl was on the stage. By and large they were lovely open-minded people and an awful lot of fun to be with.'

We left it there, with the definite promise that more discussion was possible.

****

Henry was transferred to our local hospital where we could visit him. It took a bit of time, but eventually they let him out. This, I think, was for their benefit as much as anything else. A bored Henry could be a genuine pain in the rear end. Given a project, he was as sweet as pie, but left to go feral, he got up to all sorts of mischief or tried to be '*helpful*', which was absolutely maddening.

Anyway, we had him home and recovering. Before too long, he could get about on crutches and then with a stick, which meant he had carte-blanche to interfere. A couple of times, I took him down to the allotment where he was welcomed back by everyone, except Reg of course. Once installed in his deckchair, he proceeded to make suggestions about how we could improve the layout of our allotment and increase the crop yield, because some stupid idiot (me) had given him a new gardening book to read while he'd been stuck in bed.

I greeted each crazy idea with enthusiasm and then ignored it as usual. I didn't really mind. It was great to have him back where he belonged and acting almost normal again.

Of course, the big gay elephant in the room was never far away. Henry had no idea that Eileen knew about our affair. I decided it could wait until he was stronger, but he needed to know. Besides that, Eileen was nagging me to do it because she was fed up with having to pretend, and she wanted us to start planning a future for ourselves and for her.

One Sunday morning, when the sun was high in the sky and Henry was champing at the bit to be out and about, I took him down to the allotments for an airing.

Eileen packed us up some cake and we settled down in our deckchairs on the gravel in front of the shed to eat it and have our tea outside. Henry sniffed at the flower-scented air. I could see him relaxing, which was good because he had a shock coming.

He munched away happily. He was still minus a front tooth, which I found endearing, but this didn't seem to stop him enjoying a lovely slab of Victoria Sandwich, smacking his lips and singing the praises of my talented wife. He turned and gave me a gap-toothed grin. It was wonderful to see him home safe where he belonged, all happy and covered in crumbs. It made me cry a bit.

'What's up with you?' he mumbled through a mouthful of cake.

I sighed. If we had been alone, I would have kissed him, instead I said without drama, 'Eileen knows, Henry.'

He was still in cake heaven and not really catching on. 'Knows what?' he mumbled, not really listening and eyeing up the second slice.

I rolled my eyes in a silent plea for him to concentrate for two seconds and went for it. 'She knows about us, dopey!'

Somewhere inside his brain, the rolling penny dropped, resulting in a rather more than audible, 'Holy fuck!'

He stared at me in horror, the last few morsels of cake dropping from his lips. I genuinely thought he was going to keel over, eyes staring from his head like some character from the cartoons.

'It's all going to be OK,' I soothed, 'really it is.'

'Like fuck it is,' he mouthed.

He knew my feelings on dropping the 'F' bomb. I never did like it, but I let things pass. Sipping my tea and trying to control the escalating situation, I continued, 'She's known for years.'

He was listening now, and I certainly had his full attention. He was, as they say, absolutely gobsmacked. It took him a minute to get his poor battered old head around it all.

'We do need to have a very grown-up chat; you, me and Eileen,' I said.

'She wants us to get everything we need to say out on the table and into the open, because we need to agree on where we go from here. Next Wednesday evening is her suggested date, unless you have a prior engagement.'

Henry made a half-hearted quip about Eileen banging her sensible shoe on the table like Nikita Khrushchev at the United Nations and calling us to order.

Looking round to ensure we weren't being observed, I squeezed his hand. 'It can only be a good thing, Hen. A step forward for all of us,' I tried to reassure him. 'No more hiding. Isn't honesty what we always wanted?'

He gave me a 'rabbit in the headlights' look. He was clearly terrified so I joked, 'Look, even if she does bean you with a rolling pin, I promise I will still love you. I'll apply a sticking plaster and clean the blood and brains off the walls if necessary.'

He didn't think it was at all funny, so I took him home.

'Don't come in,' he said. 'I need to have a long hard think about what this all means, and you need to go indoors and hide any blunt instruments!'

I knew what he was getting at. Longing for decades that we could come out of hiding and be a proper couple was one thing, but the practicalities of doing it were something entirely different. Also, he was worried that Eileen, as the wronged woman, might arm herself with some domestic object and finish off what the Newcastle muggers had started.

Despite my best assurances, Henry gave Eileen and me a wide berth for days, until she cornered him in the alley by the dustbins where he couldn't escape.

'Pack it in and stop being a complete arse about things, it's upsetting George,' was apparently her chosen phrase, and furthermore avoiding the issue was getting us nowhere. She told him more than plainly that, 'This isn't the time for hiding, because we have all done that for far too long. It's a time for honesty and respect, and for thinking about the rest of the family besides us three and the wider aspects of revealing all to the world.'

When she got going, my Eileen would give Mohammed Ali a run for his money. Henry gave in and agreed to talk, and Eileen promised, tongue in cheek, to keep the rolling pin in the drawer.

Chapter 17

We sat in our neat, tidy kitchen, the scene of many a domestic drama over the years. The big, loud clock on the wall above the AGA ticked away the minutes, like an ominous beetle gnawing into our lives.

Funny how the common spaces in a home are the ones that get to have the drama. I suppose it is because arguments or acts of charged emotion tend to happen at unscheduled moments. Nobody pencils in '*bloody great life changing row - Thursday 3 p.m. living room*' do they?

Someone will say something innocuous over a coffee, or a cheese and pickle sandwich, and that will tip into all the other things that have been building up over months, or even years, which will light the bomb.

The board had changed, and the players had moved without anyone else noticing. What we needed to do now, was to work out how we finished the game.

To our grandchildren, we were a condiment set of three, not four. Nana and Poppa with an opa, but no oma. Salt and pepper with a German mustard pot. Only Clara, the beautiful and fragile vinegar jar, was missing. Smashed so long ago that they hardly remembered there was one, except for an empty space in the holder. I had no idea how we were going to tell them and their parents that we had all been living a lie.

The three of us sat together round our kitchen table, eating a Chinese takeaway (on blue patterned plates, not out

of the cartons, of course) before we discussed the matter in a
'*polite, civilised*' fashion.

Everyone ignored the elephant, like we had been doing
for decades.

I had a headache and a sinking feeling that the truth
was not going to be terribly pleasant. Henry was quiet, too,
pushing his chop suey around with a less than enthusiastic
air.

Eileen finished her sweet and sour pork balls by stabbing
at the last one viciously with a chopstick, which did not bode
well for the future.

'Right then, boys, can I go first?' she asked without
warning.

Take the enemy by surprise was always a favourite tactic
of hers.

As usual, she was direct and to the point. With Eileen,
you never had to wonder if she was pursuing some hidden
agenda or secretly having a bitchy old dig, because she always
came straight out with what she wanted to say and no
messing about.

'Go ahead,' I told her, looking over at Henry who
nodded.

He seemed a bit green around the gills. I wondered if it
was nerves or the chop suey.

'First I want you both to know that I am not in the
least bit bitter or hurt about the way things have turned
out.' She took a deep breath. 'I will admit that once upon a
time, I could cheerfully have brained the pair of you, but that
was years ago, and things were different. No, actually, I was
different then. I know you love each other, and I really do

want you to be together. To be honest, shedding this load we have all been carrying for decades would be a bloody relief, but I don't think this is the right time to tell everyone...'

Henry began to drum his fingers very slowly on the table. *De-dum, de-dum, de-dum, de-dum.* A sure sign of irritation. He was still in a fair amount of discomfort from his injuries and liable to be a mite tetchy if things were not going his way.

'It's OK, Hen,' I soothed, hoping he would keep a lid on things.

'Just hear me out, Henry, then you can have your say,' she said in a commanding tone, looking over at me as if to say, *'Keep your impulsive boyfriend under control or else'.*

Henry shut up but I could tell he wasn't happy. He poked his fork around in the rapidly congealing Chinese and huffed a bit. He looked at me for support, realised he wasn't getting it, then he growled the word 'traitor' under his breath.

I was in no-mans-land and liable to get shot in the arse by both sides, with nowhere to run for cover.

I thought it was important to hear what Eileen had to say. She was a sensible woman who always thought before she spoke, so I said, 'Go on, Eileen, we are listening.'

Henry gave us both daggers.

Eileen continued, 'I know this must be disappointing for you, after all the time you have waited to be together, but it isn't just us that we have to think of, is it, Henry?'

Henry was now looking at the clock on the wall above her head, he wouldn't meet her gaze and it was obvious he intended to ignore her.

She sighed and ploughed on regardless saying, 'We have a shared family and they have lives and friends and colleagues too. This isn't going to be about how they react to our surprising news; it is about how people will react to them.'

With an odd sinking feeling in the pit of my stomach, I realised that she was absolutely right, we were the centre of a storm that would rain on everyone in our wider world; what a sensible woman she was.

She lit yet another cigarette and continued, 'You two read the proper papers just as much as I do. This dreadful, dreadful news about all the poor gay men dying from this illness in America is making people go most peculiar and paranoid. Now it's come over here and I'm really scared for the pair of you and for the family. Not that you will catch it; as far as I am aware you two only have eyes for each other, thank goodness, but it won't be seen like that.

'Do you want our children, and grandchildren, to have their lives made a misery, by stupid ignorant people? Do you want Terry and Claudie's marriage put under more strain? His business is hanging on by the skin of its teeth as it is, like your shop, Henry. Do you want customers to go elsewhere?'

Henry grunted under his breath, which showed that he was distinctly unhappy but listening; it was a start. Eileen looked to me for support. I shrugged; we both knew that nothing short of a minor earthquake could shift Henry when he was in one of his stubborn moods.

Eileen put on her extra patient face and said quietly, 'Think about it. Once we let our news out of the box, there is no putting it back in. I know you want to stop hiding and be a couple, loud and proud of who you are, as they say now, but it's a really bad time to be coming out of the closet, and I have a feeling it is going to get a lot worse before it gets better.

'So, I think we need to wait for a bit. You know how it is; homosexuals have always been an easy target because they dare to appear different, and anything different scares stupid people. Now they have this illness to use as an excuse.'

Some papers were already calling it the 'gay plague' and all those idiots who'd thought 1967 was the beginning of a new era of Sodom and Gomorrah, fire and flood etc. were patting themselves on the back and saying to their mates, '*I bloody told you this would happen once we got that poofters charter!*'.

She stubbed out her cigarette viciously into a saucer. 'If you kick something's head in you don't have to be afraid of it for a while, which makes the ignorant feel powerful and righteous.'

Not for the first time that evening, I marvelled at the way she had handled a distinctly tricky situation with calm good sense. Getting Henry to see it that way was going to be an entirely different challenge and not one that I relished.

She put her hands up. 'That's it, I have said my piece, well most of it anyway. I know it is disappointing, Henry, but it's how I feel about things, and we agreed to be completely honest with each other. It isn't you two I have a problem with, it is the rest of the world, and the three of us have always agreed that family comes first.'

She gave us both a questioning gaze and asked, 'So, what do you two think?'

Henry stared out of the window as if he very much wanted to be somewhere else, anywhere but in that smoky, takeaway scented kitchen.

'George, what do you think?' she asked, lighting up again.

Reluctantly, I nodded and said, 'Yes, you have a point. We don't want the boys, big as they are now, to be excluded from parties by ignorant parents or getting into fights at school. It is a bad time, and I think we should wait a bit and see how things go. What about you, Hen?'

Henry's face was tired, full of shadows. Some were faded bruises, but the rest were made of disappointment and, if I am being honest, a fair bit of pique.

He waved a hand, dismissive and slightly bitter. 'Oh whatever. The pair of you seem to have decided on things quite nicely without any input from me. I'll just hang around and kick my heels for another 30 years, shall I? Until you tell me that it is OK to start living my life in the way I want to live it, with the man I want to live it with.'

My heart went out to him; for a not very patient person he had been amazing, but he had obviously had enough. He was still recovering from his Newcastle beating and the constant pain he was in had drained him.

'Don't be so down, Hen, it will happen,' I said, taking his big paw in my own and squeezing slightly. It was the first time I had been affectionate with him in front of Eileen.

It wasn't as if we were hiding anymore, and she didn't seem to mind.

'I did mention that I hadn't quite finished,' she said. 'I have a suggestion that may make you feel a bit better about things, Henry. I think we should become a trio.'

I remember that I looked up in abject panic only to hear her say sharply, 'Don't be disgusting, George. I said trio, not threesome! I'm not talking about anything remotely kinky here, just that we could come to some agreement where we present our usual face to the world with an entirely different arrangement behind the scenes.'

It was a brilliant idea, and I felt a lot brighter, I hoped Henry thought so too.

'You two will be the couple and I will be your supportive friend. How does that sound, Henry? I know it isn't perfect, but it is a whole lot better than you two sneaking around all the time and me pretending it isn't happening.'

Henry remained stubbornly silent, but he nodded, and I felt his fingers touch my palm. We were making progress.

Eileen sighed and said, 'Of course, we would all have to be a bit discreet regarding visitors and the family and suchlike, but otherwise you two get to spend a lot more time together, and I get a bit of peace and quiet without this one and his muddy allotment footprints all over my clean floors.' She moved her head in my direction to indicate it was me she was talking about, and I was almost 90% sure that she was kidding.

Henry seemed to be a bit happier. 'OK,' he said, somewhat wearily, 'if it suits George then it's OK with me. Georgie?'

They both looked at me, waiting for an answer. What could I say but, 'Yes.'

I felt both guilty and relieved; both of them were strong stubborn personalities, and they were giving ground and compromising, just for me.

****

It took a bit of time to get used to the new arrangements. I ate dinner alone with Henry most nights, but sometimes I ate with Eileen and at least once a week we all ate together.

It seemed to work most of the time. Staying overnight was a bit of a trauma for me. I was used to sneaking around and it felt very odd to say openly, 'See you tomorrow then, dear,' as I popped next door for the undoubted delights of Chez Henry.

The first time it happened was unplanned and I returned in the morning, shoes in hand so as not to make a noise on the gravel when coming in. I felt horribly guilty, like some randy old tomcat who had been out on the tiles all night.

Eileen was in the kitchen making breakfast. She raised an eyebrow, winked in a knowing way and silently handed me a cup of tea, with a smirk a mile wide written right across her face. I went beetroot poked my tongue out and said, 'Oh shut up!'

She shooshed me and then she said kindly, 'It's early days, George. Things will get easier with time.'

She was right, they did get easier, and we settled into a pattern of life that we could all live with. Nobody was saying it was perfect, or even ideal, but between the three of us there was honesty, which was way better than things had been before.

Shortly after this, prompted by Henry, we made a joint decision to make a monthly donation to the Terence Higgins Trust, one of the first UK charities set up to help people with AIDS. It was our way of supporting a community who had no idea we were even members.

I retired at the end of the year. I should have gone earlier but they'd wanted me to stay on to see the new chap settled in. There was a do in the canteen, speeches were made, and I was duly parcelled off with some garden centre vouchers and a rather lovely gold watch, which I knew I would never wear.

To be fair to my old firm, they were never stingy when it came to leaving presents. Lots of people popped down to the office to say 'cheerio George' and to ask me what I was going to do with all my free time.

Edward Seymour did his usual royal visit to the plebs from the giddy heights of the top floor. He was also about to retire. True to form, he purred, 'Not many of us left from the good old days, eh, Potter.' The prat!

After his statutory five minutes with the great unwashed were up, he wished me well and asked, 'So what are you planning to do with all your free time then, George?'

For once he even got my name right. Perhaps it was written on the back of his hand or something.

I said I was looking forward to spending more time in the garden, and he smiled and said, 'Splendid,' then he shook my hand.

It was obvious from the vacant look on his face that he was thinking, 'Of course you are, you boring little worm.'

I found it difficult to adapt. I got up the same time as I usually did, whether it was at Henry's or at number 13, but

I didn't have to put my suit on. Eileen was generally out and about doing her chores, and Henry was off at the shop. I soon realised that I was hopelessly out of sync.

At first it was like being on holiday, except that the break was endless. Henry didn't understand how out of joint I felt. He had his own business, and he could have tottered on until he was 90 if he wanted to. Nobody was going to call time or force him into slowing down.

Retirement was always going to feel a bit weird. After all, you spend most of your adult life being governed by work. There is a rhythm to your day, and you go with the flow like a heartbeat. Weekends are when you have a rest. Suddenly there's nothing to take a rest from and you are expected to throw away the past 40 years or so and magically accept the change. It's one hell of a shock to realise on a Monday morning that you're no longer as relevant, or indeed useful, to the world as on the previous Friday evening.

I learned pretty quickly that Eileen also had a distinct pattern to her life. She did all sorts of things I'd never known about because, for over 40 years, I'd left her at eight every morning and had come home at six after getting on with my own day. She often had friends round and she went to over 60s wheelchair keep fit twice a week.

I wished we still had a dog so I could walk it for something to do. Briefly, I considered offering my services as a dog walker. In the end, I took up swimming to keep fit and to stop me getting all podgy and slow. The lovely Victorian swimming baths had shut and I had to go to the new leisure centre, which was awful. There were no pretty

Victorian tiles; no icy plunge pool or massage, just sleek modern efficiency which was sterile and uninviting.

Henry promised to find some bookshop jobs for me to do, just to tide me over until I established a new routine for myself. I was not at all sure I could stop myself from tidying up the unruly piles of books everywhere. He thought it added atmosphere - I thought it added dust!

I found out all sorts of things that I never knew about the running of the house. When I left home for work every day these things just happened. I had always wondered who cleaned our windows, because it wasn't me. Then I met Bert, a cheery old soul, who chuckled,

'Been doing your windows since 1950, Mr Potter.'

This seemed entirely possible as he appeared to be approximately 103 years old! Eileen told me they had a long-established routine. When he got to the top middle bedroom, she left him a cup of tea and a piece of cake on the sill.

She also said, 'He's a cheeky beggar and he once made an improper suggestion to me, after one too many sherries at Christmas.'

Intrigued, I asked, 'Go on then, what happened?'

She grinned and said, 'All cake and tea privileges were withdrawn, followed by the abrupt slamming of the bedroom window. They were not restored until he apologised, and he never tried it on with me again.'

I remember thinking, t*here goes a very brave man!*

Chapter 18

As your life story draws nearer to its conclusion, inevitably things speed up. Once you stop work and your family grows up you have less to write about.

The 1980s slid by fairly peacefully as I recall, as much as it could in Margaret Thatcher's brutal Britain. We became used to the way we were living, the new regime became familiar and comfortable, and none of us gave it very much thought.

Beryl's husband, Charlie, died. He was found sitting bolt upright, dead as a dodo in his big, polished chair at the bank. It was his heart, of course. Too many fat cigars and running around in the Jag instead of getting in a good walk every day had made him all furred up inside. His father, Alf, had gone much the same way at a similar age.

The outcome of Charlie's sudden demise had unseen consequences for Beryl, because it turned out he had left her with little besides half his pension and the house.

Everything has been frittered away on grand holidays and ridiculously awful furniture. There were debts that had to be paid, and it left her in a pretty poor position financially.

After we had talked her out of her lunatic scheme to run a boarding house, I suggested a sensible plan.

'We split the house into two flats,' I proposed.

'You could sell them and buy somewhere smaller, investing the difference to give you an income. What do you think, Beryl?'

She was flicking through the pages of a glossy magazine at the time and not taking much notice.

Eileen nudged her and sizzled, 'Oh for God's sake, Beryl, put down that rag and pay attention. George and I are trying to help you out of the mess you are in.'

Eventually we got her to agree. She didn't have an awful lot of choice if I remember correctly.

Eileen and I paid for the plans to be drawn up to help her out. Quite frankly, it was a bloody nightmare; mainly because Beryl was most unhelpful, escaping meetings for the hairdressers and spending cash that she didn't have, racking up more debts.

After months of planning offices, permissions and revisions of plans, we were finally getting somewhere when madam had other ideas. One morning, she phoned to inform us that she was going to live in Spain.

'I'm going to play golf all day and have a laugh, instead of staying here being all miserable and cold. Charlie wouldn't have wanted that. A gentleman friend has offered me his apartment at a very reasonable rate so I'm off to the sun.'

Eileen almost dropped the phone in astonishment. 'What about the plans we had drawn up?' she asked, squeezing the receiver like she wished it was Beryl's neck.

'Oh,' came the reply, 'another gentleman friend has offered to buy the house. He knows planning permission or whatever you call it has already been granted, so he gave me a very good price. It seemed a pity not to accept it, Lena, but do thank George for all his trouble. Ta ta, dear.'

The line went dead, leaving Eileen completely thunderstruck on the other end of it.

When I thought back over the many times we had helped Beryl out, it made me very angry. I consoled myself with the fact that in Spain she would be out of reach. If she got herself into a mess, then it was her problem, not ours.

I wanted to wring her scrawny neck, but Eileen said I would have to fight her for the privilege of doing it. The sisters didn't speak for weeks, but they made it up in the end, and Beryl flew off to the sun and out of our lives, or so we thought.

Over the following few years, she got herself into all sorts of scrapes financially and emotionally and we were always called upon to sort it out, because that is what families do. Some people are givers and some are takers. Beryl was neither of these - she was a bloody grabber with both hands.

Henry shut his bookshop doors for the last time in 1994. He decided it was all getting too much for him and he rather fancied taking things easy, pottering around on the allotment instead of leaving me snoozing in bed to go to work every day.

One foul, winter morning, when I saw no reason at all to relocate from under his duvet, he looked out of the window and growled, 'Bugger this for a game of soldiers, Georgie.'

I had secretly been hoping he would retire so we could spend more time together, but it was a decision he had to make for himself. He sold most of the stock and the rest remained to decorate the coffee shop that moved in after him. The new owner was his old assistant, Lindsey. She asked him if she could call it '*Henry's*'. He was flattered and, of course, he said yes.

He found it tough to adapt because it takes a bit of time to wind down. I was the same at first, but I soon learned to fill up my days with interesting things. People say that a good retirement means they don't know how they found the time to go to work. It is true. I swam, played bowls with Eileen, and I was on several committees - life was good and I intended it to stay that way. Eileen, on the other hand, decided we needed to shake things up a bit.

The weather was mild, and she asked me if I would like a trip to the park - just me and her. We had a splendid afternoon, feeding the ducks and talking about old times when we used to bring the kids and then the grandkids for a run about.

We sat by the duck pond and had a tea. It came in a nasty Styrofoam cup with a lid on it. Not at all like when Judy had run the café and we'd had proper china.

We sat in the sunshine for a bit then she took my hand and said, 'Thank you for looking after me, George.'

I gave her fingers a friendly squeeze, because I knew that there was something in the wind.

She got a bit teary and said, 'I think it is high time we came out of the woodwork, George. Helena will be getting her PhD in August so they will all have flown the nest.'

Helena had gone off the rails a bit after university the first time round and it had taken her some time to sort herself out. She caused her parents, and indeed her grandparents, many sleepless nights before she was done rebelling. There were drugs involved, and it isn't something I want to dwell on. Music was her way back to the world and to us.

I suppose I had grown very used to things being the way they were, and it was quite a shock. Eileen proposed that we should tell everyone after the fuss of the graduation had died down. She suggested we start with Terry and Claudie and see how that went, then tell the rest of the family. I said I would have to talk to Henry but, yes, I thought we were ready for it if she was.

Then she mumbled, 'I have to tell you something a bit difficult.' She blushed.

I had never seen her do this in over 50 years of marriage. Then she told me she had found someone, another art lover apparently, a chap from the stroke club she went to. It was, according to her, completely platonic, not that it mattered at our age anyway.

Apparently, they had been seeing each other for a while, and they had decided to throw caution to the wind and move in together, like young people do nowadays. She didn't want to tell me any more than that, but she promised that I could meet him once everything was settled.

She described him as an old-fashioned sort of a gent. A widower with no children and, like her, he used a wheelchair. The fact that Eileen was married had caused him all sorts of moral problems because he was a man of faith and would not entertain the idea of breaking up someone else's marriage. So, she'd told him that I had a boyfriend who lived next door and that we had in fact been living a double life for years.

Blimey, I thought, Henry and I were not going to be the only cats among the pigeons. It was a proper shock. Of course, I was happy for her, but a tiny bit of me was sad that she would no longer be my wife after 54 years. We had become really good pals, the three of us. A tight-knit group who enjoyed each other's company enormously. She let us be us, and we allowed her to be herself without any pressure or expectation. She said once that she had learned through me what it was to let somebody get close to you, and she wanted to spend her final years enjoying it.

We both knew that Terry, out of everyone, would be the problem. He was fiercely protective of his mum because he loved her a great deal and he knew how much she had done for him. Oh, I knew he loved me too, but his first few years had been spent exclusively with Eileen, and they had a special bond.

We finished our tea, and I put the cups into the bin. When I came back, Eileen was grinning like a loon.

'What?' I asked.

She smiled and teased, 'Vera B and Muriel Wellington are probably going to explode like a couple of gassy old boilers when they hear the news, that the eminently respectable Potters at the end of Radcliffe Road have been living in a love triangle for years, and they hadn't got wind of any of it.'

I joked back, 'We will need a decent supply of earplugs for when you tell Beryl.'

Eileen laughed. 'Oh yes, dear. I'm rather looking forward to being the scandalous one for a change. I wish I could see her face.'

The whole family knew that when surprised, excited or outraged, Eileen's whiny sister could reach a vocal pitch that was only audible to dogs.

I was, of course, worried and anxious for the road ahead. I wanted to stop lying and be with Henry for everyone to see, but I knew that the price of this freedom might well be the loss of my son.

I talked it through with Henry and it seemed to be a done deal. Come September, the balloon was going up. When the dust had settled, number 13 would be going on the market, and Eileen and I would be taking a 50-50 split to fund our new lives. Henry suggested that we also sell number 11 and start afresh as a couple somewhere down at the coast. He got very excited, as you would expect. I hoped he could contain himself for a bit longer because we did not want to overshadow the graduation.

He started making all sorts of crazy plans, although he knew full well that there were choppy waters ahead.

I could hardly blame him. After all, he had waited the best part of 40 years for us to be together building a home. The thought of choosing curtains together, while not exactly thrilling, was a definite step in the right direction.

So that was that. The winds of change were blowing and who knew what was going to happen next. Of course, we had to get to September first.

****

One sunny morning, when we were sitting in the car waiting for Henry to come out of the dentist, I asked Eileen, 'Got any thoughts about your birthday this year?'

She nodded enthusiastically and said, 'Oh, could we have a trip down to the coast, George? Just the three of us?'

I replied, 'Wouldn't you rather spend it with Ted?' as I had found out he was called.

She said, 'No. I want to spend it having a laugh with you and Henry. Maybe next year, when things have settled, we could make up a foursome.'

I nudged her with my elbow and teased, 'Well look at you, Eileen Potter, getting all liberal in your old age, suggesting a double date with your husband and your fancy man, you shameless hussy.'

She poked her tongue out at me and replied, 'I don't see why on earth I shouldn't bring my fancy man, dear, after all you will be bringing yours.'

Then she thumped me on the arm as Henry got back into the car and said, 'Anyway, less of the old-age jokes, you cheeky beggar!'

We set off for home, with Henry wondering what on earth we had been doing while he'd been at the hygienist.

On a beautiful July morning, we set off in Henry's car. There was no rush because the day was our own. Eileen had packed us up a picnic and we sang all the way to the coast, songs from our youth mostly. We were carefree and ridiculous, and we didn't give a fig.

By the time we arrived, we were more than ready for lunch on the beach, and it was truly glorious weather. Eileen's chair was fine on the hard sand by the slip, and we had a marvellous time.

Henry said, 'Eileen, you look like Britannia ruling the waves in your chariot.'

She got very silly and demanded a sandcastle in her honour, so we saluted her and set to work.

If I remember it right, everything got a tiny bit competitive, but she loved it and, complete with a hat made from my newspaper, she joined in the fun, issuing building instructions with regard to the size of battlements etc. Finally, she demanded we fill the moat and we both took one of the large containers that had held the sandwiches and set off in a race for the sea.

As we trotted back, Henry kept nudging me so that I spilt my water. Of course, that kind of foul play demands revenge, so I responded likewise.

By the time we reached her majesty, we were both soaking and didn't have enough water left to fill an egg cup, so we all had a slice of birthday cake instead.

It was such a happy day. We came home slightly sunburnt and in high spirits. It was like being six again.

Eileen clapped her hands and said, 'Ooh that was fun. I don't think I ever enjoyed a birthday more. Thank you, boys.'

We stopped for a drink, because the old days of no booze were long gone. Eileen enjoyed a lager and lime and a packet of crisps as much as the next woman.

When we got back, Henry went for fish and chips, Eileen installed herself in front of the telly to watch Corrie, and I went to give the allotment plants a good water - and to write in my journal.

I had already decided that I would be staying over at Henry's, which I often did. It had been a splendid happy day, and I wanted to feel extra close to him.

At 5.30 the next morning when it was already light with just a few lingering stars remaining to be chased away, I was out in the back garden. Everything smelt fresh and newly washed by a spot of rain that had fallen about three o'clock.

I had not been to bed, and our fish and chip supper was residing in its paper in the bin, perfuming the kitchen with vinegar. Henry was fast asleep on the couch, and I didn't want to wake him if I could help it because we had had a very long evening.

My Eileen had passed away, suddenly but peacefully in front of her beloved Coronation Street. It was Henry who'd found her, when he'd got back from the chippy. I'd still been scribbling away.

He'd called out, 'Do you want yours on a plate, Eileen, or out of the paper?' Not getting an answer, he'd gone to check she was OK - and of course she hadn't been.

He'd met me at the back door, and I distinctly remember that he'd said, 'Don't go in yet, Georgie. Sit down here for a bit. There is something unpleasant that I need to tell you.'

After the bomb had been dropped and I had cried a bit on his shoulder, we went in to see her. She was curled up on the sofa in the front room, with her slippers on and a birthday glass of champagne going flat on the table beside her. I like to think she had dozed off after a lovely day out and slipped away.

Unlike Beryl, Eileen had very dainty feet. It was one of the things I found endearing about her. I also noticed that she had caught the sun on her nose.

I kissed her forehead and said, 'Goodbye, old girl.'

Henry covered her with a blanket, and we closed the door. I don't remember a lot more; shock I suppose.

It was all very dignified and professional. The doctor came and then the undertakers did what they needed to do. Of course, we had to ring Terry and the rest of the family. I steeled myself to phone Beryl in Spain. My sister-in-law was a hard woman in many ways, but she had, on occasion, been known to have full-blooded hysterics.

She took it pretty well, all things considered. There were more than a few tears from both of us, and she said to let her know about the funeral as soon as we could, so that she could book a flight.

Eileen and I had become good friends. I told Terry honestly that his mum had been in splendid form when she'd gone, tired but happy and waiting for a fish supper. She would have appreciated the neatness of dying on your own birthday. Exactly 77 years from start to finish.

I kept expecting to hear her chair on the parquet flooring in the hall. Sometimes the tyres squeaked as she rounded the tricky corner by the stairs. One of the familiar domestic sounds that you miss when someone goes. They are the noises that echo most when you are missing someone.

It took me a few days to face going into her room, with its art books and the desk in the corner. Henry had built it for her as a birthday present when she'd been 70, just the right height and with enough drawers for all her bits and bobs.

Because it had once been the dining room, there were French doors that led out into the garden. One look at the battered wooden board that she'd used as a ramp to give her access made me cry again.

Being a widower took a bit of getting used to. People were very kind. She had a lot of friends, and we had lived in Radcliffe Road for an awfully long time.

My goodness, you are kept busy when someone dies. I was pretty fit for my age, but I felt completely wiped with all the organising and people calling round. There is such a lot of admin to be done when someone goes. Terry and Claudie were marvellous, running me all over the place; so were the grandkids. They all took their turn to drive Pops to his various appointments when they weren't working.

The priest called in to discuss the details of the service. I wanted to make it a celebration of Eileen's life, but the Catholic church had other ideas on that score. Playing the music from Coronation Street was very much frowned upon, so we used it at the wake instead.

I had to dig out Eileen's certificates, which she'd kept in a Victorian tin hat box in her wardrobe, all tucked away neatly. We were no different to most families in that way. Eileen had always said that she'd chosen the box because it was metal with a tight-fitting lid, which might just save something if the house burned down.

Everyone has a 'place', a box or a bag, where the bits get kept. Not a filing cabinet, just something simple to gather the important stuff together. Life insurance, premium bonds, birth, death, and marriage certificates, the normal stuff.

I had the family round for tea, and we had a good old rummage through it for what was needed. Eileen's birth certificate for a start and her pension details and national health number.

Terry was amazed to learn his mother had a middle name, because she'd never told him. It was Leonora, after a friend of her mother's. Miss Eileen Leonora O'Connor, who'd became rather briefly Mrs Eileen Kelly and finally plain old Mrs Eileen Potter. I told the family that she didn't mind the name Leonora at all. She'd just thought it was a bit fancy and it didn't suit her.

Of course, certificates were not the only things to come out of that hat box. A whole load of family secrets came out too. Helena found an envelope containing the certificate of Eileen's first marriage to Arthur and some newspaper cuttings about his accident. It was a painful time and Eileen never really wanted it mentioned, so none of the grandkids knew she had been married twice. Along with this came the birth certificates of Sally Frances Kelly and of Elizabeth Mary Potter, and Lizzie's death certificate.

The younger generation were vaguely aware that their dad had a sister who'd run away, but they'd had no idea that she wasn't mine, or that we had another child who'd died within hours of her birth. They were Eileen's secrets, and she'd locked the pain away with the box.

Even today, when so many years have passed, I wonder what our Lizzie would have been like had she lived. Today they call it '*Down's Syndrome*', but back then there was a really horrible name for the condition. I will not sully these pages by writing it.

With the funeral just around the corner and Beryl on her way from Spain, Henry and I got stuck into some housework, because Eileen would not have wanted the house looking mucky.

Henry, bless him, was hoovering with gusto and true German efficiency while I was dusting the family photographs that we kept on the piano. It wasn't really a piano, we just called it that. It was actually a long, low table, that sat perfectly under the lip of the bay window. Funny how people used to keep things they didn't really like, just because they fitted the room.

Terry had cracked his head open on it when he'd been six, and Eileen had me file the corners down to make it safe. It was not a pretty object and so she always kept a white cloth over it.

They were an interesting group of snaps. Four generations of our family. People who had never even met each other, gathered together on display for visitors to admire. There was a large, framed photo of my parents on their wedding day in 1917, Dad in his dog collar and Mum in an empire-line dress, cleverly cut to disguise the fact that I was well on my way into existence. There was also a photograph of Eileen's parents at their wedding in 1913. They looked so young, and they had absolutely no idea that within a few short years their world would be torn apart forever.

Eileen always said she was glad that they'd had a few happy memories. Every time I looked at it, I was struck at how much Eileen looked like her father. The same eyes and the same determined chin. Beryl was a perfect blend of the two, but Eileen was her daddy's girl. A little windfall apple who had never met the tree she'd fallen from.

Other photographs showed the grandchildren and there was one tiny picture of our wedding. Eileen in a smart-looking brown suit and a hat with a feather in it, and me in uniform with my hair flattened down. We were standing on the steps of the town hall, which was the registry office in those long-ago days. Dave Robinson was my best man.

There were also photographs of the two of us as children. One of Eileen as a chubby bald grinner sitting on her mother's knee, with a curly-haired Beryl standing up next to them, holding a rag doll in one hand. It was the only photograph that she and Beryl ever had taken with their mother. I suspect it was done especially to send to their father at the front.

There were two infant photos of me, both taken in America when I was very young. One made me look a bit like the famous shot of Christopher Robin Milne, the child from Winnie the Pooh, all big eyes and a glossy pudding bowl haircut that was popular for small boys in my childhood.

Eileen always pointed out how well dressed I was. Smart leather boots, a stripey jumper and knickerbockers. She used to tease me and call me a *'lucky little posh boy'* because I was standing next to my pride and joy, a red pedal racing car. It was an absolute beauty, and it came from a famous department store, via some relative of my father's. Dennis, my teddy, was sitting in the car and we were wearing matching bow ties made especially for the occasion.

Eileen was right. I was a much-loved only child. My first few years were nothing but happiness, in the centre of a safe and secure world that I never thought to question - until it was no longer there. When the wind did blow into my life, it was bitter. It took my mother away and left the stutter behind.

The second photo was one that used to live on my father's desk, because it amused him. In it, I was wearing one of those checked hats with ear flaps and determinedly towing a loaded sledge through the New York snow.

My dad told me that I had packed up all my belongings in some fit of childish temper and set off for my granny's house, where I intended to reside. As Granny was at home on the farm in Suffolk, I was in for a bit of a walk. I remember nothing, except the snow, which seemed very deep at the time.

Eileen never had a childhood birthday party or a cake, so I always tried to make the day special in some way. I forget the number of times I dragged the kids off to the allotment to pick birthday or Mother's Day flowers for their mum. I have fond memories of the pair of them sitting at the table in the shed, lost in furious concentration, as they each made her a wobbly card.

We always put everything on the tray when we brought her breakfast in bed. She would make a big fuss and play at being surprised, like mothers always do, although the noise they made coming up the stairs would have woken the dead!

My favourite picture was not that old - 10 years or so. We'd become great supporters of an organisation that helps people who have been disabled by a stroke. Henry and I both did our turn on the committee. The photograph was taken at a fundraising fancy dress ball for the local branch. The three of us went as the Marx brothers; Henry as Chico, me as Groucho complete with silly moustache, and Eileen as

Harpo, sitting in her wheelchair, dressed in my raincoat and a blonde curly wig honking an old car horn. In the photo, we were all roaring with laughter.

It was a joyous photograph, and we won a camera as second prize. Eileen told me later that she found it easier to enjoy herself when she was being someone else. Terry and Claudie still have a copy of that one on their real piano at home.

Dusting the photos made me happy and sad all at the same time. Happy because of the memories they brought and sad because I would never be able to chat to Eileen again. I remember thinking, *Right, George Potter, that is enough, old lad.* I was getting all sniffy and it wouldn't wash, because I had a great deal to do. My late Mrs would never have approved of the self-indulgence when there was work to be done.

The funeral went well. I suppose there are few that go wrong. Beryl came over from Spain. I'm not saying she wasn't upset at losing her baby sister, but she didn't half milk the grieving relative bit. Lace and a heavy veil was the order of the day, topped off by an enormous hat that made her look like a freshly picked mushroom.

I could almost hear Eileen whispering to me, *'Oh God, here we go. The circus is in town. Who the hell does she think she is?'*

Terry did the eulogy. He broke down about halfway through, and Martin got up and finished it for him. Helena did a reading from some poem Eileen had liked. I just hoped that wherever Eileen was, everything was ready and in order when she got there.

Lots of people came. Friends from her various clubs and charities. I got to meet Ted, who introduced himself to us as a '*good friend*'. He seemed nice and a bit younger than I was expecting. He asked me to accompany him to his car. Terry, who was dealing with a sniffling Vera at the time, hardly noticed him.

We had a brief chat about Eileen, and I asked him what he intended to do with the rest of his life. He was planning to return to his native Ghana, where he had a house, and live out the rest of his days in the sun, not doing very much if he could help it, except paint, because he liked painting.

He shook my hand and said, 'Don't leave it too long, George, go and enjoy the life you and Henry have left because we never know, do we?'

He got into his car and left. I waved him goodbye and went back to the funeral.

Beryl got all squiffy and cackled away with Vera for most of the evening. It looked for all the world as if Endor was missing its third witch. Muriel Wellington was away on a SAGA holiday to Crete - I'm sure she would have made up the set!

John Wellington came. He'd left Muriel years ago, for a widow with three children who was doing a bit of cleaning at his school, and then they'd had two of their own.

Muriel got herself a job when John went - well she had to. For many years, she worked in the perfumery department of a large store. You know the sort of place I mean? They are brightly lit and full of well-dressed, well-made-up ladies for whom life had not turned out exactly as planned. She took up with an alarming succession of younger men and eventually settled down with a long-distance lorry driver named Mick.

Henry did not attend the funeral. Obviously, he was going to come because he was very close to Eileen and he wanted to support me, but a couple of days beforehand, he'd had a phone call from his sister, Anna, in Germany, to tell him their younger sister, Erna, was in a bad way and she wanted to see them before she died. Nobody had spoken to Erna since she'd married that Nazi sympathiser in 1943.

Henry had said, 'I don't see why I should go when you need me here and, anyway, we haven't exchanged so much as a Christmas card in over 50 years.'

He'd told Anna on the phone, 'I can't forgive her. She broke Mother's heart and drove Father into an early grave.'

Anna, a sensible and dignified woman replied, 'Well we may not have liked her choice, but we can't help who we fall in love with, can we, Heinrich dear?'

Anna knew all about me. Henry had told her when he was having his breakdown after Clara died. In the end, with a bit of pushing, he went to Germany. He was glad he did, and his sister went to her rest reconciled with both siblings.

Eileen went to glory on a beautiful summer afternoon with the roses in full bloom. As I stood alone by her grave, I could only think, *Goodbye, old girl, I am really going to miss you.*

Chapter 19

A whiff of autumn and seasonal change was in the air at the allotment, and I was burning leaves when Henry arrived with a book in his hand. It had a red paisley cover instead of a blue one like my own diary.

Eileen had left Henry all her recipe books. Both the printed ones and the handwritten notebooks - the ones she'd written when she'd been a girl learning to cook in that house in Ireland.

'This is Eileen's diary,' Henry told me. 'I found it among the books. Of course, I didn't read it. There was an envelope sticking out of it and a note inside saying, "Henry please burn this for me, regards, E", so here I am.'

He did a little German bow, snappy and from the waist, then he tossed the book into the flames. We sipped our mugs of tea and had a thoughtful moment as we watched it return to its literary gods.

'She called it Doris,' he mumbled, 'just like you called yours Dave. It was written on the cover in biro.' He tossed a few more leaves onto the fire, and I turned away because the smoke was making my eyes water.

'Doris and Dave,' I said, 'we obviously had the same idea. Perhaps she needed a friend too? Such a shame it took us so long to realise that we could have confided in each other.'

When Eileen had been dead for six months, certain ladies in Radcliffe Road decided that I was fair game. As far as they were concerned, I had my own house, a bit of money in the bank and most of my original teeth, which made me a prime target for their attentions.

It started as kindness. Casseroles and cakes appearing on the doorstep, that sort of thing. Then they appeared with notes tied to the handles, saying, *'Come round for tea'* or *'I make a decent Sunday lunch if you are feeling lonely, George'.*

Vera was the worst offender. She took to stalking me like some beast. I could not leave the house without bumping into her, and she started wearing this awful red lipstick in an attempt to ensnare me with lust. Vampy scarlet might have been the thing in her younger days, but, quite frankly, it made her look like she had just taken a bite out of the postman's leg. She was as bad as Eileen for the ciggies and she pretty much lived on coffee once rationing had ended, so her teeth were the colour of sand. It was horrific.

I don't want to be ungallant, but Vera was an awful woman. I never thought she was a particularly good friend to my wife, yet they'd been buddies for decades. I had asked Eileen why they had remained friends, and she'd told me quite plainly that, 'It's always better to have Vera inside the tent peeing out than the other way around, George.'

I think she meant it was better to have Vera gossiping to you rather than about you.

Vera had always had a thing for me, which Eileen had thought was terribly funny. As I mentioned once before, she'd made a drunken pass at me during our Coronation Day party in 1953. I'd had to run for my life when she pounced. She was horrible sober, so imagine how terrifying the gossipy old witch was plastered.

Henry and Terry thought it was hilarious. My son took to calling me the 'Radcliffe Romeo'.

'Bad luck, Dad,' he teased. 'She's got a face like a bag full of spanners, but at your age you should be lucky anyone is chasing you at all.'

I gave him the two-finger salute and grumbled, 'It isn't funny, Terry.'

'Yes, it is,' he said. 'Mum would have wet herself laughing at the terrified look on your face.'

Henry chimed in with, 'I always thought she looked more like a discarded flip-flop—all yellow and hard.'

Then they both collapsed into fits of laughter again.

Later, I told Henry I could always put the word around that he was feeling lonely. This made him go pale and shut him up. I had to have a word with Vera in the end. I indicated that her attentions were flattering, but unwanted, especially at our age. She huffed off, obviously wondering which of her fellow jackals had beaten her to the carcass.

She needn't have worried. What happened next ruined all her ideas of making me a notch on her awful, posture-sprung bedpost. Henry let the cat out of the bag, and it was not some cuddly tabby. It was a great hairy thing that rooted through the bins of our lives, revealing every hidden secret.

We had been working on a plan to tell Terry and Claudie privately and calmly that we were an item. We knew full well it was going to release a tsunami of emotion. I hoped that they might appreciate a bit of time to come to terms with the situation, before they told anyone else about it.

Of course, it didn't happen like that thanks to the excitable German big mouth I'd attached myself to all those years ago. He stirred up a storm and we had to sail through it together, taking others along on the voyage.

He apologised for opening his mouth, but he couldn't undo the damage. I mean, it was never going to be a picnic, but blurting everything out was a serious error. He'd got over excited at the prospect of us being together after his long years of waiting.

He was talking to Claudie one day in the garden, after they had done a bit of weeding and needed a coffee. They were sitting in the shade of a tree chatting about this and that, when the conversation turned to relationships.

'Are you lonely, Dad?' she asked. 'You have been on your own for a very long time and I worry about you. Or is there a secret someone you haven't told us about?' she teased.

Henry went red, and she said, 'Papa, you are blushing. Come on now, don't be shy, tell me all about your secret love.'

He threw caution to the wind and replied with tears in his eyes, '*Liebchen*, I have something very important to tell you. You are right, there is someone. I have not been honest and for that I am most sorry.'

'Don't be shy,' she said, intrigued. 'Come on, tell me, Papa, I would love to meet her.'

He was in with both feet by this point and he couldn't get out, so he took her hand and said, 'I have been in a relationship with a wonderful man for well over 30 years. Yes, you heard me right, your Papa is coming out into the world, and he wanted to tell you first, but he didn't quite know how to start the conversation.'

Claudie was, of course, stunned by this. Henry said she was really very sweet. She put down her cup and flung her arms around him saying, 'Oh, Dad, it's OK. Why on earth didn't you tell me? I would have understood. Did Mum know?'

'No, I was never unfaithful to your mother, Claudie, not once,' he replied.

(This was technically true, as we were not intimate in that way until after Clara's death.)

She asked, 'Can I meet him? It would be wonderful to make him part of our family.'

He sighed and told her, 'He is already a part of our family, sweetheart. It's George.'

Claudie stared at him for a moment, unable to believe her ears. This was closely followed by total disbelief, a meltdown, and a tearful phone call to Terry to tell him to, 'Get his arse down to Radcliffe Road pronto or else!'

Henry had waited a long time for me to be free so I couldn't be angry with him, but it might have been polite to ask me if I was ready for the bomb to drop!

In the blissful oblivion of the shed, I was sitting at the table sorting out the lifted spring bulbs, completely unaware that Henry had just pulled the pin on all our lives.

The first thing I knew about it was when Terry appeared in the shed doorway, blocking out the light. He flung himself into my dad's old armchair and asked me straight out, 'What the bloody hell has been going on here, Dad? What is all this rubbish Claudie has just been telling me, about you cheating on Mum for years and having a long-term thing with Henry? Is it true? Please tell me it isn't.'

I began to shake. I could see my hands moving in front of me as the dam began to break and 30 years of hidden guilt came flooding out. In the end I nodded and stuttered, 'Yes it's true, son.' I was completely caught off guard and very near to tears.

For a full minute there was silence. I looked at him and, for the first time, I realised how much like my father he was getting. We always thought he was the dead spit of Eileen's pa. In build he was, but facially he had started to look like my dad, without the wonky teeth. He was older than either of our fathers had been when they'd died.

He put his head in his hands and spoke through his fingers saying, 'I always thought that Claudie and I were lucky. Most people we know have elderly parents who are a pain in the arse most of the time. You two have always been a delight to have around, and now this.'

He took a long deep breath; it reminded me of how Eileen used to be when she was trying to keep her temper, a last-ditch attempt at control before the meter ran out and everything turned to red.

'Bloody hell, Dad, I don't know who you are anymore. Not the man who gave me my moral compass, that is for sure. I never knew you to tell a deliberate lie, except when I was a kid and Mum sent me to the shed for a walloping. You used to give me an apple and a good talking to instead.'

'Now I find you have been lying to all of us for decades and cheating on Mum into the bargain, in the most sordid, deceitful way. How could you do that to her, Dad?'

He thumped his fist down hard on the table, which made me jump; I was a bundle of nervous guilt anyway.

'All these years and none of us had a clue. How stupid were we?! When it was going on under our very noses for decades. You made fools out of us, your own bloody family. How could you do that to us, Dad?'

'It was society that made us deceitful, son,' I replied.

He wasn't really in a listening mood and who could have blamed him? I found my voice and I told him, 'I fell in love, Terry, head over heels and for the first and only time in my life. I'm truly sorry you are hurt, I'm sorry we had to lie, but I won't apologise for loving Henry, if that is what you want.'

He made it very clear in return that he was disgusted with me for doing the dirty on his mum. He was also confused, sad and very angry, which was only natural. He got out of the chair and stood in the doorway again, saying, 'Jesus I need some fucking time to process this. Don't call me, OK, because I really don't want to talk to you at the moment.'

Before he left, he turned and gave me his parting shot. 'I just want to make things crystal clear, Dad. I'm not angry about the whole gay bit of this, OK? At least, I don't think I am. For a start, I haven't even had time to unpack that particular box yet, and secondly nobody ever came out to me before.

'What a mess,' he muttered, tapping like a mad thing with his right foot, as if it were a conduit for his emotions. 'How the hell we tell our kids that both their grandfathers have just come out of the closet holding hands, I do not know.' Then he left.

I let him go because there was nothing more to be said. I stayed in the shed for an hour or more, biting my nails and staring out of the window at the clouds. I had this bit of old twine in my hands that I kept winding through my fingers like a rosary. The sky had fallen in, and I knew full well that I was the one who had smashed it. It was Henry who'd tipped over the hornets' nest, but we all had to deal with the stings, of which there were many, and they hurt.

Terry refused to talk to me; relations between Claudie and Henry were better but not great, and then Beryl waded in from Spain with her larger than average stilettos flying. She was a size seven, extraordinarily large for a woman of her frame and height. Terry must have phoned her to ask if she'd known, which obviously she hadn't. She put the phone down from talking to him then she picked it up again to give me an ear bashing. She had a shrill voice at the best of times, as I have previously mentioned. If she was angry, it rose to a pitch audible only to dogs and fruit bats! She was extremely miffed at me for messing her sister around, and even more miffed at Eileen for not telling her.

So, I was in everyone's bad books. Henry developed a rather truculent attitude to the whole family. He reckoned they could, '*go and stuff themselves*', if they couldn't accept us. I think he meant '*get stuffed*'. He still got it wrong sometimes. Anyway, he didn't mean a word of it. He was just as upset as I was underneath it all, but he was trying to put on a brave face.

It was never going to be easy telling our children that we had been in love with each other for more than three decades, but I had hoped we could tell them privately and with tact, not blurt it all out.

Terry kept his distance. Claudie popped in now and again, but she felt torn between loyalty to her husband and love for her dad. All sorts of things were stirred up in her, things about her past. Henry had always been her security, until he'd told her he had been deceiving her since she was a young woman. There were several tearful conversations. I kept well out of the way because it was something they needed to work through together.

It was difficult to imagine being someone who had no real idea about their past. Always wondering about who they are; a ship without an anchor to ground them. We all need one of those and the certainty of knowing where we come from. In the mirror, I always saw my father looking back at me.

Claudie had no idea of who she looked like, no memories, not even a photo. All she'd had in the world as she'd been growing up were Henry and Clara. The bonds between them were incredibly strong. Clara had cut them both adrift when she'd gone under that train, but no matter what, Claudie always had Henry. She might have been a grown woman, with a husband and three adult children, but those old ties were tight. Her rock had crumbled a little and she had to find a way to deal with him not being perfect.

Everything was one almighty mess, and I had no idea if we would ever find our way back to each other. I could only hope we would.

The next thing that happened was Henry dropping his second bomb and we became, as they say now, 'out' to the world.

It was nothing dramatic; I mean we didn't paint a couple of rainbows on the front door or anything like that. I was all for keeping things low key until the family dust had settled, but Henry was having none of it. We had a few words, more than a few actually. I was completely lost about making our relationship public, in view of the current situation vis-à-vis Terry and Claudie. Hen said he wanted to shout it from the rooftops and the family could take a running jump. As usual, I was in favour of a more cautious approach.

Henry rarely lost his temper. He got the grumps occasionally, but going totally bananas at me was not something he did. He didn't shout, what he actually said was, 'Are you ashamed of me? Because that is what it damned well looks like. Christ, George, you know I love you. I tell you often enough. How much longer do you want me to wait?' Then he walked out, and he didn't come back until the next morning.

I sat up half the night until, exhausted, I fell asleep in a chair in the front room. When I woke up, unshaven and stiff, with the telly still on, I heard the back door go. Henry wasn't coming in - he was going out again. I found him sitting in my garden, drumming his fingers on the scabby wooden table we always kept outside the back door.

'I didn't want to wake you,' he said, sipping from a mug of coffee.

He offered it to me, and I took a swig, although he always made it way too strong for my taste. We sat opposite each other on a cool, grey morning. Rarely had we been further apart.

He looked down at an imaginary spot between his shoes, then he apologised for his outburst, and I said it was OK. He told me he had spent most of the night in the pub followed by walking around the streets like a stupid, drunken old man. He took my hand and said, 'Georgie, sweetheart, I have done something terrible.' He mumbled, 'God I am a hot-headed old idiot sometimes.'

I asked him what he had done that was so bad, hoping it wasn't anything that we couldn't undo. He sighed and told me, 'I was drunk and, on my way home to you, I knocked over Vera's milk bottles as I went past the flats on the corner. She stuck her head out of a window and asked me what the hell I was doing? I think I ended up telling her you were the love of my life, and I wanted to shout it from the rooftops, but you wouldn't let me. Now the whole world will know about us. Sorry.'

Well that most definitely couldn't be undone, but it solved the problem of how to tell people about the change in our lives, because Vera Bulstrode, in her prime, was a human megaphone. After that there was nothing we could do except wait for whatever fallout was heading our way.

The British are a funny nation. Some people avoided us, others were supportive, and the rest pretended that nothing had changed. I imagine we were the subject of a fair amount of gossip around the dinner tables of Radcliffe Road, mainly because Radio Vera would no doubt have been broadcasting around the clock.

One of our neighbours, a nice young chap, knocked on the door and gave us some leaflets. He said, 'I know some people if you ever want to talk about how you feel. It can't have been easy coming out at your age.'

We thanked him and added that we were fine and probably a bit long in the tooth for counselling, but we appreciated the offer. He shook his head and said that nobody was too old for a sympathetic ear, if they needed it.

It was good to know that there was help available. Henry and I had to work everything out for ourselves, because there had been no advice and support way back in 1961, not even a helpful leaflet to read.

We had a truly miserable Christmas, which we spent together with no contact from the family, and a lousy birthday where Henry tried way too hard to make it a special day for me.

Terry turned up one day in the spring, when I was at the allotment digging out all the rubbish and generally preparing the ground for a new season. Henry was out doing our shopping. He had promised to bring me a doughnut if I finished the digging before he got back.

Without a word, my son poured himself a cuppa and he sat down outside in Henry's deckchair. The kids had painted our names on the back of them years ago, just for a laugh. '*Opa*' and '*Poppa*' in blue and red. The paint had faded with the years, a bit like us.

Terry looked drawn and dark around the eyes, not surprising really. We were all exhausted. I parked myself opposite and put my mug on the rusty upturned oil drum that we had used as a table for years.

We sat not speaking for a while, letting the dust settle, I suppose. I realised that I was unshaven and rather muddy, but it didn't matter, because neither of us cared. At the time I was thinking about growing a beard, but Henry didn't like it much.

It was me that spoke first. 'How have you been, son?' I asked him, just for openers really.

He waved a hand and said, 'Oh, OK. Busy as usual.'

It reminded me so much of when he'd been a teenager. That state of wanting to give in and make it up, but still hanging onto the shreds of anger, like a tattered old coat that you should have ditched long ago. Something in you clung to it, as if the rage you felt was security against further emotion.

'How about you?' he asked, slurping tea.

'Oh, you know, pretty good considering.' I shrugged, knowing it was a barefaced lie.

It was our longest time without communicating since he'd been five years old. Even at university he'd phoned every Sunday from the call box at the end of the road. When he'd been in the army, he'd always kept in touch by letter or card.

'And Henry?' he asked, clearly wary of opening a wound.

I took a swig from my mug then replied with, 'Oh, you know Henry. Henry is always Henry; he's ok. We are getting used to living together and making a few plans for our future.'

Terry wiped his mouth with the back of his hand, and he took the chocolate biscuit I offered him. He'd always had a sweet tooth. Keeping him out of the biscuit jar had been a bit of a herculean task when he'd been a boy. At the age of

10, before the hormones had kicked in and turned him into a gawky beanpole, he'd gone through a phase where he was very nearly circular. More silence and a gentle munching of biscuits filled in for awkward conversation.

'Not like your mother's,' I ventured, waiting for the blast.

He grinned. 'Yeah, they were amazing. God how I miss those little chocolate and peppermint ones she used to make.'

His face crumpled, creased like the empty biscuit wrapper he was holding in his hand. 'I miss her too, Dad.' He wiped his eyes. 'And I miss you.'

'Me too,' I told him, my voice cracking. 'More than I ever thought possible, son. I never meant to hurt her, Tel, or you, truly I didn't.'

He nodded, tears streaming down his face as he said, 'I know you didn't, Pa.'

It was messy, both of us howling, with red eyes and runny noses. Luckily, it was a weekday, and the allotments were pretty quiet. Nobody around but us. He got up and we gave each other a snotty hug, then he took another biscuit and asked with a smile, 'Come on then, how did it start? You know, between you and Henry, I mean. Did your eyes meet among the broad beans and suddenly you couldn't live without each other? Or what? Because I need to know, Dad.'

So, I told him. Oh, not the intimate details, of course, I just said, 'We got very close, very quickly. Best pals we were, but underneath we both began to realise it was more than that; the feeling was growing stronger every time we saw each other. It was bloody terrifying because we could have been jailed.'

I smiled at the memory and said, 'Henry kissed me when we were playing chess and then he walked out because I told him I wasn't that sort of a chap, but I wasn't being honest with him or with myself. In the end, I had to admit that I was in love with him and it all went on from there really, son.'

He asked me some questions about his mum, and I tried to answer him honestly, but kindly. I didn't mention Ted. After all, he was only just coming to terms with his father having a boyfriend. I didn't think he was anywhere near ready to know that his mother had had one too.

Terry left when Henry turned up, but only after he had eaten my doughnut. He told us to take care of each other, then he had wandered off, licking a stray bit of jam from one of his fingers. We watched him drive away and Henry put an arm around my shoulders and whispered, 'See, it will all be OK, Georgie. It is just going to take a bit of time.'

A few hours earlier I would have disagreed with him, but I was starting to think, or at least hope, that those weeds in my garden might turn out to be flowers after all.

****

I hardly lived at number 13 anymore. Once it was sold, that major part of my life came to an end. In time, we would be forgotten and the Potters of Radcliffe Road would cease to exist, along with all the people who'd lived there with us.

Another sudden change happened in our lives - Red Reg Braithwaite died. One of my allotment neighbours, Hugh Jones, who was our GP, told me. 'You know how he was, George, all piss and vinegar. He was ranting and giving full blast to some kids who were playing ball against the side of his house when it happened. He dropped like a stone. Nothing to be done. He was dead before he hit the ground, to use a cliché! To be honest, he had been living on borrowed time for years, and he never took his damned blood-pressure pills.'

I knew exactly what he meant about Reg and the piss and vinegar. He was never one to take advice, but he really loved to give it out. I think he became a parody of himself in the end. The crusty old colonel bellowing orders that everyone ignored. His position as chairman of the allotment association had become a bit of a joke, but he wouldn't move aside and let someone with fresh ideas have a try. I guess it was the last bit of power and status he had left, so he'd held onto it with all he'd had. Sad really.

That often happens to people like Reg. They cannot cope with the fact that they are no longer relevant, and it turns them into tin-pot tyrants. On every committee in the land, every residents' association, neighbourhood watch or local historical society, you will find a Reg, clinging on to past glories.

He'd been foul to us when he'd found out that Henry and I had moved in together. We'd found a sign pinned to the shed door one morning. In his large round handwriting it read:

Honeymoon Suite, please knock
entrance for deliveries around the back!

I was determined to go and sort things out with him. I remember I was absolutely livid and stuttering away like an enraged chicken. 'That's it, I'm bloody having him for this,' I ranted, scrunching up the sign and stamping it into the mud.

Henry seemed amused, but it wasn't funny.

'OK, so what are you going to do when you get there, sweetheart?'

'I'm gonna bloody thump him, that's what, right on the end of his big red nose!'

Henry raised a quizzical eyebrow. 'And then what?'

I hadn't thought that far. 'I don't know, and stop being so reasonable,' I growled. 'That's my job.'

Henry sighed; I could tell he was holding in a laugh.

'Did I ever tell you how adorable you are when you are angry? Now calm down, slugger, Reg is well over 80 and you are no spring chicken. One of you will break a hip or something. Ignoring the notice will drive him crazy, you know how he is.'

Reg and his rampant homophobia, accompanied by his constant search for commies, hippies, druggies, and anyone with origins that happened to hail from anywhere outside the home counties, were the stuff of legend.

Henry, being German, was always going to be on the top of the hit list. To find out that he had been harbouring a couple of extra (in his words) 'pansies' on the allotments all those years was, in his eyes, tantamount to treason. I'm surprised he didn't order us from the shed with a pitchfork and burn us.

As one of the longest serving plot holders, I was asked if I wanted to be chairman. I turned it down because I knew that we would be moving on before long. Anyway, the last thing they needed was another old man slowing everything down and keeping them in the past.

I thought they should give it to someone younger, who could bring fresh ideas to the table. It made me very conscious of the fact that, quite soon, I would have to start a new garden somewhere else.

Chapter 20

We went out for Sunday lunch with the family, our first social engagement as an officially 'out' couple. Things were thawing a bit and, mercifully, we were all on speaking terms again.

Because it was still early days, we decided that we would go out to eat on neutral ground. It would have been beyond weird at home without Eileen there, because in a sense she would have been looking over all our shoulders. Probably telling us we needed our heads knocking together to put some bloody sense into them, I expect.

We decided on a decent hotel where the food was good. Everybody sat around being ridiculously polite and making stilted chit-chat, carefully avoiding the elephant in the room, which of course was Henry and me.

The grandkids, who were all adults, had obviously been warned to avoid the taboo subject of the gay grandpas, if at all possible, but it couldn't be avoided forever.

It felt for all the world like we were on some sort of trial. We were guarded in case we upset someone, and I know they were feeling the same. I had pre-warned Henry to keep his trap shut, but, as usual, he found it difficult.

I heard him mutter, 'Oh, stuff this,' under his breath before he stood up. Holding my hand, he made a little speech, while I battened down the hatches for yet another storm.

'Family, I love you all, but I have had enough of this,' he said.

'Either we stop treading on eggshells and get back to taking the piss out of each other and having a good time like we normally do, or I am going, because it is killing me watching us all being so damned polite.'

He looked at Claudie. 'I know it has been a shock and I'm sorry about that, but we have to get past it. George and I are together, and we are staying that way. We are not hiding or apologising any more, because we already did that bit, since before most of you were born. We didn't mean to hurt anybody.'

He looked down at me and smiled before he continued, 'We are two tired old fellas who love each other very much and want to spend the rest of their years together. You can be part of our new life and let us be a part of yours, or we can go and live that life without you in it, which would probably kill both of us. Your choice. Now I am going to the bar to get another round in before dessert arrives.' Then he squeezed my fingers and stalked off.

I remember the silence that fell. It lasted until Martin piped up with,

'Pops, are you absolutely sure you want to live out the rest of your days with old Opa bossy knickers?'

I shrugged and joked that it was part of his charm, and we all laughed. A bit nervously, it must be said, but the ice was broken and things felt easier. We ended the meal on better terms than we'd started, so for once Henry and his big mouth had been bang on the money.

We found a house. After months of searching, we were getting a bit fed up, but we finally cracked it. Situated down a sandy lane that led to a rocky beach, with three bedrooms and two bathrooms; one downstairs for when we couldn't manage the stairs anymore.

I sold number 13 and Henry had an offer for number 11, so we were on the move. Selling both houses and only buying one gave us a comfortable nest egg with no money worries for the future. I knew I would miss our old place, both the domestic dramas and the happy times. We were both excited and looking forward to our new life together. A fresh start at an age when many people have stopped.

Operation 'Move Opa and Poppa" got underway. The whole family was mobilised to shift us into our new home. We could not breathe for helpful people trying to make sure we were efficiently dispatched to our new pad.

Henry went a bit nuts with the packing tape, and I feared I might be next if I stayed in one place for too long. So, I said goodbye to number 13, and we set off to start a new life in our house on the coast.

Henry could not wait to move, but I found it all a bit traumatic. On our final morning, I took a last look round, wandering through the empty rooms, patting things. I know it was silly, but I had lived there since 1946 and every bump and scratch or mark on the wallpaper meant something. We never had got the dents out of the door frame in the hall, where Terry used to crash his toy cars into it. When we'd come to look around with a view to buying, I still had a tan from fighting in the desert. Terry had just turned six and Sally had been ten. Eileen was pregnant with Lizzie.

We looked at number four as well as number 13, Radcliffe Road. Number four was bigger but a bit too expensive. We were lucky to have a choice of any, because there was a terrible housing shortage after the war; so many houses had been bombed out and there was rampant profiteering.

I had the money my dad had left me. It was way more than I expected, and we needed somewhere urgently. Sally was getting too big to share with her little brother, there was a new baby on the way, and we were all getting on each other's nerves in the cramped, rented flat that had once been Eileen and Arthur's place.

The kids went to explore the garden, and we looked around. Eileen checked every cupboard in the kitchen, and I had a good look at the joists in the attic. My old boss at the architects' firm had warned me to always check the roof and to look for any cracks in the walls. We had just been through a war and hidden bomb damage was not unthinkable.

Eileen loved the place immediately. It occurred to me that this was the first time she would have had a home to call her own. She asked me, 'Can we afford a lovely big place like this, George?'

I told her, 'It will be tight, but yes I think we can do it, with something left over for a rainy day.'

We put in a cheeky offer, quite a bit below the price they wanted, and we got it because we were cash buyers. The other people who were interested had yet to get a mortgage. So we moved in with not much but hope for the future.

Terry's second front tooth came out on our first morning in that house. He looked like a tiny vampire, and it cost me a shilling. The memory makes me smile because he was terribly worried that the tooth fairy wouldn't know our new address and that he might get missed out. I explained that tooth fairies were magic and knew where all the good boys and girls were. Eileen scolded me for filling his head with rubbish. I replied, somewhat wearily, that she could spend the night soothing his anxiety if she wished, but I would rather sleep!

We worked hard to get the place if not how we wanted it, at least fit for habitation. Eileen made temporary blinds, because they took up less material than curtains, and cushions from fabric she'd had from before the war, and I got on with the preparation for decorating. Every night after I came home from work at my new job, I was up a ladder somewhere, peeling off old paper ready for when there was some in the shops, or painting the kids' bedrooms with the only colour we had available, two large cans of a sort of creamy off-white that we found in the shed. If it belonged to the last inhabitants, they never used it. The place was pretty depressing and hadn't been touched since the first war, I reckoned.

The hardest task was the bathroom. That was painted woodchip paper and it was a pig to shift. In the end, Eileen came up with the rule that anyone having a bath had to scrape a bit of paper off when it softened in the steam. A fish slice was provided for the job. The kids loved that and as a reward they got to write their name or draw a picture in pencil on the bit of wall they had uncovered, and date it. Someone new would soon be revealing our artwork and wondering who'd drawn all the flowers and the toy cars way back in 1946.

Somewhere under the tiles are two portraits. We drew them when Eileen was busy with Sally's homework, and she had decided that I could be trusted not to drown Terry. We chipped off a large bit of paper. Terry drew me and I drew him. I wrote his name underneath and he wrote, *'Mi dady'*. The spelling was a bit rough, but the meaning was crystal clear. After years of war and separation, we belonged to each other. I had to wipe my eyes on the towel.

The children were fitting in at a new school and Sally was working on sitting her 11+, so it was a busy time for all of us. We had been through a period of extreme anxiety and enormous disruption. Terry, as a war baby, knew nothing else. He understood air raids, but bananas and oranges were a mystery to him.

For me, it felt good to be building stability for the future; a career, a family, and a home. I had no idea of what that future would hold of course; none of us did.

The last thing I did before I left 13, Radcliffe Road was to walk down the hall with its wooden parquet floor. Eileen had always kept it polished. Behind me, I heard my footsteps echo, but there was no umbrella stand, no colourful rug and no mirror that I had straightened my tie in every day for 50 years, just emptiness. My time in Radcliffe Road was at an end so I shut the front door with a final click and walked into my new life without turning back.

****

We arrived at the coast and were duly deposited in our new home with its hideous green wallpaper and lurid blue bathroom suite. Things were in a proper pickle, but we had a bed, and Claudie found us the kettle. We phoned for an

Indian takeaway as soon as they had gone for the night. It was a bit of a gamble because we had no idea where the good places were.

It tasted OK, but we were too exhausted to finish it. We crawled into bed and slept like a couple of logs. Neither of us could be bothered to hunt for pyjamas, we just tumbled in and that was that.

Next morning, Terry rang to say he was on his way and would be with us in an hour. Henry rolled over and kissed me good morning, which was lovely, then he promised me he would do the same thing every day of our lives from now on. He was dead right about it being 'our' lives. There was to be no more waiting in the wings for the performance to begin, or indeed a rehearsal; we were on stage and what was more we were sharing a dressing room!

Henry got up and threw on some clothes, but he couldn't find one of his socks, and he picked up mine because they were the same colour blue. My feet were small compared to his great hooves, and he waggled his foot in the air and hopped about a bit with my tiny sock on the end of his toes, which for some reason we both found extremely funny. I hoped that it would always be like this, filled with the normal daft stuff that people who live together do every day.

I lay dozy and comfortable while he pottered about downstairs to find his essentials box where there were two mugs, a knife, some teabags and the special German coffee his sister had sent him. He had been filling up this box for weeks. It contained our toothbrushes, toothpaste and loo roll, as well as other things he thought we might need, like breakfast cereal, spare pills and showering things. Oh, and a box of lightbulbs, just in case the previous owners had taken them.

I quipped, 'I have seen less well-organised military invasions.'

Henry replied, 'I'm German. We are good at this stuff, and I've had donkey's years to plan for it.'

He brought everything up on a tray he'd found down the side of the washing machine, along with a daffodil that was growing by the back door. There were Danish pastries he had secreted away for our first morning. We clinked mugs and drank a toast to our new lives as a couple.

We chatted for a bit about how it felt to finally be together. Everything smelt funny, the house was unfamiliar and not quite ours yet. Not surprising - only a day ago it had been someone else's home.

The shower upstairs was set too high up for either of us. Whoever lived there before must have been very tall. The en-suite was perfectly clean, but Henry insisted on thoroughly bleaching the lav before either of us used it.

'If I am going to share DNA in a bathroom, I would rather it was yours and not some random stranger.' Sometimes he was hilariously German.

We had agreed to each bring only one non-essential item from our old lives. I'd chosen my father's armchair from the allotment. It got recovered and went into the study. Henry had brought his carpentry things, and Claudie had inherited Eileen's table with the legs back on. It had been my mother's and my grandmother's before that; no doubt one day it will be Helena's if she wants it.

We had a new sofa and some chairs on order, and we made do with the battered old ones until they arrived.

On our second morning, we were very nearly caught in flagrante. We were, as they say, christening our new home. It was a gentle, geriatric roll in the hay and we were rather enjoying ourselves. We quite forgot about the time, until Terry arrived in the hall and yelled up to see where we were.

Panicked, I called back, 'Just getting dressed, Tel. Could you pop to the shop for some milk, please?'

Mercifully he did. If it had been thirty seconds earlier, I do not think I would have had the breath to answer him.

Henry collapsed laughing and we felt like a couple of youngsters almost caught at it on the sofa by someone's dad! Sending my son, who was in his 50s, off to the equivalent of the pictures was pretty funny. Henry, leaning back on the pillows, grinned and said, 'You should have given him a fiver.'

I kissed him and replied, 'OK, Casanova, now which one of us is going to leg it downstairs to empty the fridge before Terry finds out that we had plenty of milk in all the time?'

I also remember that Henry smirked all morning as we were busy unpacking our boxes and I had to try to keep a straight face when he kept waggling a £5 note around.

Young people think the idea of anyone older conducting horizontal shenanigans is stomach turning and not something you would ever want to think about. '*Get out the brain bleach*', as the teenagers say. A bit of geriatric slap and tickle, if you are up to it, is probably quite healthy. After all, as they used to say in the music halls: A Little of What You Fancy Does You Good!

We settled in and started on our garden. There was a veg patch, but it needed a darn good sort out. We planted roses to remember our wives. Henry chose a yellow climbing rose for Clara, and I went for a large, scented pink for Eileen.

Henry ordered me a greenhouse. He'd always promised he would buy me one as a moving-in present, but it was about much more than that. All those years when we'd met in secret at the allotment, the shed had been a place to hide - at first from my troubles with Eileen, and then it had served to give us a bit of privacy to be together. So, my new greenhouse was symbolic of us not hiding anymore, because everyone could see us inside it.

Of course it had to happen; we had a first row, a big one which was unusual. It is funny how the smallest things can make the most noise. Henry wanted us to have a yellow front door – yellow! I wanted blue to reflect the fact that we were near the beach. Neither of us were prepared to give in.

I told him Satan would be putting on an extra thick jumper before I ever said yes to yellow, and for extras, I called him a stupid, stubborn, pig-headed German idiot with zero taste. Henry told me he wanted the world to know we had arrived, and that daffodil was a lovely colour. Then he called me an uptight, English, public-school twat and walked out to go and buy a can of his filthy paint.

He came back with a bucket-load, and I did my best to ignore him. I was hoovering and listening to Wagner. I had my headphones on, so it was easy to pretend he wasn't there. By lunchtime, he had finished stripping the door and was preparing to put on his first coat of the muck.

I took him out a coffee and he accepted it with extremely bad grace. We circled each other for a bit, eventually I gave in and said he could have yellow if it meant that much to him. He nodded and we gave each other a hug to say sorry. We sat on the doorstep with our mugs and went thoughtful for a bit.

We compromised in the end - we usually did. We had a daffodil-coloured front door, which was far more subtle when it dried - thank God! Our back door, which faced the sea, was pale blue. Our dustbin ended up striped with both colours because we had some left over. Terry bought us an engraved slate, which hung on a nail outside the porch. It read *'Number 3 - George and Henry's house'*. I think it was his way of saying, *OK, I accept you.*

We had a housewarming garden party for our old friends and to introduce ourselves to the neighbours. Terry helped us out and we used his barbecue. The weather was good, and we all had fun and a lot to drink. Some people from Radcliffe Road came up and some from my old work, including my old friend, Joan, who I was delighted to see.

I took a breather and watched everyone for a bit. Henry was having a ball, chatting to people and showing them the garden we had both worked hard to knock into some kind of shape. He had been up hideously early, checking that everything was in order and bustling around in the kitchen wrapping fish in silver foil, muttering about the burgers and prodding away at the tiramisu. I'd had to insist that he took a break before the mayhem began or he would have exhausted himself before the guests and the family had arrived.

It occurred to me how much everything had changed over the years that we had known each other. We were far more relaxed—not just me and Henry, but everyone.

In 1958, a barbecue in the garden would have been unheard of and considered decadent, if not a trifle odd, when you had a perfectly good cooker indoors, and everyone would have arrived suited and booted in their Sunday best. I supposed that life is a more or less permanent state of change. We were old but we could still move with the times, all be it slowly.

When everyone had waved goodbye, we left the carnage for the morning and went to bed, tired but content. I was asleep before Henry had even finished in the bathroom. I really don't remember much, to be honest, except him kissing me goodnight, which he always did, on the back of my neck. I think he said something about us finally being where we always wanted to be, but I couldn't be entirely certain. We settled down and slept in until late, entirely at peace with our new world.

****

When we got the chance, we took our first holiday together. Henry was adamant that he would not go anywhere that did not accept us as a couple. He was right, of course. They did not deserve our tourist dollar, and they didn't get it. We indulged ourselves a bit, but we did not spend money like water. We managed to travel in comfort, although the cost of insurance was eyewatering, because we were old, which put a damper on things.

Those first few years together were among the happiest I ever knew. We planted a beautiful garden and watched it grow, but there came a time when we had to admit it was getting too much. We could bimble about and do pots and such, but the heavy work was beyond us. At well over 80, I was thin and wiry as a bit of old string, but no longer strong. Henry had problems with his back, so he was of no use. We did our sums and decided to employ a gardener.

I did not want to give up my gardening completely. It had always sustained me and was a source of much pleasure. I gained real satisfaction from looking out on a neat plot after a hard day's work. Eating your own veg tastes good, but the digging was for a younger man. Henry had a hover mower for the grass, which made things very much easier.

Apart from getting on in years, we were a contented couple of old coots. We rarely argued and when we did, it never lasted for long. Occasionally one of us would do something that really upset the other, but we soon made it up. All in all, we were ridiculously happy.

In 2005, I had a fall in the garden. I slipped and broke my hip. It hurt like the blue blazes, and they carted me off to the old folks' wing at the hospital, where all the other old codgers went to get fixed up when they snapped a twig. I am mortally ashamed to tell you this next bit. The fall was so damned painful that I peed myself like a toddler and then I had to lay in it for half an hour until Henry found me.

Humiliating, that's what it was. People talking about me, and even to me, like I was deaf or gaga. I wasn't even allowed to pee on my own at first. I had the embarrassment of having a plastic tube shoved up my you know what and piddling into a bottle. I am an easy-going chap as a rule, but there are some things that go well beyond the pale and having your meat and two veg rearranged by a stranger in a uniform is one of them, unless you are paying for the privilege.

Old age is horrible. Inside you feel as good as ever, but outside the paintwork is getting a bit chipped. I think it is as much about how people see you and how they treat you as it is about you getting old. I was not doddery. I'd slipped because it was wet.

Henry drove me mad. He kept fussing like I was about to die or something. In fact, the whole family were making me crazy with their smothering. I will admit to turning into a cranky old bugger for a while. I think I was really quite scared. It was the first time my independence had been threatened, and I didn't like it one little bit.

Enforced resting of my ancient bones had unintended and far-reaching consequences. Henry had to go to Germany to see his sister, Anna, who was ill. I couldn't be left alone because of my hip, so the grandchildren took it in turns to move in with me for a few days. There had obviously been a family discussion about 'keeping the old boy busy' and Helena suggested a bit of genealogy to keep me amused.

She pointed out that it was unusual to have such a big gap in your family tree and I guess she was right. Apart from my dad's date of birth and his father's name, I knew nothing about his history. If you grow up with a thing you don't tend to question it too much. We wondered if he was adopted, or the shameful product of some illicit Victorian liaison, but they were just guesses, so we set off to find out who and what kind of Potters we were.

Helena was a big help because she was just as curious as I was. She kindly fetched my big old suitcase down from the attic. It contained all my father's papers. It had come with us from Radcliffe Road and, as far as I knew, it had not been opened since 1940. Old Ma Beavis had packed it with everything from Dad's desk after he'd died, although I would have bet the farm on her having a good nose through it first. I'd never had the heart to open it before.

We found it to be neatly ordered into bundles, letters, bills etc. It was very exciting to find all this, and I rather got the bug. Over the next few days, using letters and the 1901 census, we pieced together the details of my father's life.

I had suspected that the Potters would be reliable, worthy, God-fearing and just a bit dull, but I was wrong. For a start, my dad wasn't even English.

He was American, born in New York to an American father and a Canadian mother, Hettie (née Palmer). They eloped to Baltimore, and later came to London with my infant father, their only child, in tow.

Mr George Potter Senior was ambitious, a man of business with several stores to his name. He sold innovative household goods imported from the States, mechanical potato peelers, non-stick pans, egg timers that let you decide how done you wanted your egg, the sort of thing any aspiring Edwardian housewife was desperate to own, and he made money.

My dad was sent to Winchester to make him as British as possible and to rub off any rough Yankee edges. The idea being that he would finish his education, go on to Oxford or possibly Cambridge and then join the business, hopefully snagging some titled girl from the shires along the way. The Potters were realistic. Nobody was expecting him to snaffle the daughter of an earl or anything; they weren't rich enough for that. The well-bred offspring of some country squire would have to do. His future was all planned out before he could walk.

As so often happens, my father had other ideas. The letters spoke of the terrible rows when dad told them he was going into the church. His father was a modern man of business and had no time at all for religious mumbo jumbo. He threatened to cut his wayward son off without a shilling, if he carried on with his lunatic scheme. Dad said, '*fine*', stuck two metaphorical fingers up to his father and went off to join the church. They never spoke again.

In early 1918, my dad wrote to his parents to tell them he had married and had a baby son named George. He reached out to them and said they were welcome to visit whenever they liked and he enclosed a studio photograph of the three of us, with me in the starring role of blanket-wrapped bundle of joy. The letter was marked return to sender, although I noted that the envelope had been slit open.

That was it really, a good old family bust up, and a young man who wanted to do things his own way were at the heart of the mystery. In 1919, a solicitor wrote to tell my dad that his father had died of the Spanish flu, and his mother had returned to New York and wanted a reconciliation, which explains our time there.

I found some notes from Hettie, thanking them for coming for dinner and calling me a bonny young fellow. She was amused that I had taken to calling her Granny, which explains another mystery. I must have been walking to her house across Central Park in the snow, rather than to my other gran in Suffolk.

I have vague recollections of visiting a large house and garden, which I think must have been hers. She died in 1921, just before we came home. Most of the shops were sold and Dad took a modest proportion of the money, enough to pay for my education and to purchase an annuity and a house for when he retired. The rest he gave to charities for ex-servicemen and other worthy causes. He was indeed a good man.

The last bundle contained a guarantee from FAO Schwartz for my pedal car and the telegram Beryl sent to say Terry had been born. There was also a letter from Bishop Bob, who was my godfather. He wrote to say he was delighted that Dad was thinking of settling down again and that he hoped to hear the vicarage full to the rafters with noisy little Potters running about, because it had been quiet for far too long.

Fancy me being half-American with a spoonful of Canadian on the side! I suppose to many people it was no big deal, but my whole identity had changed within a few days, and it took a bit of getting used to. I had always assumed I was as English as Marmite or Yorkshire Pud! I was stunned for a while and I cried a few tears for all the half brothers and sisters I never got to have, but I was also happy for Dad. When he died, he was planning to build a life with someone new. After I had packed it all away, both mentally and physically, I got back to my own life because, although the past tends to follow you around like your coat tails, you cannot let it take the lead.

****

2008 was quite a year for us. We both turned 90 and we celebrated knowing each other for 50 years. There were no presents as such. At 90, neither of us needed anything except each other. Both of us had retained our marbles and generally our health was pretty good too.

Henry suggested, 'Let's go out. Somewhere posh and ridiculously expensive. We can afford it, anyway, putting up with me for 50 years deserves a bit of a treat, don't you think?'

I joked, with my tongue firmly in my cheek, 'A bag of chips in front of the telly would be fine, as long as we are together, but yes I do need some compensation for you being such a giant pain all these years, so let's do it.'

We booked a posh hotel, and he surprised me with a champagne trip in a private box on the London Eye because I had always wanted to have a go on it.

We had a moonlit view of the Thames, St Paul's, and the Gherkin, as they call it, all lit up. We sat on our bench and held hands while the attendant stood discreetly with her back to us. I imagine she did it every day for proposals and such like, but I bet she didn't get a couple of 90 somethings too often.

Thinking about it, 1958 was also the year I started my diary, the one where all these memories come from. Dave had been there before Henry was, so I have been scribbling away for a long time. As I have said before, when I go, Dave will be placed into the coffin with me. We will depart together in a blaze of glory; a Viking chieftain and his faithful retainer, consigned to the eternal flames or some such nonsense.

****

In the autumn of that year, a most extraordinary thing happened. The morning seemed a perfectly ordinary one. We had breakfast and Henry went for his walk. He usually took a stroll along the front and stopped for a coffee and sometimes an iced bun. He was type 2 diabetic and not really allowed buns, sometimes guilt overtook him, so he would bring the other half home to me. I always forgave him.

This particular day, I waited for him to walk past the living room window. He always waved as he went out of the front gate, but for some reason he didn't, but I didn't think too much of it.

I was in the kitchen when I heard him come back. He was talking to someone on the front step. I assumed it was the postie, our regular chap at the time was quite chatty.

Anyway, he came back into the kitchen and stood hovering in the doorway, filling the space because, by this stage, he was getting quite wide.

I could tell by the look on his face that something was up. My mind automatically leapt to TV shows where the police turn up to tell you about a dreadful car crash or something equally awful. He was odd. He beckoned me to come into the living room with a, 'Hold my arm, George, and don't argue, because you have quite a shock coming and I don't want you to fall and hurt yourself, OK.'

Since I'd broken my hip, Henry had become a wee bit overprotective. I didn't want an argument, so I took his arm without question or complaint. We went through to the lounge where a tiny white-haired lady was sitting on our sofa. Vaguely I wondered if she was from the social services, come to check if we had gone gaga and needed putting in a home or something.

'Hello, Dad.' She smiled.

I fell backwards, and Henry guided me into a chair. Our Sally, the girl who'd run away in 1957, was sitting in front of me. It wasn't like the movies. I didn't recognise her immediately and we didn't fall into each other's arms in a tearful burst of long-delayed reconciliation. For several minutes, I could not say anything at all. I was far too shaky, and my heart was going like the clappers while I tried to take it all in.

Henry, frowning over his glasses, looked down and asked, 'Did you take your pills this morning, George?'

I shook my head, and he fetched them for me with a glass of water. He looked over at Sally with a less than kindly eye and said, 'He's rather shaky these days. His heart does not take to stress very well.'

I knew Henry Muller almost as well as I knew myself. What he was really telling her was, *'Couldn't you have phoned or sent an e-mail or even a letter first, you selfish cow? Can't you see what you have done to the old boy?'.*

I patted Henry's hand to say I was fine, then I asked for a cup of tea. It was really to get Henry out of the room for a minute, and he damned well knew it.

'Nice to see you,' I stuttered out. Daft, but it was all I could think of after 50 years.

Sally got up and came over to me with her arms out and we both started crying. She said, 'I'm so sorry, Dad. I didn't mean to give you such a shock.'

As if that was going to cut it after five decades of silence.

Henry brought in two mugs of tea and then he left, telling me rather sternly, 'If you need me, call my mobile, and I'll come straight back, you hear?' Then he raised his hat to Sally and walked out of the door.

Of course, Sally asked, 'Who is that chap, Dad? Only he seems a bit territorial?'

I thought she might have asked about her mother first, but anyway, she didn't. I answered her simply and honestly with, 'Henry is my partner, Sally, we fell in love not long after you went and we have been together ever since. Your mother both knew and accepted the situation.'

I cannot recall exactly what she replied, something banal I expect like, 'Wow, things sure have changed around here, Dad!'

I was unsure as to what she had been expecting. When she left, Macmillan had been Prime Minister, I'd been straight, and Bobby Sox and Hula Hoops had been all the rage!

I wasn't going to fall at her feet in gratitude for turning up after half a century of making us worry. I surprised myself. I had always thought that I would welcome her back with open arms. During the many sleepless nights she'd given me over the years, and all the Christmases and birthdays, I would gladly have sold my soul to be able to tell Eileen that her daughter was fine and not in an unmarked grave somewhere.

I had grown old not knowing where she was and I guess the wounds ran deeper than I had realised. Anger doesn't always melt away when you leave it to fester. Sometimes it sets like concrete.

Eileen went to eternity not knowing if her daughter was alive and that hurts more than I can say. A single card would have put her mind at rest. She was a good mother, and she deserved so much better.

Sally had not been a part of our family for so long that we had all changed beyond recognition. I'd always thought she was the missing piece in the puzzle. I realise now that the jigsaw of our lives was, in fact, perfectly complete and she was the piece that didn't fit anywhere. To be frank, her picture was no longer on the box.

As she had declined to ask, I said, 'Your mum died in 1994. She is buried with your dad. I can give you details if you want to visit the grave. I am being buried with Henry when my time comes.'

She gave me a tight smile and said, 'How cute.' Which spoke volumes.

Then I went for the biggie, the 'Where have you been all these years and why didn't you get in touch?' question.

'Canada,' she said, quite casually.

Over the next half an hour, she told me a bit about her life. She had married and divorced twice and was now the mother of four grown sons and grandmother to a shed load of grandchildren that she rarely saw. To be honest, she didn't seem that bothered.

Apparently, she'd decided to let God back into her life after her second marriage had gone west. She explained, without regret, that she left us because she couldn't stand living in a house with two people who thoroughly depressed her with their failed and sterile marriage. She'd longed to be free to live her life as she wanted, with no input from us. Sally had never written or phoned because she'd been worried that we would try and track her down.

Then she dropped the grenade, saying, 'Auntie Beryl paid for my ticket, didn't she tell you? She did promise she wouldn't let on, but you know what her and mum were like, thick as thieves when they weren't trying to murder each other.'

I was truly staggered. All those years Beryl had let Eileen suffer and had never said a word, because she'd promised. Some promises are made to be broken, and this was definitely one of them.

There was a lot of Beryl in Sally. The hard, selfish parts anyway. I'd always thought that, come what may, Beryl had always had her sister's best interests at heart. It seemed not.

I couldn't pick up the phone and scream at Beryl, much as I wanted to do it. A few years earlier, we'd had to mount a rescue mission to bring her back from Spain because she was showing definite signs of dementia. She was still living, but she didn't know who she was most of the time, let alone anyone else.

Sally told me she only wrote to Beryl once a year, just to let her know she was fine, then when she was settled, she gave her the slip as well. How kind!

She worked in the same office for almost 40 years before she retired and she brought her kids up in the small town where she made her home. For the most part, her life had been busy. Bringing up four boys pretty much single-handed left her no time for dreaming.

She still painted and enjoyed walking and skiing, as well as other community-based activities. She seemed content with her lot, although to me it seemed that she had left grey domesticity in post-war Britain, only to run straight into its waiting arms in Canada.

We got down to the reason for Sally's visit. Nothing more than curiosity, apparently. She'd come to the UK on a trip with her church group and it had started her off in wondering about us. She had stayed on for an extra couple of weeks and had decided to grace us all with an appearance, after she had done a bit of detective work to track us down, of course.

I found the fact that she'd been in London with her church hugely funny in an odd way. Eileen had always had to drag her to Mass when she'd been a girl. Sally vowed that as soon as she was old enough, she would never enter a church again. How ironic that one of the things that drove her away from us should be the very thing that brought her back.

We swapped e-mail addresses and made vague promises to keep in touch, but I never thought it would happen. Too much water had passed under the bridge, and we had nothing in common, except a few memories.

She told me in a rather blunt way that my 'surprising lifestyle choices' did not sit at all well with her religious beliefs.

I replied with an equal amount of honesty that loving Henry was not a 'lifestyle choice'. He was the right and only person for me and I was not going to apologise to her for that.

I think she was a bit taken aback, but I had learned to stick up for myself in the 50 years since we'd last met and I was not going to be lectured on who I could or could not love, especially by her.

When she left, she gave me a brief hug and then she walked out of the door without so much as a look back over her shoulder, just like she had all those years ago. I guess her curiosity had been satisfied and she had no further need to stay. As usual, we were expendable.

I shed a tear or two, but not for long. There was a bit of me that would always love her and be her dad, but you can't keep hold of your children once they grow. You just hope that they will want to stick around, or at least like you enough to visit and invite you to be a part of their lives.

As she had asked about Terry, I phoned him to arrange for them to meet up, but he flatly refused to see her. That was entirely his choice. He had his own family, and he made it quite clear that he didn't need anything from his sister. He was still angry and bitter, and who could blame him.

Sometimes life is not kind. It isn't a soap opera with a happy ending around each corner, no matter how much we might want it to happen. I don't have a lot more to say on the subject because to this day it still makes me profoundly sad.

The following year, I asked Henry if he would do me the honour of accompanying me to our first Pride march. The encounter with Sally had disturbed me, and I had a need to show the world who we were, and to be surrounded by other people like ourselves.

So we went, to watch all the young people being happy with who they are. We also went to represent people like us; the silent, married ones who were made to feel ashamed and had to hide themselves away from a free and colourful world for so very long.

Henry wore a rather jaunty, rainbow bow tie and a Panama hat with a coloured band; one of our grandchildren went online and found me a sleeveless rainbow coloured pullover. The music was a bit loud at times. Henry had to turn his hearing aid down a notch or two, but we enjoyed ourselves enormously.

I wondered if there was a place for the frightened people who could not fight for their freedom, because they would have lost everything, including their liberty. A parade of elderly people in cardigans shuffling along on sticks and Zimmer frames with placards saying *'Here we are, at last'*. In this inclusive community, I am sure they would have made a space for us too. After all, gay people get old and crumbly. They don't stay beautiful forever, because they are human beings, just the same as anyone else.

Afterwards, we had a splendid afternoon tea, then we tottered off home and left everyone else to dance the night away.

As a much belated 90th birthday surprise from Terry (some things never change) we went swimming. It was all a bit mad at over 90. The hilarious bit was, we went to the old baths. You know, the ones I used to go to when we lived in Radcliffe Road. When the leisure centre was built, they stayed boarded up because nobody knew what to do with them and the council slapped a preservation order on the inside. When the new cinema had been built in front of them, they'd sort of got forgotten.

Terry told us some company that bought up old lidos had completely refurbished the inside. There is a vogue for these places; people like the idea of swimming somewhere glamorous and 'retro', whatever that is. We just called it old fashioned. They even opened the place with someone dressed as the mayor from 1880 cutting the ribbon.

I must say, they did a jolly good job. What was terribly scruffy, had been reborn with all the late Victorian charm intact. They'd even kept the funny individual changing cubicles with their own showers, where you had to pull on what looked like a lavatory chain to start the water off. So much better than the communal ones at the leisure centre, which made you feel like you were at school.

We went to the session they did for old folks. Extra lifeguards, in case we croaked mid-swim, I supposed. Henry and Terry came in too. It was nice and warm, and the light filtering down through the glass dome took me right back. Something special about the columns and tiles everywhere; it made you feel like a Roman emperor paddling about.

Of course, the Swansea Cruncher was long gone. Dilys, with the gorilla knuckles, gave up the massaging game decades ago. Afterwards, we had lunch in their rather swish restaurant; I think it used to be the old boiler house where they'd kept the coke for heating everything up, and a man called Trevor, who'd only had one eye, used to do odd things with spanners.

It was a real treat, and I was secretly delighted that my lovely old baths had outlasted that horrible leisure centre.

Chapter 21

I am reaching the end of my story. Just a few short years to go to bring me up to date. I want to tell you what happened to us, some of it was sad and other bits were beyond joyous.

One afternoon, we were pootling around in the garden, just tidying up. Henry dropped to one knee. I honestly thought he was having some sort of seizure—not entirely out of the question at his age. Then I realised he was holding a box with a silver ring in it. I was speechless.

Henry smiled and then he mumbled, 'Marry me? For God's sake say yes, Georgie, before I get stuck down here.'

'Yes of course I will,' I replied. Then I hauled him up so that he could sit on the garden bench to get his breath back.

He held my hand and squeezed it tight before he said, 'I thought it was about time I made an honest man of you, after all these years.'

We drank our tea, ridiculously happy, like we were kids who had just got engaged, instead of two wrinkly old giant tortoises pottering about together and nibbling on our greens.

We had talked about a civil partnership just to get our financial affairs in order, but we had never really pursued it further. The fact that our kids were married to each other made everything a whole lot easier. Considering where we'd started, it was a damned fine way to end.

We didn't need a piece of paper to tell us we belonged to each other, but validation in law and a ceremony to say to the world *'here we are, old and creaky, but proud of loving each other'*, was going to be amazing.

Henry and I became official life partners on Saturday 5th June 2010, which was Henry's 92nd birthday. We wanted to look smart for the occasion, but a new suit each seemed rather an indulgence, so we had ties made in matching grey spotted silk. Mine was the traditional sort, and Henry, as usual, went for a bow. I wore the gold tie pin that Mark Windlesham had left me. I'm sure he would have approved.

Henry and I sat in our front room all gussied up and looking smart, waiting for our ride to the registry office. He was nervous, prowling about in his newly acquired wheelchair and looking out of the window to see if the car had arrived, and I was oddly calm, a strange swap of personalities.

I asked him gently, 'Are you OK? Not getting cold feet or anything?'

He rolled his eyes and said, 'George Andrew Fielding Potter, I have been waiting for this since 1958, and wild horses won't stop me now. I was only worrying in case the car breaks down, or we are attacked by rampaging dinosaurs or some other crazy happening that prevents us from getting to where we need to be.'

I replied with a wink, 'We could always get there on the bus, and I have a rolled-up newspaper to deal with the dinosaurs, so you can stop fretting.'

Henry laughed and said, 'Oh, fair enough then.'

I straightened his bow tie for him, and he kissed the top of my head and told me he loved me very much. Our lift arrived and we went off to get hitched, with half the road waving and wishing us well.

I managed to get from the car to the registry office under my own steam and Martin pushed Henry in his chair.

The room was full with friends and our ever-expanding family, which now included several great-grandchildren. Claudie, pencil slim as always and tanned from a recent trip to the sun, looked lovely in dusky pink.

We did the ceremony with me standing and Henry sitting down. It wasn't too long. We held hands the whole way through and exchanged our rings. When the registrar pronounced us as one, Henry had tears in his eyes. He got up from his wheelchair and hugged the stuffing out of me, which set everyone else off. I held his arm, and we tottered outside together in a hail of confetti, like a couple of young things just starting out, instead of two creaky old 92-year-olds. It was a magical day.

Terry took some lovely photos, and a woman from the local paper turned up and took a few more. I guessed we would be a feature in next week's edition.

I hadn't forgotten Eileen. After all our differences, she'd turned out to be a truly giving and remarkable person. In our later years, we'd become very loving friends. I was thankful that we'd shared so many laughs and good times together. If you had told me I would say that when I started the diary, I would have laughed myself silly.

Henry was in charge of the wedding cake. He had been rather secretive about it. I thought it might be in the shape of a garden shed, but it turned out to be a whole allotment full of tiny vegetables and us sitting in our deckchairs holding hands. Jamie, who was always very arty, had done all the modelling and Claudie had made the cake, with a lot of supervision from Henry who was way beyond baking anything himself. How Eileen would have enjoyed making that one!

Of course, we had a do in the evening as well. Nothing ornate, a meal and a few short speeches. There was a surprise one from Henry. I had been wondering what he was up to because there had been a certain amount of scribbling going on and, typical Henry, he was never terribly subtle about hiding it.

He thanked everyone for coming and for accepting us into their lives as a couple. He mentioned Clara and Eileen, then he looked over at me and winked as he joked, 'It's been the best birthday present ever, even if the package took more than 50 years to arrive.'

I remember quipping back, 'The wrapping is a bit knackered,' and everyone laughed.

We couldn't do a first dance as Henry, who was tired, found it almost impossible to get out of the chair. Terry and Claudie did it for us by proxy. They danced to Nat King Cole singing *Unforgettable*, the song we had heard as we'd fallen in love with each other, all those years ago in the allotment shed.

To be honest, I was slightly nervous about our wedding night. I'd been jumpy the first time round, if I remember rightly. We were both over 90 and Henry was ill, so I didn't expect to be getting up to much more than a cuddle, but I was wrong! OK, it wasn't exactly a night of lustful debauchery; that bus had left the station quite some time ago.

Henry and I had a glass of champagne and went to bed. Teeth cleaned, pyjamas on, all the usual, oh and, of course, at our age a pee was essential. A precursor to the umpteen other visits we would make before the morning. Anyway, Henry came out of the bathroom, and I was in bed. He was wearing nothing but his old gardening hat, a bow tie and a smile, like he had that first morning together. I mean, he was leaning on his frame, to which he had attached a couple of ribbons, and he still had his slippers on, but the thought was there.

I laughed and laughed, and then I said, 'You will catch your death of cold, and I am not explaining that outfit to the undertakers.'

He got himself into bed and he whispered into my ear, 'Take your pyjamas off, Georgie, because this is our wedding night. I want to feel you naked in my arms one more time.'

I raised an amused eyebrow and said, 'You saucy old beggar.'

Then I did what he'd asked because it meant so much to him. We lay together warm skin on warm skin. I could smell his aftershave, the one he'd always been so terribly fond of. Spicy and sweet. A bit like faded memories, I suppose.

'Well then, sexy, so what do you want to do now?' I asked.

He kissed the back of my neck and murmured, 'I do love you. Now go to sleep, Georgie.'

I remembered the first time he had said it, in that cold little flat above his bookshop way back in 1961. I had gone there to tell him our friendship was over and I'd woken up with him sleeping beside me. I was a whole new person, a stuttering middle-aged man in love who had just broken the law and his marriage vows, and he didn't care a fig about either of them.

It was lovely to feel his arms around me, and I have to admit that I cried a bit, but only when he was asleep. We both knew that one of us, probably me, would soon be waking up alone.

At least Henry and I could chat to each other. We still had our shared memories. We were lucky because we were both still dealing from a pretty full deck.

Eileen's sister, Beryl, had been nowhere near as lucky. She existed in a twilight world where her hair was cut short to help with washing, and she shuffled around the home in a pair of tartan granny slippers that she would have consigned to the dustbin before they were out of the box 10 years before.

****

On Henry's birthday and the first anniversary of our civil partnership, we got some bad news, which left us trying to come to terms with the fact that he would not be around for very much longer.

There were few treatment options, so we decided it was better to make the most of the time we had left. It was difficult for him. Sometimes he made jokes, stupid ones about not buying him socks for Christmas because he wouldn't get the wear out of them. It helped to keep the pain away for a bit longer, because what was coming was too bloody awful to think about.

He kept remembering the crazy things he'd always wanted to do. Water-skiing, for heaven's sake! What on earth made a 93-year-old man who'd only learned to swim the dog paddle at 55, think of water-skiing? He'd missed the boat on that one - literally.

Once, he told me he'd always wanted to do an abstract painting. That was hilarious, given his views on modern art. A stick man ended up abstract when Henry did it, because he could not draw for toffee.

He was not up to swimming with dolphins or climbing Ben Nevis, but he asked if we could go and see the Northern Lights. The family came along, and it was quite a trip. We also went to his boyhood home because he said he wanted to sit in a coffee shop, eat German cake and hear his native language spoken all around him one last time. Simple stuff really.

We stayed with his nephew, Ralf, who always called Henry 'Uncle Heinz', which made me think of baked beans and bottom burps. Ralf, a doctor, was very good with him and it made me feel a bit easier knowing we had a medic on hand. We did the whole café thing. The cake was truly amazing and, believe me, I know an excellent bit of cake when I taste one.

The Northern Lights were fabulous. We oldies watched them from the picture window in our lodge. It was far too cold for my thin bones and certainly too much for Henry. I put my arm around him, and we sat wrapped together in the same blanket, speechless at the beauty of it all. Henry fell asleep still holding my hand.

It was an odd, sad feeling to think that these experiences would probably be our last. I couldn't help thinking, if you are going to take him anyway, do it now, God, while he is so happy. I had stopped believing in the Almighty in 1947, but you never knew who was listening.

When Henry woke up, I said, 'Come on, sleepy, it's bedtime.'

We tottered off to bed, just two tired old fellas ready for a good night's sleep, filled to the brim with the wonders of the day.

****

On Christmas Day that year, I was awake early because Henry had had a restless night. He was downstairs in what used to be the study. He never meant to wake me, but he was in pain, and he cried out quite a bit, often in his sleep. I had been shown what to do. There was usually a nurse with him for part of the day, but it was Christmas, and I'd told her we could manage.

Jamie was going to cook Christmas dinner for us, and I thought I might grab an hour's kip myself while the others looked after Henry. At almost 94, I got very tired, but I was painfully aware that in a week or two I would not have anything to wear me out, except grief.

Everyone who could make it was coming for dinner because Henry wanted it that way. We promised to help him get washed and dressed, if he was feeling up to it. If not, I was going to eat my Christmas dinner in his room with the door open, so he could see what was going on and help him pull a cracker, because he loved them, although he never did understand the point of having stupid jokes.

He told me he needed to look smart, but everything was falling off him. I'd sobbed like a baby in private after we'd had our dress rehearsal. It was the bow tie that did it. When I tried to tighten it up for him, it had sagged, and it hung like a dead butterfly from his skinny throat, which upset him. He called himself a useless old bag of bones and pitched the tie into the bin in disgust.

He so wanted to look his best for what we all knew would be his last Christmas and his final family occasion. He had a dark-red cardigan and a soft-blue shirt all ironed and ready to go, but the tie was very important to him.

Looking back, I think he felt it connected him with the Henry we all knew and loved, not the tired old man in a wheelchair. For a brief time, he wanted to forget and appear to everyone as he had always appeared. Opa always wore a bow tie and Poppa didn't. That was the way we would be remembered.

When I had finished blubbing, I got on the phone to Helena, an absolute whiz with a needle. She was of course Nana Eileen trained, and she knew her stuff. She made him an elasticated one with reindeers on it.

We had an exhausting day, but a good one. Henry got up and dressed for Christmas dinner, although he ate practically nothing. Helena, good to her word, had made the bow tie and it fitted fine. He was so happy lost among the noise of the children, I had to go into the kitchen for a bit of a sniffle.

When Terry came out to find me, I was looking out of the back door into the garden and trying to pull myself together a bit. He didn't ask me if I was OK, because obviously I was not. The weather was most unseasonable for Christmas Day, slightly cloudy but rather mild. Henry had been hoping for a bit of snow, but it was never more than a vague possibility.

My son and I had spent many moments like this in times of crisis, silently supporting each other. He handed me a bit of kitchen roll and I blew my nose, noisily.

'Come and have a drink, Dad,' he said. 'Henry will be wondering where on earth you have got to.'

Henry wasn't wondering anything. He had nodded off, still wearing his yellow paper hat from the cracker. Martin took a photo on his phone to show him later to make him laugh.

Before he did it, I saw him discreetly touch Henry's skinny old wrist, just to make sure he wasn't photographing a corpse, I suppose. He was a theatre nurse, but he served his time on geriatric, and I guess it became a habit with snoozing old people.

When Henry woke up, we did presents. There was a surprise for both of us. A taped message from Rory, Helena's oldest who was on his gap year in Australia. He looked well and was enjoying his new-found freedom.

I went on a trip at that age, way back in 1936, although we didn't call it a gap year or anything. I went hiking with a friend. We had a marvellous time, released from the fetters of our parents and from school. We drank quite a lot of beer and took photographs of each other doing silly things. Just boys really, with no idea that within a few short years we would be fighting as men.

Every Christmas we took a family photograph. It wasn't formal, we just sort of piled in and set the timer to take a snap or two. We gathered around Henry's wheelchair. I stood behind him and put my arms around his neck with my face next to his. The little ones were all sat on the floor at his feet, some of them still covered in trifle. We Potters ranged in age from well over ninety down to three and a half. Two of our great-grandchildren had a mum from Nigeria, another was half Japanese, and they in turn had a couple of gay great-grandfathers who were married to each other. One of us was German and the other half American. Most of the family spoke at least two languages. We were a modern liberated multicultural family—how wonderful!

Nobody was saying things were perfect, but when I thought back to the repressed way we'd lived in 1958, it made me shudder.

I slept downstairs, in case Henry needed me. Terry and Claudie had offered to stay and give me a hand, but I said I could manage, and to be honest, I was treasuring the last precious days we would have together. They were not far away, at a Premier Inn, so they could come round if I needed them.

Henry woke up about 4.30. He said he wasn't in too much pain, and he wanted to talk for a bit. It was cold so I got into bed with him, and we lay together just chatting about the day and the funny things the kids had got up to. When he said he felt sleepy, I told him to turn over then I curled myself around him until he drifted off in my arms.

He always used to feel bulky and I was the slim one, but I could feel every one of his ribs. I was going to slip back to the sofa, but I decided to stay. Close and warm, I dozed off and I slept better than I had done in months. We were still out cold when Terry and Claudie arrived. They had made tea and bacon sarnies before either of us surfaced!

I left him to go to a charity football match with Terry and Martin. Martin was playing, although he was well over 40. I sat in a deckchair, wrapped up like an extra Christmas parcel placed on the side lines. Claudie had a bit of quality time with her dad, just the two of them. They only watched telly, but it was important they did things together.

Henry went downhill quite suddenly. He drifted in and out like a boat at sea. Sometimes he came into harbour for a while, but the stays grew shorter, and I knew that he was getting ready to sail away for good and leave me alone.

I was dozing in the chair when I felt Henry tap my hand. I kissed his thin fingers and he called me '*schnecke*', which was his soppy pet name for me. It is German for snail, because I curl myself up into a tight ball when I sleep. At least I used to; I'm a bit arthritic to do it these days. I can vividly remember the first time he called me it. I was having a blissful sleep on the Monday morning, after that first weekend together at the flat. I felt a kiss on my shoulder and a voice had whispered, 'Hey, *schnecke*, you are going to be late for work.' I was most definitely late, but it was worth it.

Neither of us said much. Henry, because he couldn't manage long conversations and me because I didn't want him to know how much it was killing me to see him suffer. We had had our lives, and it was time to take a bow and leave the stage before they dragged us off with a great big hook. I wished that I could go too. I didn't want the pain of not having him around, but death rarely does you the favour of carrying you both off together. I stayed with him, just holding hands, the two of us alone for the last time.

His eyes closed and his breathing began to slow, then the life drained out of him. It was as gentle and as peaceful as he would have wanted. For a while, I failed to realise that I still had hold of his fingers. Letting go was just awful. I knew I would never feel his great big paw in my smaller one again. I am sure he would have made a brilliant pianist, but we would never know.

He had wanted to hang on until my birthday, but it wasn't to be.

The night after his death, although I was exhausted by sadness and grief, I found sleep to be impossible. My tired old brain was buzzing with memories. That is the one thing you do have when you are about a zillion years old - you have your memories. That's if you are lucky enough to still have someone to share them with and that bastard dementia hasn't stolen them away from you.

I kept expecting Hen to walk through the door and ask me if I wanted tea. The place was too tidy, except for all the medical equipment, which they had promised to come and collect.

Hen could be infuriating and funny and messy, and a whole host of other Henry things, that I knew I would miss. Mostly, I missed being loved and being able to love him back. For over 50 years, he'd been a constant part of my life, even if a lot of that time we'd been hidden beneath a cloak of respectability.

I guess the pain of loss is the price we end up paying for the joy of love. We made the best we could out of the life we were given, and that is all you can say for any partnership.

My life became foggy. I couldn't see a way forward and there was no going back. I was surrounded by our children and shared grandchildren, yet I felt entirely alone. In the middle of the night, I woke and I knew he was no longer there, but in an odd way he was always with me in my head. We grew old together, and death is what happens to old people. Sometimes it happens to young people too, but mostly it happens to the old ones, like me and Henry.

We had outlived our time and seen great changes, some good, some bad, and that is in the nature of things. I did not think I wanted to go on too much longer without Hen. I felt tired with life, and I wanted to leave the living to the next generation.

Terry and Claudie asked me to live with them, but I preferred an old folks' home where I wouldn't be a bother, and they could come and visit me while I crumbled away in an armchair.

Henry's funeral was the 10th of January. I threw up in the sink through nerves and grief. The doctor gave me some pills, but I didn't like taking them because they made me feel all disconnected from life. However, on that horrendous day I needed them, because I didn't want to feel anything. I wanted to be an unthinking zombie and not let Henry down by blubbing. My suit was neatly pressed, as was my shirt and tie. I looked as smart as paint on the outside, but the inside was falling apart.

Silly, I know, but I remember putting Henry's bow tie into my pocket so that I could feel close to him. There were a few drops of his favourite aftershave left so I was wearing that too. Funny how taste, touch and smell can bring you just as much comfort as sight, probably more, because they tend to linger in the memory long after vision has departed.

I asked if I could be alone for half an hour. I needed a bit of time to gather myself together. I had hardly been on my own since he'd gone. Everyone was terribly kind, but I wanted to think about Henry for a bit.

Our house was full. The family were downstairs, including some who had come from Germany. In a minute, I knew that Terry would be up to make sure I was OK and to tell me Henry had arrived for his final journey. I did not want to look at the coffin as we followed behind in the car because I knew for certain it would make me cry, and as I said before I didn't want to let myself, or Henry, down.

An odd memory came floating back. A timid boy in a rather jazzy blue sleeveless pullover kept saying, 'It's just the empty chocolate box, Georgie, all the good bits have been eaten.'

I heard Terry's footsteps on the stairs, and it was time to say goodbye. The grandchildren put flowers on the coffin for themselves and their children. Claudie put yellow roses on for her and Clara, and Terry got up and put a red one on for me. I couldn't do it. He realised it was way beyond me, so he squeezed my arm and did it on my behalf.

I would dearly have loved at least one flower to have come from our garden, but it was the beginning of January and there was nothing to cut, so it had to come from the florist. Hothouse grown, I expect. Hothouse flowers are sad, unnatural beauties. They know nothing of the wind or rain, just an endless false summer, with a pair of clippers at the end and no butterflies.

Everything was over swiftly, with relentless efficiency and before I knew it, they were playing Nat King Cole singing *Let There Be Love*, which was one of his favourites. Henry had chosen it himself. Silly, but sometimes when he was feeling a bit daft, he would dance me around the kitchen to it.

I knew that soon the house would go on the market and my life, or at least the things in it, would start to disappear. It was an odd feeling. I didn't want to look at anything that reminded me of Henry because it hurt, but at the same time I couldn't let them go. There were memories attached to things we'd bought and had done together. Getting rid of them was an admission to myself that he was dead and didn't need them anymore, even stupid stuff like his clothes.

He'd driven me mad with his socks. Every night, I used to put my socks and undies into the laundry basket like a good, tidy boy. Henry rubbed his foot along the carpet like a bull about to charge, until each sock came off in a ball, then he would leave them there and for good measure drop his pants on top of the pile. Oh, how I wished he would do it one more time – but he couldn't, could he?

Chapter 22

We found me a home called '*The Cedars*'. It was brand spanking new and still smelled of paint, which to my mind was better than cabbage. Old people places always smelled of depression and boiled cabbage, goodness knows why. It isn't as if we lived on the stuff.

I didn't take much with me. Photographs, a few personal items, a suitcase with my clothes and of course Dave came too. I had my own room, but there were always care assistants popping in and out to see if we wanted anything. It was nice, but way too hot for my taste. I found that the early mornings, when the heating was off, was a good time to write. I was missing Henry terribly. I know it was his time to go, but there wasn't a day that I didn't long to hear his voice or to chat with him, like always. I couldn't even put his photo up because it made me cry. Sometimes I talked to him just for comfort. There are many people here who mutter away to themselves, so I didn't think one more was going to make a difference.

Being in a home is like primary school. Apparently, old people don't know what is good for them. A quiet read is not nearly as healthy as the enforced torture of handicrafts. I created a collage of garden flowers. It was made from bits of torn up magazine, like I was five. The activities coordinator said it was lovely. I observed quietly and somewhat sourly on the phone to Terry, that perhaps Claudie might like to put it up on the fridge. He laughed and teased that he would get me a packet of gold stars, and I told him exactly where he could stick them.

Some young people came in the evening, to do a sing along with us, mainly old stuff. There were lots of songs from WWI, like *Pack Up Your Troubles*. I find it all a bit strange that they think we will like songs from before most of us were born. At 94, I am one of the oldest here and I wasn't even a year old when the 'Great War' as they called it then (because obviously we didn't know there would be a sequel) had finished.

Lately, I had been wondering what it was going to be like when I died? I wasn't thinking of jumping off the roof or anything like that, not that I could have managed the stairs anyway. It was just that with Henry gone, and me being ancient, the possibility of it happening seemed likely.

I was not maudlin about it. I just wanted it to happen sooner rather than later, that is all. When you get to my age, you are tired of everything, especially the being old bit. The world has moved on, and this time I was not sure I could keep up. I was the limpy, old buffalo at the back of the pack, fodder for crocodiles or whatever the hell it is that chases them on those endless David Attenborough programmes.

I hoped death would be kind to me and finish me off in my sleep. It is probably the best anyone can hope for in the end; pain free and not completely gaga like Beryl.

Anyway, I hope the afterlife is much cheerier. It's all I have to look forward to, and I do. Maybe it is a great big afternoon tea party with a sign saying *'Welcome George Potter'* and all the people I have ever loved and lost will be sitting round and chatting away to each other nineteen to the dozen.

Eileen will have made the cakes, and Henry can pour the tea. Mum and Dad, and Dave Robinson, and Mark, and lots of other people will be there. Maybe Henry's naughty old Uncle Friedrich can come along, because I bet he could tell us a few stories. The one person I hope will not be there is our Lizzie. Babies should get another chance at life, don't you think, because they were diddled out of it the first time round.

I like to think she was reborn and that she was happy somewhere, but this is just an old man's fancy, because he cannot ever stop loving his lost little child. We only had four hours together, but she will always be my girl.

Time to stop for a bit, I am getting tired and probably quite tiresome. Anyway, I need a pee, and you have pretty much had the story of my life, from soup to nuts.

****

Dear reader as yet unborn, I have a bit of quiet time to add a few final notes before the ritual torture known as exercise hour. We have a jolly time doing gentle physical jerks sitting down, which is stupid.

I would rather be outside working on my assigned patch of flower bed. It is like Colditz in here sometimes, or perhaps Wormwood Scrubs Prison would be an appropriate expression. Maybe I should start to dig an escape tunnel. I could put soil in my pockets and transport it past the guards for disposal, like they did in that old film.

Henry would have laughed himself silly at me grumbling away like this. Elderly people grumble a lot. All we have left is to blame life for making us so bloody old and useless. Anyway, before they drag me out kicking and screaming...

Oh dear, it sounds like the storm troopers are coming for me. I can hear the music starting up, and, now I am fully recovered from my UTI, I have no excuse, so I'm off to wave my arms around, like a lovely sunflower or some such crap.

Last time I wrote, I completely forgot that I'd been going out on a day pass, for afternoon tea - brain going a bit soft I expect. I didn't feel very hungry - I rarely do - but I nibbled at a scone, and I had a cup of tea. I missed Eileen's scones, especially the cheese ones, which I used to eat with butter and her homemade jam made with raspberries I grew on the allotment. Jam and cheese might sound a trifle odd, but they were lovely.

I miss Henry most of all. The last few months have been very hard. Feeling empty most of the time, when I want to share a joke or a memory that nobody else except Henry would understand. The people here are kind, but it isn't my home, our house, with Henry beside me.

There is more acceptance now than there ever has been. When I think of all the years we had to hide our love for each other, and of Henry's poor Uncle Friedrich, herded into a camp, where he was forced to wear a pink triangle with all the other homosexuals and treated in the most barbaric way imaginable... I will not call it inhumane, because that means not human like, and it was bloody human beings who did these terrible, terrible things. He died, you know, in a camp, that lovely man, starved and beaten down just for wanting to love in the way he wanted to love. It makes me weep, not like an old man, but like any sane person who has any feeling in him at all.

I think I will stop writing for good now. I will print you out so you can get sealed up in the time capsule and tell the future what it was like for men like me and Henry, and Mark and Friedrich.

Then I will take a nap. With any luck I will have a dream about Eileen's food, in the kitchen with her and Henry. I will probably start to drool at the thought of a lovely plate of egg and chips. I'm in my 90s, I dribble when I am napping anyway, so who would know.

Best wishes, dear future reader. I do hope you find my story interesting.

I told it with an honest voice and, hopefully, I missed out most of the boring bits.

My regards to 2112,

George.

Epilogue

Dear future reader, as my dad called you, my name is Terry Potter, and I am adding this note to finish off his story. He can't do it himself because he died a few days ago. It was all very peaceful. He was ill for a couple of weeks and then he slipped away from us.

I have come to clear his room. I need to take his story down to the time capsule committee who are waiting for it and to collect Dave, later re-named '*Dog Eared Dave*', his beloved diary where he made all his notes.

Dad was most insistent that Dave was going to go with him in the coffin, and I need to get him down to the undertakers.

My dad was a good man, who worked hard and loved his family. He never wanted to be a liar and an adulterer, but society made him into one. I made my peace with what he did to my mother years ago. I won't forget, but with time comes forgiveness and Mum, it seems, was happy for them. She mellowed with age, and she became quite a laugh. Who would have guessed that was going to happen?

Most of all, Dad loved Henry and Henry loved him back. He always said they were two halves of the same cup waiting to find each other, and he was really only half a person after Henry went

When you read this in 100 years, I hope the world is a more accepting place and nobody has to hide who they are. Who knows, we can only hope it will be so.

I am attaching a photo because they asked me to find one of dad to put in the capsule. I chose this snap of the three of them dressed as the Marx brothers, because they are all laughing.

Proof that if you can laugh at yourself, you can survive pretty much anything, and they did.

Terry.

About the Author

Betty Valentine lives in the Channel Islands.

This is her 4th published book, and she hopes that she has a few more in her because she enjoys writing.

When not writing she is someone's wife, mum, sister, daughter, mother -in law and granny.

For more information about our books and services,
please visit
www.greencatbooks.com[1]